ONE DEADLY SAFARI

A AGATHA ROYALE MYSTERY
BOOK 4

ELLA ANDREW

BACKSPACE
PRESS

First paperback edition April 2025

Backspace Press

Houston, Texas

Cover design by Backspace Press

ISBN 979-8-9932530-5-3 (paperback)

ISBN 979-8-9859898-7-8 (ebook)

Printed in the United States of America

1

LUGGAGE, LAUGHTER, AND CHAOS

Agatha Royale stood in One Deadly Chapter Books & Brew, her mystery bookshop tucked into the heart of Bristol Lake, rearranging a display of Agatha Christie novels for the third time that morning. At thirty-nine, with hazel eyes that missed nothing and light brown bangs that refused to stay put, Agatha had rebuilt her life from the ground up after a painful divorce and being laid off from her job as a librarian. The shop had become her refuge—a haven filled with fictional crimes, curious locals, and the occasional very real mystery.

After solving a few puzzles that even Sheriff Salinger couldn't crack, Agatha had earned a bit of a reputation in town. Not that she'd ever call herself an *amateur sleuth*—that sounded far too dramatic. She preferred the term "observant bookshop owner with trust issues."

Mike, her miniature schnauzer and self-appointed security detail, waited patiently by the front door, ears perked and leash nearby.

"Okay, okay," she said, straightening the last book for the fourth time. "We're going."

THE NEXT MORNING, at 93 Knob Hill, Agatha sipped a lukewarm cup of coffee as she zipped her final suitcase shut. Her half-finished manuscript was carefully tucked into her carry-on—along with three pens, two notebooks, and a level of writerly optimism she hadn't felt in years.

"I'm not coming back until I've written at least one good murder," she muttered, folding her sunhat and tucking it into her suitcase before checking her watch.

Mike stood by the kitchen door, tail wagging in that hopeful, ready-for-anything way he had.

Agatha opened the door to let him out, wincing as cold air hit her face. Heavy gray clouds loomed overhead. "Of course," she said, frowning. "Because why wouldn't a snowstorm try to sabotage our connection in New York?" She glanced at the list on the counter. Passport? Check. Plane ticket? Check. Emergency chocolate? Check. Agatha was officially in route to Botswana for the Savuti Scribe Safari writing retreat—a chance to escape, recharge, and finally finish her mystery novel.

Assuming nothing...murderous happened along the way.

LATER THAT MORNING, Agatha, Emma, and Mike stood on the sidewalk in front of One Deadly Chapter Books & Brew, waiting for Lorraine to meet them before they headed to the airport. The cold air bit at their cheeks as Agatha's hair whipped across her face in the wind. She tucked a strand behind her ear with a sigh and shifted from foot to foot to stay warm, glancing down at Mike, who sat patiently by her side.

Emma tapped her foot impatiently, her eyes darting up and down the street, her breath visible in the chilly air. "What's taking Lorraine so long?" Emma checked her watch. "Our ride will be here in fifteen minutes." She sighed in frustration.

"It'll be okay, Emma," Agatha said, double-checking Mike's crate to ensure he'd be comfortable for the flight. "Oxford Hill Regional Airport is only forty-five minutes away."

Five minutes later, Lorraine finally appeared around the corner, limping heavily as she struggled forward. Her flushed face glistened with sweat, despite the chilly morning, and her hair, tangled and sticking to her forehead, added to her disheveled appearance. Her wrinkled clothes looked like she had just battled a windstorm, and her eyes had a defiant glint, as if daring anyone to comment on her state. She lugged two large vintage suitcases—faded blue-green with white stitching—and clutched a small vanity case in one hand. Her purse hung awkwardly from her shoulder, while her other hand tried to keep everything from falling apart. Mud stained her white pants at the knee, and the heel of one shoe dangled precariously. Lorraine was, quite simply, a walking disaster.

"Mon dieu, help me, please," Lorraine gasped dramatically, the vanity case slipping from her grasp and nearly hitting the ground before she caught it.

"What in the world happened to you, Lorraine?" Agatha ran over to help, grabbing the vanity case while Emma took one of the bulky suitcases. "And what is this?" Agatha raised an eyebrow at the small, retro vanity case. "Did you stop at an antique store?"

Lorraine, exasperated but still managing to maintain her usual charm, sighed. "This? Oh, this suitcase set was my mother's, thank you very much!" She paused, catching her breath, then added with a chuckle, "At this point, I wouldn't be surprised if it's cursed."

Eliza, Gladys, and Dawson, who had come to bid the trio farewell, rushed over to rescue Lorraine.

"I was rushing," Lorraine continued, "and my heel got stuck in the cobblestone." She held up her broken shoe. "I stumbled, fell, and bam! Mud everywhere." She gestured to her once-white pants, now stained. "And of course, I couldn't leave this vanity case behind," she said, clutching it dramatically as if it held her entire life's secrets.

Even in the middle of the disaster, Lorraine found humor in the situation. She opened the vanity case, pulling out a compact mirror and lipstick. "I mean, at least I still have my essentials," she said with a grin before bursting into laughter.

Agatha, Emma, and the others couldn't help but laugh along with her.

Soon, the three of them were in the car, finally on the way to the airport.

Eliza stood on the sidewalk, waving them off like they were leaving forever. I'll miss you guys," Eliza sobbed dramatically, dabbing at her eyes.

Celeste came out of the store briefly to say, "Have fun, Agatha, and don't worry about the bookstore. I've got everything under control."

Agatha smiled in gratitude and waved goodbye.

Dawson waved goodbye and as he got close to the car window he said, "Ms. Royale, enjoy yourself and stay out of trouble over there!"

Agatha gave a playful salute. "Yes, sir!" As the car pulled away from the curb, she leaned back in her seat, a smile still playing on her lips. The familiar excitement of a new adventure mingled with Dawson's words. "I'll certainly stay out of trouble..." she whispered to herself as she watched the scenery pass by through the car window.

∾

THE NEXT MORNING Agatha stood in line at Johannesburg Airport, her eyes darting nervously between her luggage and Mike's travel crate. Emma was a few paces ahead, chatting animatedly with Lorraine, who was waving her arms in exaggerated movements. Agatha tried to calm herself. After all, it was just a short layover before they caught their next flight to Maun.

"Agatha, ma chérie, are you sure Mike's sorted?" Lorraine asked, glancing back with that signature French flair in her voice. Her tone carried that unmistakable blend of maternal concern and dramatic fussing she reserved for moments when she thought extra attention to detail was needed.

"Of course he is!" Agatha said, putting on her best confident face. She gave a reassuring pat to the crate—though, at that moment, she couldn't see the little snout she expected. "Mike's right here. Aren't you, boy?"

The crate was silent. Agatha frowned, her heart skipping a beat as she peered inside. The crate was empty.

"Agatha, what—?" Lorraine leaned over, her eyes widening. "Where is Mike?!"

"Oh no..." Agatha whispered, scanning the airport frantically. She was suddenly certain that she had seen a baggage handler carry a crate that looked suspiciously like Mike's towards the luggage conveyor belt.

"Did you put Mike with the luggage?!" Emma asked, her voice cracking with a mix of panic and disbelief.

Agatha opened her mouth, then closed it, realizing the only possible answer. "It... may have happened."

Lorraine couldn't help herself. She burst into laughter, doubling over at the absurdity of it. "Mon Dieu, Agatha! You've sent Mike on a worldwide adventure! I hope he sends postcards."

"This isn't funny, Lorraine!" Agatha exclaimed, her face

reddening. "What if he ends up... I don't know, in Madagascar or something?"

Emma pulled out her phone and began dialing furiously. "We have to find him before we board our next flight. Oh, Agatha... how do you manage these things?"

"It's a talent," Lorraine added with a grin, her French accent making 'talent' sound all the more sarcastic. "Un talent très unique, très chaotique."

The airline staff weren't much help either. Agatha could only watch as a young attendant stared blankly at her before saying, "The dog? Oh yes, it may have been routed to Windhoek, Namibia. Or possibly Lusaka. We're looking into it."

"Namibia?" Lorraine cackled, "Quelle aventure! You know, Mike always did have a taste for adventure."

Agatha groaned, rubbing her temples. "This is not happening. I can't believe I lost my own dog in an airport."

"Look on the bright side," Lorraine said, still chuckling. "At least you didn't send him to Antarctica."

"Not helping," Agatha snapped, but her lips twitched despite herself. There was something absurdly comical about the situation, and Lorraine's carefree attitude made it difficult to stay upset.

The next few hours were a mix of frantic conversations with airline personnel, Lorraine and Emma trying to keep Agatha from completely breaking down, and periodic reassurances from the staff that "all would be sorted by tomorrow." They moved from counter to counter, each new attendant offering a different story about where Mike might be. One even suggested he might have been mistakenly put on a flight to Cairo.

"Cairo?!" Agatha's voice was shrill now, her eyes widening in horror. "Why would Mike go to Cairo?!"

"Perhaps he's off to see the pyramids," Lorraine mused,

clearly enjoying herself. "Mike, the intrepid explorer, toujours en mouvement!"

"Lorraine, if you don't stop making jokes, I swear—"

Emma stepped in, placing a calming hand on Agatha's shoulder. "Deep breaths, Agatha," she said softly. "We'll figure it out. Mike's a tough little guy, remember? Plus, you've got all of us helping."

After much back-and-forth, it was clear they would have to continue to Maun and stay the night while waiting for Mike to be located. They reluctantly checked into a modest lodge, and Agatha spent most of the evening anxiously calling the airline for updates.

The following morning, just as promised, a very ruffled Mike —with fur sticking up in random directions—was brought to their hotel in Maun. He gave Agatha a long, unimpressed stare before happily bounding up to Lorraine, who was ready with a treat.

"See, Mike?" Lorraine said with a wink, "I knew you were tough enough to survive a little adventure. Plus, now you've got a stamp in your passport!"

Emma knelt down, scratching behind Mike's ears. "We missed you, buddy," she said, her voice filled with warmth. "You certainly had us all worried, but we knew you'd find your way back."

Agatha sighed in relief, rubbing her temples as she muttered, "Never. Again."

Lorraine laughed, "Voyons, Agatha. You have to admit, it adds a bit of excitement to the trip."

"I could do without that kind of excitement," Agatha grumbled, but her tone was lighter now, the tension slowly ebbing away.

Emma smiled. "This will make quite the story for your next book. You can call it 'The Case of the Missing Schnauzer.'"

Agatha couldn't help but laugh. "Only if I make you two the prime suspects."

"Guilty as charged," Lorraine said, raising her hand. "But only if I get a heroic redemption arc."

"Deal," Agatha said, shaking her head. She looked down at Mike, who was now contentedly munching on his treat. "But seriously, no more adventures for you, okay?"

Mike barked in response, his tail wagging furiously. It was almost as if he was saying, "No promises."

2

TURBULENCE AND TIME TRAVEL

The sun was just peeking over the horizon as Agatha, Emma, Lorraine, and Mike arrived at the small airfield. Their excited chatter died down as they caught sight of their transportation. Parked before them was the Savuti Scribe Safari plane–an aging DC-3 that had clearly seen better days.

Lorraine's face fell dramatically. "Mon Dieu! Is that our plane or a museum piece?"

The silver fuselage glinted in the soft morning light, its patchwork of repairs and visible rivets telling tales of countless adventures–and misadventures. While the vintage aircraft certainly had character, it also looked like it had survived every mishap imaginable.

Agatha patted Lorraine's arm reassuringly. "Come now, it's got charm. Think of the stories it could tell."

"Oui," Lorraine muttered, eyeing the plane suspiciously. "And I fear we might become its final chapter!"

"I thought we were flying, not time-traveling!" Lorraine exclaimed, clutching her vintage vanity case like a life preserver.

Her carefully crafted French persona slipped as her expression morphed into a mixture of horror and disbelief.

Agatha tried to hide her smirk. "Look at it this way, Lorraine —if we crash, at least it'll be a memorable chapter in your memoir." She nudged Emma, who stifled a laugh.

"Mon Dieu! I can't believe we're flying in that... that relic!" Lorraine muttered, shaking her head as she eyed the plane like it might suddenly sprout fangs and devour them whole.

Mike seemed more excited than anxious, barking cheerfully at the aircraft and wagging his tail. Agatha couldn't help but think that Mike's judgment of the plane was probably more reliable than Lorraine's at the moment.

The rest of the passengers trudged forward, their luggage in tow. A man in a pilot's jacket greeted them, his enthusiasm barely masking the airplane's ominous creaking. "Welcome aboard, adventurers! We're taking you straight to Savuti in style —classic, vintage style, mind you!"

Once inside, the old-fashioned seats were narrow, and the interior looked like it belonged in a history museum. The smell of old leather and aviation fuel permeated the air, adding to the vintage atmosphere.

Nigel Thompson, a publisher and writer, who was also a passenger on this journey, waved enthusiastically from his seat near the entrance. "Isn't this exciting?" he called out, his eyes sparkling with genuine enthusiasm despite the nervous grip he had on his laptop. "It's like stepping back in time!"

Nigel was a larger-than-life figure, both in stature and personality. His brightly colored silk scarf fluttered as he gestured, paired incongruously with a tweed jacket that looked a size too small. His thinning silver hair was carefully combed back, though a few rebellious strands refused to stay in place. Known for his flamboyant style and penchant for drama, Nigel had built a reputation as a daring publisher who wasn't afraid to ruffle feathers.

In recent years, however, Nigel had ventured into writing. Unfortunately, his career as an author was less than stellar. While his books received moderate attention due to his fame, critics often dismissed them as formulaic and uninspired. Still, Nigel approached his new endeavor with unshakable optimism, proclaiming himself an 'expert in storytelling' at every opportunity.

Though admired for his charm and business acumen, he had his share of detractors. Rumors swirled about questionable financial dealings and cutthroat tactics in the literary world. To his critics, Nigel's vibrant personality masked a ruthless streak, but to those who loved him, he was an irresistible force of nature. His booming laugh and relentless enthusiasm could brighten even the dreariest room.

"Stepping back in time, indeed," murmured Agatha under her breath as she exchanged a glance with Emma. She wasn't sure whether to find his boundless energy endearing or exhausting.

Eleanor Price, a sharp-tongued literary critic already seated inside, rolled her eyes at Nigel's excitement. "More like stepping into a death trap," she muttered, loud enough for others to hear.

Eleanor was a figure who commanded attention, though not always for the right reasons. With her angular face and steely silver hair cut in a precise bob, she exuded an air of authority that few dared to challenge. Her tailored suits, always in muted tones, reflected her no-nonsense demeanor.

As one of the most feared critics in the literary world, Eleanor had built her career on scathing reviews that could make or break an author's reputation. Her sharp wit and brutal honesty had earned her both respect and resentment in equal measure. While some admired her for her uncompromising standards, many viewed her as a bitter, vindictive figure who took pleasure in tearing others down.

Despite her professional success, Eleanor had a knack for alienating those around her. Her penchant for pointing out flaws, even in casual conversation, ensured she was rarely invited to social gatherings outside of professional obligations. Yet, Eleanor seemed unfazed by her reputation, wielding her words like weapons and thriving in the power they gave her.

Agatha, observing her from a distance, couldn't help but wonder if Eleanor's barbed tongue had finally gone too far. "She's not exactly making friends," Emma murmured, leaning close to Agatha.

"No," Agatha agreed, her gaze lingering on Eleanor. "And that might just be her downfall."

"Oh, fantastique," Lorraine groaned. "We're going to crash in style." She struggled to heave her vanity case up the narrow metal staircase, getting into a loud argument with the flight attendant about why her precious cargo couldn't sit in her lap during the flight.

Agatha took her seat next to Lorraine, who was still complaining under her breath about how she was not "built for time-travel aviation."

Emma was seated just across the aisle, her eyes twinkling with amusement at the unfolding drama.

Eleanor wasted no time loudly voicing her displeasure, her sharp comments slicing through the cabin's excited chatter. "This is utterly absurd," she declared, her voice dripping with disdain. "I can't believe Savuti Scribe Safari expects us to tolerate this... this flying museum piece."

Nigel, ever the optimist, leaned forward in his seat, unde-terred by Eleanor's biting criticism. "Oh, come now, Eleanor! There's something undeniably romantic about flying in such a historic aircraft. Just imagine the tales it could tell if it could speak!"

Eleanor's eyes narrowed dangerously as she turned to face him. "Romantic? More like reckless and foolhardy. I'd rather not become another chapter in its colorful history, thank you very much."

Nigel's enthusiasm dimmed slightly, but he pressed on with the determination of a man trying to sell ice to Eskimos. "Where's your sense of adventure, Eleanor? This is precisely the stuff great literature is made of!"

"Great literature, perhaps," Eleanor sniffed, her nose wrinkling as if she'd caught a whiff of something unpleasant, "but absolutely terrible travel experiences. Some of us prefer our adventures safely bound between book covers, where they belong."

Agatha watched this verbal tennis match with growing interest, noting the palpable tension crackling between the publisher and the critic. She caught Emma's eye and raised an eyebrow, silently communicating that this trip was shaping up to be far more intriguing than they'd anticipated.

There was clearly more to this group than met the eye, and Agatha's detective instincts were already tingling with curiosity.

The pilot's cheerful voice crackled over the intercom, sounding far too enthusiastic for the situation. "Buckle up, dear passengers! We're about to embark on an adventure. First stop, turbulence over the savannah!"

Lorraine let out a dramatic gasp that would have done credit to any Parisian stage. "Turbulence? Mon Dieu! I'm not emotionally equipped for turbulence!" She looked around for sympathy, but Agatha merely rolled her eyes, fighting back a smile.

"You'll be fine, Lorraine," Agatha said, patting her friend's arm reassuringly. "Think of it as research for your future bestseller—'Surviving a Rickety Plane: Adventures with a Flamboyant Pilot, an Irate Critic, and an Overly Enthusiastic Publisher.'"

As the engines roared to life, rattling the cabin like an over-sized maraca, Lorraine gripped her armrests with white knuckles. Her precious vanity case sat awkwardly between her feet, threatening to escape at any moment.

The plane wobbled into the air, eliciting a squeal from Lorraine as she squeezed her eyes shut, her French phrases mixing with unintelligible muttering in a linguistic parfait of panic.

Eleanor, not to be outdone in the complaints department, now turned her razor-sharp commentary on the state of the aircraft itself. "There *better* be some kind of onboard service on this flying relic—or do we just flap our arms and hope for the best?"

Across the aisle, Lorraine shot her a sideways glance over the rim of her sunglasses and muttered, "Mon dieu... it's going to be a *very* long flight."

Meanwhile, Nigel was practically pressing his nose against the window, his childlike wonder seemingly impervious to the plane's alarming shakes and rattles. "Oh, look at that view! Simply marvelous!"

The pilot, clearly in his element, swayed with the plane like a conductor leading a very unsteady orchestra, calling out reassurances that did little to calm anyone's nerves. "Just a bit of turbulence, folks! Think of it as nature's massage chair!"

Suddenly, the plane hit a particularly vigorous patch of turbulence, sending Lorraine's vanity case on an impromptu journey down the aisle. Lorraine let out a shriek that could have rivaled any opera diva, scrambling after her prized possession with a desperation that was both comical and touching.

"You should have just left that case in the cargo," Agatha

called out, barely suppressing her laughter at the sight of her usually composed friend crawling down the aisle.

"Oh, non, non, Agatha!" Lorraine's voice rose to new octaves as she retrieved her case, staggering back to her seat like a drunken tightrope walker. "This case is irreplaceable! Unlike my sanity, which I fear has already abandoned ship—or plane, as it were!"

Emma burst into laughter, and even Agatha had to hide her growing smile behind her hand. The situation was too ridiculous not to find amusing.

Nigel, caught up in the moment, began narrating the scene as if he were crafting the next great African adventure novel. "And there, amidst the turbulent skies over the vast savannah, our intrepid heroine battled not only the elements but her own vanity case..."

Eleanor shot him a glare that could have frozen the Sahara. "If you don't stop that incessant narration, I'll give you a real cliffhanger to write about."

Despite the continued complaints from Eleanor and Lorraine's dramatic antics, the tension in the cabin began to soften. It was hard to take the situation too seriously with Lorraine acting as if each bump might be their last and Nigel treating the whole experience like the adventure of a lifetime.

Agatha couldn't help but think that this motley crew might just make for an interesting story after all—assuming, of course, they all survived the flight.

As the plane settled into a smoother flight pattern, Agatha wondered what other surprises this safari had in store for them. With this eclectic group of personalities, she had a feeling that the wildlife wouldn't be the only source of excitement on this trip.

"You know," Emma leaned across the aisle, her voice low, "I

think this might be perfect material for your book, Agatha. A mystery set on a rickety plane over the African savannah?"

Agatha chuckled. "With Lorraine as the reluctant heroine?"

"I heard that!" Lorraine huffed, still clutching her vanity case. "If I'm to be a character in your book, Agatha, at least make me glamorous. And on solid ground!"

Their conversation was interrupted by Eleanor's sharp voice. "Excuse me, but is there any chance of getting a decent cup of tea on this flying relic?"

The flight attendant, a cheerful young woman named Sarah, approached with a smile. "I'm afraid we only have instant coffee, ma'am. But I can add some hot water to make it extra strong!"

Eleanor's face contorted in disgust. "Instant coffee? On a writers' retreat? This is an outrage!"

Nigel, ever the optimist, chimed in. "Now, now, Eleanor. Think of it as an authentic experience! We're roughing it, just like the great explorers of old!"

"I didn't sign up to be a great explorer," Eleanor snapped. "I signed up to critique literature, not endure culinary torture."

Agatha exchanged an amused glance with Emma. The tension between the critic and the publisher was palpable, and she couldn't help but wonder about the history there.

As if reading her thoughts, Emma whispered, "Ten quid says there's a story between those two."

Agatha nodded, her detective instincts already kicking in. "I'd bet my typewriter on it."

The flight continued, punctuated by Lorraine's dramatic gasps at every slight turbulence, Eleanor's constant complaints, and Nigel's enthusiastic observations about the landscape below. Mike, for his part, seemed to be thoroughly enjoying the adventure, his tail wagging every time the plane dipped or swayed.

As they neared their destination, the pilot's voice crackled over the intercom once more. "Ladies and gentlemen, we're approaching Savuti! Please fasten your seatbelts and prepare for a landing that'll make you wish you'd packed your sense of humor!"

Lorraine groaned. "Mon Dieu, does he think he's a comedian?"

"Well," Agatha said, patting her friend's arm, "laughter might be the best medicine for your aviation anxiety."

As the plane began its descent, the vastness of the African savannah came into view. Even Eleanor seemed momentarily silenced by the breathtaking landscape.

With a series of bumps and jolts that had Lorraine muttering rapid-fire French prayers, the plane finally touched down on the dusty airstrip. As it rolled to a stop, a collective sigh of relief echoed through the cabin.

"Ladies and gentlemen," the pilot announced, his voice filled with theatrical flair, "welcome to Savuti! Please exit carefully, and don't forget to thank our lovely DC-3 for not falling apart mid-flight!"

As they disembarked, Agatha couldn't shake the feeling that this was just the beginning of a very unusual adventure. With a critic ready to critique everything in sight, a publisher bursting with enthusiasm, a dramatic friend on the verge of a nervous breakdown, and a mystery writer's instinct telling her there was more to this retreat than met the eye, she knew one thing for certain: this was going to be a safari to remember.

3

A COZY WELCOME WITH AN OMINOUS VIBE

The group arrived at the Savuti Safari Lodge just before noon, the African sun high and unforgiving in the cloudless sky. Agatha, Lorraine, and Emma stepped out of the dusty Jeep, immediately feeling the full force of the Savuti's midday heat. The lodge loomed ahead of them, a far cry from the luxurious retreat they had imagined. The wood-framed building looked weathered, as if it had been forgotten by time, its thatched roof sagging under the weight of the elements.

Lorraine was the first to speak, pulling off her oversized sunglasses and squinting in the harsh light as she glanced around with a skeptical eye. "Luxury? More like rustic with a touch of regret," she muttered, brushing off the dust that had already begun to settle on her dress. "Très rustique, if you ask me."

Agatha gave a small, resigned smile as she followed Lorraine and Emma toward the lodge's entrance, grateful for any respite from the midday sun. Inside, the open room was dimly lit, a stark contrast to the bright exterior. A few flickering lanterns hung from exposed beams, struggling to illuminate the space.

Mismatched wicker chairs were scattered around a communal table that had seen better days—its surface scratched and faded, a testament to the countless guests who had come and gone.

"Oh là là! Is this where you're supposed to find your muse?" Lorraine gasped, dramatically placing a hand on her forehead. "The only thing I'm inspired to write is a strongly worded complaint!"

Agatha ran her hand over the uneven wood, her fingers brushing against a splinter.

"You're here for the writers' retreat, right? Maybe we can turn this into a metaphor," Emma said, her tone trying for optimism but falling short. "You know, something about rough edges and hidden charm."

"Hidden being the key word," Lorraine muttered. "Bien caché."

At the far end of the lodge, a small bar was tucked into the corner. Bottles of liquor, some with faded labels and others completely unlabeled, lined a dusty shelf. A lone bartender stood behind it, staring vacantly ahead.

Lorraine raised an eyebrow. "Courage," she muttered, heading toward the bar. She inspected a bottle, wiped her finger over it, and grimaced at the dust that came off. "I've seen cleaner bottles at a marché aux puces."

Agatha looked puzzled for a moment.

Lorraine sighed. "A flea market, ma chérie. Though I doubt even those would stock such... questionable spirits."

Agatha shook her head, her gaze drifting to the far corner where a couple of guests had already gathered. A small fire crackled in the pit outside, sending a soft glow into the open space. Around it, the faces of the other retreat-goers flickered in and out of the firelight—Eleanor Price sat stiffly on one of the wooden benches, scribbling something into her notebook. Across from her, Naomi Ndlovu sat in near silence, nervously biting her lip as though afraid Eleanor might critique her existence.

"Well, at least there's some charm to the fire," Agatha said, more to herself than anyone else.

Lorraine returned with a glass, sniffing the contents cautiously before taking a tiny sip. She made a face. "Charm doesn't quite make up for what passes as gin here. It's a bit... dubious," she said, wrinkling her nose. "Douteux, as they say in Paris."

Emma, always the optimist, grabbed a plate from the small buffet table and examined the meal. "Stew. Could be worse."

Lorraine raised an eyebrow. "Ma chère, if that's what you call optimism, I'm worried for you," she said with a dramatic sigh. "Je suis inquiète—absolutely concerned—for your definition of looking on the bright side."

Later that evening the group moved toward the outdoor fire pit, where Nigel Thompson was already holding court. His flamboyant outfit—a wide-brimmed hat, bright scarf, and flashy bracelets—caught the glow of the flames, giving him a theatrical air. He gestured grandly as he spoke, his voice carrying over the crackling fire.

"And so," Nigel was saying, "I told them: darling, if you're going to write about love, you need passion. Without it, your work is as dry as this... well, this place." He laughed at his own joke, while the others offered half-hearted chuckles.

Lorraine eyed his flamboyant outfit with a mix of amusement and horror.

Agatha took a seat beside Lorraine, who immediately leaned in and whispered, "look at that ensemble. It's like a carnival exploded on him. I can't decide if I'm impressed or terrified."

Just then, a gust of wind sent a small cloud of dust swirling around the fire, causing everyone to squint and shield their eyes.

Lorraine let out a dramatic gasp. "Parfait! Not only are we in the middle of nowhere, but now we're being attacked by the elements. I should have brought my hazmat suit instead of my sunhat!"

Nigel, unfazed, continued his monologue. "Ah, yes, nature at its finest!" he declared, raising his arms as though embracing the dusty inconvenience.

Eleanor Price looked up from her notebook, her eyes sharp. "Less about nature, more about substance, don't you think? Or is substance too much to ask from someone who specializes in commercially packaged bestsellers with questionable authorship?"

Nigel's face flushed red. "I'll have you know, my books have touched more lives than your scathing reviews ever will. At least I'm contributing something positive to the literary world."

"Positive?" Eleanor scoffed. "Is that what we're calling it now? Flooding the market with vapid, self-indulgent nonsense?"

Naomi Ndlovu, who had been quietly observing, suddenly spoke up. "At least Nigel's work reaches a wide audience. Unlike some of us who write for a select few and call it 'art'."

Eleanor's gaze snapped to Naomi. "Ah yes, because quantity always trumps quality, doesn't it? Tell me, Naomi, how many of your 'wide audience' readers can actually comprehend the themes in your work?"

Naomi's eyes narrowed. "Are you implying my writing is simplistic?"

"If the shoe fits," Eleanor replied coolly.

Agatha, feeling uncomfortable with the growing hostility, tried to change the subject. "Perhaps we could discuss the workshop schedule for tomorrow?"

Eleanor turned her sharp gaze to Agatha. "And you are? Ah yes, the bookshop owner. Tell me, dear, what qualifies you to be at a writers' retreat? Selling books isn't quite the same as writing them, is it?"

Emma, ever supportive, jumped to Agatha's defense. "Agatha's knowledge of literature is vast. She's more than qualified—"

"And you?" Eleanor interrupted. "The sidekick? Or are you here to serve refreshments?"

Lorraine, who had been uncharacteristically quiet, spoke up. "Now see here, you pompous—"

"Ladies, gentlemen," Victor Reynolds' calm voice cut through the tension. "Perhaps we've all had a long day of travel. Why don't we take a step back and remember why we're here? To inspire and support one another."

The group fell into an uneasy silence, broken only by the crackling of the fire. Agatha couldn't help but notice the lingering glares between several members of the group. Nigel was still seething, his knuckles white as he gripped his drink. Naomi had pulled out her phone and was furiously typing something, occasionally shooting glances at Eleanor. Oliver White, who had remained silent throughout the exchange, was watching everyone with an unsettling intensity.

As the group began to disperse for the night, Agatha overheard snippets of hushed conversations:

"She'll regret those words..." "...can't believe the nerve..." "...time someone put her in her place..."

Agatha felt a chill that had nothing to do with the evening air. The tension was palpable, and she couldn't shake the feeling that this retreat was a powder keg waiting to explode.

As the group's heated discussion began to simmer down, the sudden whir of helicopter blades cut through the evening air.

Heads turned as a sleek, black helicopter descended onto a nearby clearing, kicking up a cloud of dust.

"What on earth?" Nigel muttered, shielding his eyes.

From the helicopter emerged a striking woman in her late thirties. Her long, auburn hair was swept back in a stylish updo, and she wore a designer safari outfit that looked more suited to a fashion shoot than the rugged Botswana wilderness. As she approached the group, her stiletto heels sinking slightly into the soft ground, her piercing green eyes scanned the faces around the fire.

"Darlings, so sorry I'm late," she announced, her voice carrying a hint of a Southern drawl. "I'm Scarlett Beaumont. I assume you've all heard of me?"

Eleanor's eyes narrowed. 'Ah, yes. The 'queen of bodice-rippers.' I wasn't aware you were joining us."

Scarlett's smile didn't waver, but a dangerous glint appeared in her eyes. "Eleanor Price. Still bitter about being wrong, I see. My last book hit the New York Times bestseller list for 20 weeks. I believe your review called it 'a trashy escapade not fit for the discount bin'?"

"I stand by every word," Eleanor replied coolly.

Agatha cleared her throat, attempting to diffuse the tension. "Ms. Beaumont, welcome. We weren't expecting—"

"Of course you weren't, dear," Scarlett cut her off, not even glancing in Agatha's direction. "I'm a last-minute addition. When you're as in-demand as I am, schedules tend to be fluid. I had my agent arrange a private helicopter. Can't be expected to rough it like the rest, can I?"

Naomi, who had been quiet, spoke up. "Your 'Passion in the Savanna' series was quite popular in South Africa."

Scarlett beamed. "Of course it was, darling. My books resonate with real people, not just stuffy critics." She shot a pointed look at Eleanor.

Victor, ever the peacemaker, stood up. "Ms. Beaumont, welcome to our retreat. I'm sure we're all looking forward to learning from each other's diverse experiences."

"Oh, I'm sure," Scarlett said, her tone suggesting she doubted there was much she could learn from this group. "Now, who do I speak to about my accommodations? I assume there's a luxury suite?"

As Scarlett sashayed towards the lodge, leaving a wake of muttered comments and raised eyebrows, Agatha couldn't help but feel that the dynamics of the retreat had just shifted dramatically. The tension in the air was almost palpable, and she noticed Eleanor scribbling furiously in her notebook, her knuckles white around her pen.

The evening wound down with an undercurrent of unease. As Agatha headed to her room, the whispered conversations she overheard did nothing to settle her nerves.

Naomi Ndlovu's voice carried a hint of admiration mixed with resentment as she muttered to Oliver White, "Who does she think she is? Arriving by helicopter... though I must admit, it's a power move."

Oliver nodded, his eyes darting around nervously. "Yes, quite the entrance. But did you see Eleanor's face? It's about time someone put her in her place. These critics think they can make or break us with a few words."

From the direction of the bar, Agatha caught Nigel Thompson's exasperated tone as he spoke to Victor Reynolds. "This retreat is turning into a circus, I tell you. First Eleanor with her holier-than-thou attitude, and now this romance diva. How are we supposed to get any real work done?"

Victor's calm reply was too low for Agatha to hear, but she noticed Scarlett Beaumont lingering nearby, a satisfied smirk playing on her lips as she eavesdropped on the conversations around her.

As the group began to disperse for the night, Agatha felt a tap on her shoulder. It was Emma and Lorraine, both grinning mischievously.

"We have a surprise for you," Emma said, her eyes twinkling.

Lorraine nodded, adding, "Oui, something to make this... rustic experience a bit more bearable."

Curious, Agatha followed them to her cabin. There, sitting on the rickety desk, was a beautiful Hermes 3000 typewriter.

"We brought it with us," Emma explained. "Packed in one of Lorraine's oversized suitcases."

"I... I can't believe it," she finally managed, her voice trembling. "I've always wanted one of these. I went to a typewriter type-in when I was a kid and got to try one just like this. I fell in love with it right then."

She ran her fingers gently over the smooth metal casing, tracing the elegant curves of the machine. "I used to dream about having my own Hermes 3000, imagining all the stories I could write with it. But they were always so expensive, and there were always more practical things to spend money on."

Agatha looked up at her friends, tears glistening in her eyes. "You two are amazing," she said, pulling them both into a tight hug. "I can't believe I actually have one now. My very own Hermes 3000."

"Well, every writer needs the right tools," Emma said, beaming at Agatha's reaction.

"Oui, and now you can channel your inner Agatha Christie," Lorraine added with a wink.

As Agatha sat down at the desk, her fingers hovering over the keys, she couldn't help but feel a surge of excitement despite the tensions of the day. This typewriter represented more than just a tool for writing—it was a symbol of her dreams, her passion for mysteries, and the support of her friends.

"Thank you both, truly," Agatha said, her voice soft but filled with gratitude. "This means more to me than you can know."

As she typed out a few experimental words, relishing the satisfying click of the keys, Agatha glanced around the dimly lit lodge. The tension between the authors, the isolated location, the eclectic mix of personalities—it was almost too perfect. *If this were a mystery novel, the first body would be found any minute now,* she thought wryly.

4

LURKING SHADOWS AND DEADLY SECRETS

T he soft glow of pre-dawn light filtered through the threadbare curtains of Agatha's cabin, rousing her from a fitful sleep. The events of the previous evening —the tension-filled introductions, Scarlett's dramatic arrival, and the precious gift from her friends—swirled in her mind as she blinked away the remnants of troubled dreams.

Agatha swung her legs over the side of the creaky bed, her bare feet meeting the cool, rough-hewn wooden floor. She padded over to the small window, drawing back the curtains to reveal a world bathed in the ethereal light of an African dawn.

"Well, Mike," she murmured to her faithful schnauzer, who was already wagging his tail in anticipation of their morning routine, "shall we see what this Botswana morning has in store for us?"

She slipped on a light cardigan over her pajamas and stepped out onto the small deck behind her cabin. The air was crisp and carried the earthy scent of the bush, a stark contrast to the stuffy interior of the cabin. Agatha unlatched the gate to the modest fenced area, allowing Mike to trot out and explore.

"Don't go too far, buddy," she called softly, her voice seeming unnaturally loud in the stillness of the morning.

Returning to the deck, Agatha settled into one of the weathered chairs surrounding a small table. She placed her laptop on the rough surface, the modern device looking oddly out of place in the rustic setting. As she waited for it to boot up, she closed her eyes and let the sounds of the awakening wilderness wash over her.

The distant call of a fish eagle pierced the air, followed by the rhythmic buzzing of cicadas. Then, unexpectedly, a deep, resonant roar echoed across the landscape, causing Agatha to start.

"Was that...?" she whispered to herself, her heart racing. The sound was a stark reminder of just how far from civilization they truly were.

As the sun climbed higher, painting the sky in hues of pink and gold, Agatha sipped her coffee, savoring the rich aroma and the rare moment of solitude. The caffeine slowly worked its magic, sharpening her senses and pushing away the lingering unease from the night before.

Her thoughts drifted to the Hermes 3000, and a smile played on her lips. She longed to feel its solid presence and the promise it held, but a glance at her watch made her pause.

"Oh no, Mike! We're going to be late for breakfast," Agatha exclaimed, jumping up from her chair. "We'll have to check on the typewriter later. Emma and Lorraine will be waiting for us."

She hurried back inside, quickly changing into safari-appropriate attire and running a brush through her hair. Mike watched her with curious eyes, tail wagging in anticipation of their outing.

"Come on, boy," Agatha called, grabbing her sunhat and slipping on her walking shoes. "Let's go see what culinary adventures await us this morning."

As they stepped out of the cabin, the African sun now fully risen and warming the air, Agatha couldn't shake the nagging feeling about the typewriter. But the growling of her stomach and the thought of Lorraine's inevitable dramatic entrance to breakfast pushed the concern to the back of her mind.

"I'm sure it's fine," she muttered to herself as she and Mike set off down the path towards the dining area. "After all, who would want to steal a typewriter in the middle of the African bush?"

THE SMALL CAFÉ in the lodge was buzzing with early morning activity as guests shuffled in for breakfast. Agatha, Emma, and Lorraine settled at a corner table near the open windows, which overlooked the sprawling savannah. The air was still crisp, with the distant sounds of birds calling out as the sun slowly rose.

Agatha glanced around the room, taking in the mix of bleary-eyed tourists and smartly dressed locals. In one corner, she noticed Victor Reynolds, the quiet biographer, sipping coffee while scribbling in a small notebook. At a table near the buffet, Naomi Ndlovu was engaged in an animated conversation with Oliver White, their voices just low enough to be indistinct.

"Do you think they have anything decent for breakfast?" Emma asked, eyeing the rather uninspiring buffet setup.

"Well, I saw some croissants," Agatha said, pointing at a basket across the room. "I don't think we can go wrong with those."

Lorraine let out a dramatic sigh. "If only our dear Eliza were here." She paused. "I'm sure if she were baking, breakfast would be a hit. Alas, we must make do." She waved off the croissant suggestion. "Non, non. This morning we are going local." She stood and made her way to the counter where a small display of pastries had been laid out.

When she returned, she triumphantly placed a plate on the table, piled high with round golden balls of dough and what looked like dry biscuit-like treats. The aroma of freshly fried dough and a hint of buttermilk wafted up from the plate.

Agatha raised an eyebrow. "What... exactly are those?"

Lorraine sat down with a flourish, grinning. "Mes amies, welcome to the wonders of magwinya and buttermilk rusks."

Emma leaned in closer, poking one of the dough balls with her fork. "Mag-what-now? Lorraine, how do you even know about these?"

Lorraine's eyes sparkled with mischief. "Oh, ma chérie, I've been doing my research. I spent hours last night poring over travel blogs, local cuisine websites, and even chatted up that charming waiter at dinner. I'm practically a walking encyclopédie of Botswanan breakfast delicacies now."

Agatha raised an eyebrow, amused. "So, in other words, you have absolutely no idea what these actually taste like?"

Lorraine waved a hand dismissively. "Bah! Details, details. La vie est une aventure, mes amies!"

"La vie what?" Agatha asked, her brow furrowed.

"Life is an adventure, my friends!" Lorraine translated with a dramatic flourish. She leaned forward, her eyes twinkling with excitement as she gestured towards the plate of unfamiliar pastries. "Now, let me enlighten you about our exotic breakfast options."

Picking up one of the golden, dough balls, she held it up like a professor displaying a rare artifact. "This, mes chéries, is magwinya," Lorraine continued, her accent a mix of French and attempted African. "Or, as I like to call them, beignets africains. They're deep-fried balls of dough, crispy on the outside, soft on the inside." She took a dramatic bite and closed her eyes in exaggerated bliss. "Mmm, magnifique!"

Emma hesitantly picked one up and sniffed it. "It looks... pretty heavy."

"Of course it's heavy," Lorraine said, waving a hand. "It's le petit déjeuner. You need sustenance. None of this light and fluffy nonsense. And these," she added, gesturing to the rough, biscuit-like rusks, "are buttermilk rusks. Think of them like biscotti, but for serious tea drinkers. They're twice-baked, meant to be dunked into your coffee or tea."

She picked one up and tapped it lightly on the table with a comical 'thunk'. "Hard as a rock on their own, but perfect once you dip them. I'd say they're great for both dunking and home defense, if needed."

Agatha took a rusk and tapped it on the table lightly. "Good heavens, this could double as a weapon."

Emma eyed the rusk warily. "I think I'll stick with the magwinya. At least they're less likely to chip a tooth."

Lorraine laughed. "Oh, ma chérie, where's your sense of adventure? Now, let's dunk these little rocks and see how they transform!"

Just then, Nigel Thompson strode past their table, his face set in a scowl. He paused, eyeing their plate of local delicacies with disdain. "I hope you ladies aren't foolish enough to upset your stomachs with that local rubbish. There's a perfectly good English breakfast on offer."

Lorraine shot him a look that could curdle milk. "Some of us, Monsieur Thompson, prefer to embrace local culture rather than cling to outdated colonial attitudes."

Nigel harrumphed and moved on, leaving a wake of tension behind him.

Lorraine laughed, turning back to Agatha and Emma. "Now, where were we? Ah yes, the rusks. Dunk it or use it as a doorstop, your choice. But trust me, once it soaks up your coffee, it's delicious. A bit rustic, yes, but that's part of the charm."

Emma, still eyeing her magwinya suspiciously, finally took a bite. Her eyes widened in surprise. "Oh! It's... actually really good. The outside is crispy, but the inside is so soft and slightly sweet."

Lorraine gave her a smug look. "Of course, my dear. I know my pastries. Now dunk that rusk into your tea and embrace the local experience."

Agatha smiled as she dunked her rusk into her coffee, feeling the hard biscuit soften as it absorbed the liquid. The rich, buttery flavor bloomed as she took a bite. "You know, I could get used to this."

"See?" Lorraine said, happily munching on another magwinya. "We didn't come all this way just for croissants. Magwinya and rusks—they're the real deal. Next thing you know, I'll have you trying mopane worms."

Emma nearly choked on her tea. "I think I'll stick with the magwinya, thanks."

Lorraine grinned. "Baby steps, darling. Baby steps."

As they continued their breakfast, Agatha couldn't help but notice Eleanor Price watching their table with an oddly intense expression. She leaned in close to Nigel, whispering something that made his face darken even further. Agatha filed the observation away, wondering what could be causing such interest in their simple breakfast choices.

As they finished their breakfast, Agatha noticed Eleanor Price abruptly stand up from her table, her chair scraping loudly against the floor. The critic's face was set in a grim expression as she strode purposefully towards the café exit.

"Well, someone's in a hurry," Lorraine remarked, raising an eyebrow. "Perhaps the local cuisine didn't agree with her delicate sensibilities."

Emma chuckled, but Agatha remained silent, her eyes tracking Eleanor's movements. Just as Eleanor disappeared through the doorway, Nigel Thompson's head snapped up from his newspaper. He glanced around furtively before folding the paper with unnecessary force and rising from his seat.

"How curious," Agatha murmured, watching as Nigel followed Eleanor's path out of the café, trying and failing to appear nonchalant.

Lorraine leaned in, her eyes sparkling with interest. "Ooh, do you think there's something going on between those two? A secret rendezvous, perhaps?"

"Lorraine!" Emma admonished, though she couldn't hide her own intrigued smile.

Agatha shook her head, her brow furrowed in thought. "I'm not sure, but they both looked rather tense. I wonder if their professional disagreements are spilling over into personal territory."

As if on cue, a clatter from across the room drew their attention. Naomi Ndlovu had knocked over a glass of water, sending ice cubes skittering across the floor. As she bent to clean up the mess, Agatha noticed her hands were shaking slightly.

"Is everything alright, Naomi?" Agatha called out, concerned.

Naomi's head jerked up, her eyes wide. "Oh! Yes, yes, everything's fine. Just... just a bit clumsy this morning, that's all." She laughed, but the sound was strained and unconvincing.

Agatha frowned, wondering what could be troubling the usually composed Naomi. She stood up, decision made. "Girls, would you mind taking Mike back to your room? I think I'd like to take a short walk, clear my head a bit. You know, think about the plot of my book."

Emma looked puzzled. "Are you sure? We could come with you..."

"No, no," Agatha said, smiling warmly. "I just need a few minutes alone to organize my thoughts. Writer's block, you know how it is."

Lorraine gave her a knowing look. "Of course, darling. We'll make sure little Mike is comfortable. Won't we, Emma?"

Emma nodded, still looking slightly concerned. "Alright, if you're sure. Don't wander too far, though. Remember what the guide said about wildlife."

"I'll be careful," Agatha assured them. "I'll meet you back at the room in a bit."

As she left the café, Agatha's mind was racing. Eleanor and Nigel's hasty departures, Naomi's odd behavior – something was definitely amiss. And while she knew it wasn't really any of her business, she couldn't help but be curious. After all, as a future mystery writer, observing people and their quirks was part of her job.

Stepping out into the African sunshine, Agatha took a deep breath, enjoying the warm air and the distant calls of exotic birds. She set off down a nearby path, her thoughts drifting between the curious interactions she'd witnessed and the plot of her next novel.

Agatha trudged along the dirt path, her mind swirling with theories about the retreat's mysterious events. The plot of her mystery novel intertwined with the real-life peculiarities she'd observed here—perhaps her protagonist could stumble upon similar inconsistencies? She glanced at her watch, startled to see that hours had slipped away while she'd been lost in thought and crafting mental revisions. The late afternoon sun cast long shadows through the trees, creating an eerie atmosphere that matched her mood. As she rounded a bend, she spotted Emma and Lorraine in the distance, Mike trotting happily between them.

"Agatha!" Emma called out, waving enthusiastically. "We thought we'd surprise you with a little welcome committee."

Lorraine's eyes twinkled with mischief. "Oui, ma chérie! We couldn't let you wander these wild African paths alone. Who knows what dangers lurk in the shadows?" She wiggled her fingers dramatically, earning an eye roll from Emma.

Agatha couldn't help but smile, grateful for her friends' company. "You two are a sight for sore eyes. How's Mike been behaving?"

"Like a perfect gentleman," Emma replied, reaching down to ruffle Mike's fur. "Though he's been rather interested in that old cabin we passed earlier."

As if on cue, Mike's ears perked up, his attention drawn to something in the distance. Agatha followed his gaze, her breath catching in her throat as she noticed a shadowy figure slipping out of the abandoned cabin's doorway.

"Did you see that?" Agatha whispered, her heart racing.

Lorraine nodded, her usual joviality replaced with uncharacteristic seriousness. "Oui, it seems our little retreat has an uninvited guest. How très mystérieux!"

Before anyone could react, Mike let out a sharp bark and bolted towards the cabin, pulling free from Emma's grasp.

"Mike, no!" Agatha called out, but it was too late. The schnauzer disappeared into the darkened doorway of the cabin.

Emma and Lorraine exchanged worried glances. "We'd better go after him," Emma said, her voice tinged with concern.

Agatha nodded, leading the way as they cautiously approached the weathered structure. The wooden steps creaked ominously under their feet as they climbed onto the porch.

"Hello?" Agatha called out, peering into the gloom. "Mike?"

Silence greeted them, broken only by the sound of Mike's paws scrabbling on the wooden floor inside.

Lorraine cleared her throat nervously. "Well, mes amies, shall we venture into the unknown? Perhaps we'll find a secret passage to Narnia!" Her attempt at humor fell flat in the tense atmosphere.

Taking a deep breath, Agatha pushed open the door. Dust motes danced in the dim light filtering through grimy windows. As their eyes adjusted to the darkness, they saw Mike standing stock-still, his tail pointed straight out behind him.

And then they saw why.

Sprawled face-down on the floor, illuminated by a shaft of fading sunlight, lay a motionless figure.

Agatha's blood ran cold as she took in the scene before her. The stillness of the body left little doubt about the person's condition.

"Oh, mon Dieu," Lorraine gasped, her hand flying to her mouth. "Is that...?"

Emma nodded grimly, unable to complete the thought that hung heavy in the air.

As the trio stood frozen in shock, the distant roar of a lion echoed across the savanna, a haunting reminder of the wild and unpredictable world they now found themselves in. The eerie silence that followed was suddenly broken by a loud snap of a twig outside the cabin. They all jumped, their nerves already frayed by their grim discovery. Agatha whirled around, her heart pounding, to face the open doorway. The fading light cast long shadows across the threshold, and in that moment, one chilling thought gripped them all: Someone was out there, watching them...

5

THE TROUBLE WITH TYPEWRITERS

Agatha's eyes darted between the motionless figure on the floor and the open doorway. The snapping twig outside set her nerves on edge, but they couldn't leave without investigating further.

"We need to see who it is," Agatha whispered, her voice barely audible.

Cautiously, they approached the prone form. Emma reached out with a trembling hand and gently turned the body over. A collective gasp escaped their lips as Eleanor's lifeless face came into view.

"C'est Eleanor!" Lorraine exclaimed, her voice a mix of shock and dismay.

As they stood frozen in disbelief, Mike's insistent whining drew their attention to a corner of the room. There, partially hidden by shadows, sat a typewriter that looked eerily similar to the Hermes 3000 typewriter Emma and Lorraine had just gifted her.

"Mon Dieu, Agatha!" Lorraine gasped. "Isn't that your—"

"My new typewriter," Agatha finished, her voice hollow. "But how...?"

Emma, ever practical despite her evident shock, spoke up. "We don't know for certain it's yours yet, Agatha. But either way, we need to call the police right away. And we shouldn't touch anything else."

As Agatha stood rooted to the spot, her eyes fixed on her typewriter, Lorraine's gaze darted nervously around the room. Suddenly, she let out a dramatic shriek. "*Sacrebleu!* What is that?" she cried, pointing at a small object on a dusty shelf.

Momentarily distracted from their grim discovery, Agatha and Emma turned to look.

Perched awkwardly between a stack of crumbling books and a rusted lantern was a troll doll—one of those odd little figurines from the '90s. Its wild tuft of frizzy brown hair stuck out in all directions, and its plastic eyes gleamed unnervingly in the dim light. Time had dulled its colors, giving it a vaguely sinister air.

Lorraine's eyes widened in horror. She frantically began to make the sign of the cross, muttering, "*Au nom du Père, et du Fils, et du Saint-Esprit.*"

"Lorraine, what on earth are you doing?" Agatha asked, her tone a mixture of exasperation and confusion.

"*Can't you see?*" Lorraine hissed, still crossing herself. "That... that *poupée vaudou!* It has my hair color! *Mon Dieu,* someone's made a voodoo doll of me. I'm next!"

Despite the gravity of the situation, Emma couldn't suppress a small snort. "Lorraine, that's not a voodoo doll. It's a troll doll —from the '90s. It probably belonged to a previous guest... or got left behind during a renovation."

Lorraine paused mid-cross, her cheeks flushing. "Oh. Well, one can never be too careful, n'est-ce pas? Although," she added, eyeing the doll critically, "I must say, my hair is much more chic than that frizzy mess."

Agatha shook her head, a mix of exasperation and fondness

for her friend momentarily overshadowing her shock. "Lorraine, focus. We have a real problem here."

"Oui, oui, of course," Lorraine nodded solemnly, though she still eyed the troll doll suspiciously. "But perhaps we should... comment dit-on... exorcise this cabin, just to be safe? That doll may not be voodoo, but it certainly looks like it has some evil intentions with that hair!"

As Emma fumbled for her phone to call for help, another snap echoed from outside. Agatha moved cautiously towards the door, peering into the gathering dusk. The unseen watcher was still out there, and now they had a murder to contend with.

"Do either of you have the local police number?" Agatha asked, her voice tight with tension. "Or should we try to get back to the lodge and report this?"

"What's even the equivalent of 911 in Botswana?" Lorraine whispered, her eyes darting nervously around the cabin.

Emma shook her head. "No signal out here. We might have to go back."

"Leaving the scene of a crime?" Lorraine whispered dramatically. "Isn't that, how you say, tampering with evidence?"

Agatha took a deep breath, trying to think clearly despite the shock. "We don't have much choice. We need to report this, and quickly. But one of us should stay here, just in case..."

Lorraine, who had been uncharacteristically quiet, suddenly gasped. "Mon Dieu! What if this isn't just a one-time thing? What if there's a... how you say... a serial killer on the loose?"

The word 'serial killer' seemed to echo in the dusty cabin, making the situation feel even more dire. Agatha and Emma exchanged worried glances.

"Let's not jump to conclusions," Agatha said, trying to keep her voice steady. "But Lorraine's right that we don't know what we're dealing with here. We need to be careful. Very careful."

As if in response to her words, a floorboard creaked somewhere in the cabin, making all three women flinch in startled unison. Mike let out a low growl, his ears pricked forward.

"Did you hear that?" Emma whispered, her eyes wide.

Agatha nodded slowly, her heart pounding. The creaking could have been the old cabin settling, but what if it wasn't? What if they weren't alone after all?

Lorraine's eyes widened in horror. "Oh non, non, non! There's no way I'm staying here, ma chérie. What if Eleanor's ghost comes back for revenge?" She gestured wildly at the troll doll on the shelf. "And I am not leaving myself alone with that... that cursed poupée! Who knows what dark magic it might work while you're gone?"

Despite the gravity of the situation, Agatha couldn't suppress a small smile. "Lorraine, it's just a harmless troll doll."

"Ha!" Lorraine scoffed dramatically. "That's exactly what it wants you to think. One minute it's an innocent toy, the next it's riding around on a broom, cackling like a witch. No, thank you!"

Emma shook her head, torn between amusement and exasperation. "All right, Lorraine. You and I will go back to the lodge and alert the authorities."

"Agatha, are you okay staying here with Mike?"

Agatha nodded, her hand instinctively reaching down to pat Mike's head. "We'll be fine. Just hurry back, okay?"

As Emma and Lorraine prepared to leave, Lorraine cast one last suspicious glance at the troll doll. "Au revoir, you frizzy-headed demon," she muttered.

"Don't even think about following us!"

With that, Emma practically dragged Lorraine out of the cabin, leaving Agatha alone with Mike and the grim scene before her. As their footsteps faded into the distance, Agatha couldn't help but feel a chill run down her spine. The cabin suddenly seemed much darker and more ominous.

Mike whined softly, pressing against her leg. Agatha

scratched behind his ears, grateful for his comforting presence. "It's okay, boy," she whispered, more to herself than to Mike. "We'll be alright."

But as another twig snapped outside, Agatha wasn't so sure. It was going to be a very long day.

THE WAIT SEEMED ENDLESS. Agatha had positioned herself near the cabin's entrance, Mike alert at her feet, while keeping Eleanor's body in her peripheral vision. She couldn't bring herself to look directly at it again.

The sound of vehicles approaching broke the oppressive silence. Headlights swept across the cabin walls as multiple cars pulled up outside. Mike's ears perked up, but remained steadfast at Agatha's side.

"Hello?" a deep voice called out. "This is the police. Anyone inside?"

"Yes," Agatha called back, her voice shakier than she'd intended. "I'm in here."

Heavy footsteps mounted the cabin's weathered steps. A tall, broad-shouldered man appeared in the doorway, his flashlight beam cutting through the gloom. He had deep brown skin that gleamed in the harsh light, high cheekbones, and thoughtful eyes that seemed to take in every detail at once. Despite the late hour, his khaki uniform was well-pressed, and his alertness suggested years of experience with similar situations.

"I'm Inspector Thabo Khumalo," he announced, his voice carrying both authority and a gentle timbre that somehow put Agatha slightly more at ease. His gaze swept the room, taking in the scene with methodical precision. "Your friends told us what happened. Are you Mrs. Royale?"

"Ms.," Agatha corrected automatically. "Yes, I'm Agatha Royale."

The inspector nodded, then gestured to the crime scene techs waiting outside. As they filed in with their equipment, his eyes fell on the Hermes 3000. "That's an interesting piece of evidence," he murmured, studying the vintage machine.

Before Agatha could respond, a familiar voice rang out from outside.

"Mon Dieu! I told them not to leave you alone in here with that evil doll!" Lorraine burst through the doorway, Emma close behind her, trying to hold her back.

"Ma'am, this is now a crime scene—" Inspector Khumalo began, but Lorraine was already in full flow.

"Inspector, you must check that doll on the shelf! It has my exact hair color. C'est très suspicieux, non?" She turned casually toward the typewriter, her voice light, almost absentminded. "Isn't it strange, Inspector, that Agatha's typewriter ended up here? Emma and I had it specially delivered just last night—in my suitcase, no less."

The moment the words left her mouth, the temperature in the room seemed to drop.

Agatha froze. Emma shot Lorraine a horrified look.

Lorraine blinked, then paled. "Oh dear. I—I didn't mean it like that. I just meant it shouldn't be here. Not that Agatha— Oh, mon dieu..."

The inspector's expression remained professionally neutral, but Agatha caught the smallest twitch at the corner of his mouth. His gaze shifted to the typewriter, dark eyes narrowing as they moved from the machine to Agatha's face, studying her with renewed interest. The atmosphere in the cabin seemed to thicken, the tension palpable as the weight of Lorraine's words settled over them.

"Your typewriter, Ms. Royale?" Inspector Khumalo asked, his

deep voice deliberately measured. He pulled a small notebook from his pocket and clicked his pen, the sound unnervingly sharp in the silence.

Agatha felt her stomach drop as his attention fixed on her. What had been a shocking discovery was quickly transforming into something far more ominous. The inspector's professional demeanor couldn't mask the subtle shift in his posture—he was now looking at her not just as a witness, but as something else entirely.

"I... yes," Agatha admitted, silently cursing Lorraine's runaway tongue.

"Now, if you'll all step outside," Inspector Khumalo continued, his voice calm but authoritative, "I need to ask each of you some questions about tonight's events." As they headed toward the door, he added, almost casually, "And Ms. Royale, we'll need to discuss how your typewriter ended up here."

Agatha's stomach clenched. Somehow, she had a feeling this was going to be a very long and complicated investigation.

AT THE LOCAL POLICE STATION, later that evening... a stern-faced officer led them into separate interrogation rooms. Agatha found herself in a small, stuffy space with stark white walls and a metal table that had seen better days. Inspector Khumalo entered, carrying a manila folder and wearing an expression that made her stomach clench.

"Ms. Royale," he began, settling into the chair across from her, "let's discuss your typewriter." He placed several photographs on the table. They showed Eleanor's body, and beside it, the Hermes 3000 with what appeared to be blood spatter on its corner. "Our preliminary examination suggests this was the murder weapon."

Agatha felt the blood drain from her face. "But... that's impossible. I just received it as a gift yesterday evening."

"Yes, your friend Ms. Dubois was quite vocal about that." He made a note in his file. "The typewriter was positively identified as a Hermes 3000, matching the description of your gift."

"We don't even know for sure if it's mine," Agatha protested weakly. Khumalo's expression remained impassive. "The police already checked your room, Ms. Royale. Your typewriter isn't there."

Agatha felt as if the floor had dropped out from under her. The evidence was mounting against her with frightening speed.

"Tell me, Ms. Royale, where were you between 10 AM and noon today?"

"I was taking a walk to clear my head and think about my book." Agatha paused. "I had breakfast with Emma and Lorraine earlier - they can verify that. Then I went for a walk alone while they took Mike back to their room."

"And during this... solitary walk, did you encounter anyone?"

"No," Agatha admitted, her heart sinking. "I was deliberately seeking some quiet time to think."

"So you have no alibi for the time period when our medical examiner estimates Ms. Price was killed."

"Inspector, I wasn't anywhere near that cabin during my walk. I only discovered it when I met up with Emma and Lorraine afterward. They had come to walk back with me, and that's when we all saw someone slip out of the cabin door. Mike noticed it first and ran after the figure. That's the only reason we went to investigate - we had to follow Mike. That's when we..." She swallowed hard. "That's when we found Eleanor."

"And your typewriter just happened to be there too?" The inspector's tone remained skeptical.

"Someone must have taken it from my cabin," Agatha

insisted. "I certainly didn't bring it there. Why would I move my brand new gift to an abandoned cabin?"

The inspector leaned forward. "Let me be direct, Ms. Royale. We have a murder weapon that belongs to you, no signs of forced entry into your cabin, and no alibi. Additionally, we've uncovered some interesting information about your relationship with Eleanor Price."

"My relationship? I barely knew her!"

"According to several witnesses, she publicly criticized your presence at the retreat yesterday, suggesting you weren't qualified to be here." He paused. "That must have been humiliating."

Before Agatha could respond, there was a commotion outside. Lorraine's voice carried through the walls.

"This is ridiculous! We brought that typewriter as a gift! Are you suggesting we planned this? Mon Dieu, I can barely plan my weekly menu!"

Inspector Khumalo's expression remained neutral. "Your friends seem quite protective of you, Ms. Royale. Perhaps protective enough to help you arrange an alibi?"

"What? No!" Agatha protested. "Emma and Lorraine had nothing to do with this."

"And yet they provided you with the murder weapon." He pulled out three passports from his folder. "I'm afraid I'll need to hold onto these. None of you will be leaving Botswana until this investigation is concluded. Ms. Royale, you are our primary suspect, and your friends are being held as potential accomplices."

From the next room, Emma's voice rose in protest. "This is absurd! We're mystery book lovers, not murderers!"

"Oui!" Lorraine's voice chimed in. "The only thing Agatha has ever killed is a houseplant! And that was purely accidental!"

Despite the gravity of the situation, Agatha had to suppress a hysterical laugh. Trust Lorraine to bring up her notorious black thumb at a time like this.

Inspector Khumalo gathered his papers. "For now, you're free to return to the lodge, but don't leave the premises. We'll be watching." He stood, then added, "And Ms. Royale? I suggest you think carefully about who might have had access to your cabin last night. Sometimes the most obvious solution isn't the correct one."

As they were escorted out, Agatha found Emma and Lorraine waiting in the reception area. Emma looked pale but determined, while Lorraine had progressed from crying to muttering rapid-fire French under her breath.

"What do we do now?" Emma whispered as they huddled together.

Agatha squared her shoulders. "We find out who really killed Eleanor. Because whoever did this didn't just commit murder – they tried to frame me for it."

"Oui!" Lorraine declared, suddenly energized. "We shall investigate! Like real détectives!" She paused, then added hopefully, "Though perhaps we could stop for a croissant first? All this drama has made me hungry."

Emma rolled her eyes, but Agatha smiled. They might be suspects in a murder investigation, trapped in a foreign country, but at least they were in it together. Now they just had to prove their innocence – preferably before Lorraine stress-ate every pastry in Botswana.

6

PASSPORTS, POLICE, AND PLOTTING

The cabin felt unusually silent, the air thick with unease as Agatha, Lorraine, and Emma tried to piece together the day's events. The sharp knock on the door shattered the tension, making all three jump.

Agatha hurried to the door and opened it, revealing the tall, commanding figure of Inspector Thabo Khumalo. He stood in the fading daylight, his wide-brimmed hat casting a shadow over his serious expression.

"Ms. Royale," Khumalo began, his deep voice steady but serious, "you and your friends need to come to the lodge immediately."

"Is something wrong?" Agatha asked, her heart pounding.

Khulamo's gaze was steady, giving away little. "We're gathering all the guests to discuss the situation. Ms. Price's death requires immediate attention, and everyone's presence is necessary."

Lorraine appeared behind Agatha, her dramatic flair already on display. "Oh, mon Dieu! Is this where you accuse us all of being suspects, like in those Agatha Christie novels?" She clutched at an imaginary set of pearls. "I hope you have a good alibi, Emma!"

Emma groaned. "Lorraine, this isn't a game."

"It's not," Khumalo confirmed, his voice firm. "The lodge is now a crime scene. We'll be discussing the next steps shortly. Please come at once."

Agatha glanced at Emma and Lorraine, then nodded. "We'll be there."

As the inspector turned and strode back toward the main building, Lorraine sighed dramatically. "Well, I suppose this is as good a time as any to unveil my theory about the brooding author in the corner. Don't you think he's just a little too quiet?"

Emma rolled her eyes but couldn't suppress a small smile. Agatha, meanwhile, grabbed her bag and followed her friends out, her mind already racing with questions about the meeting they were about to attend.

The guests began to trickle into the lodge's common area, murmurs of speculation filling the air. Nigel Thompson arrived first, flamboyantly waving away the dust from an upholstered chair before settling in with an air of practiced indifference. He muttered something about the lodge's lack of modern conveniences, earning a disapproving glance from Naomi Ndlovu, who clutched a notebook to her chest and avoided eye contact with anyone.

Scarlett Beaumont swept in next, her auburn hair gleaming in the fading light. She adjusted the collar of her designer safari jacket and surveyed the room with a faint smirk. "Well," she drawled, "isn't this quaint? Like a scene from one of those gritty survival dramas."

Victor Reynolds followed, his polished demeanor contrasting with the rustic surroundings. He exchanged polite nods with Scarlett but otherwise kept to himself, settling into a seat near the bar with a glass of water in hand.

Lorraine burst in shortly after, her dramatic flair on full display as she dramatically fanned herself with a folded brochure. "Mon Dieu, this heat! Is this a writers' retreat or a test of endurance? I half expect them to hand out medals for surviving the evening."

Emma trailed behind, casting an amused glance at Lorraine before joining Agatha, who had taken a seat near the back. Mike sat obediently at her feet, his ears perking up at every new arrival.

Oliver White arrived last, his brooding presence palpable as he quietly claimed a chair in the corner. He avoided eye contact with everyone, instead pulling out a small notebook and scribbling furiously.

Lorraine's eyes darted to Agatha, and she whispered conspiratorially, "See? I told you. Brooding murderer vibe."

Before the room could dissolve further into hushed conversations and speculative glances, Inspector Khumalo entered, his imposing figure and stern expression silencing the room instantly.

"Ladies and gentlemen," Khumalo began, his deep voice steady but firm. "Following the tragic death of Ms. Eleanor Price, it is imperative that we treat this lodge as a secured crime scene. Until further notice, no one will be permitted to leave the area without authorization. This includes international departures or long-distance travel."

"What? This is outrageous!" Scarlett Beaumont's Southern drawl pierced the silence. The glamorous romance author tossed her auburn hair over her shoulder and glared at Khumalo. "I have a book signing tour to get back to! My fans expect me to be in Johannesburg by the end of the week."

Nigel Thompson folded his arms and smirked. "Oh, spare us, Scarlett. I'm sure your 'Passion Posse' can survive without you for a few days. Besides, this is far more riveting than any of your so-called steamy sagas."

Scarlett's eyes narrowed dangerously. "Careful, Nigel. I've written villains more charming than you."

"Enough," Khumalo interjected, his tone sharp. The room fell silent. "This is not a vacation, and Ms. Price's death is not a source of entertainment. Someone in this lodge may have had a motive to harm her. Until we uncover the truth, you are all potential suspects."

A nervous cough came from Naomi Ndlovu, who adjusted her glasses and stared at her lap. "B-but what if... I mean, what if it was an accident? Maybe she fell?"

Khulamo's gaze settled on Naomi, who seemed to shrink under the weight of his scrutiny. "Ms. Ndlovu, I appreciate your optimism, but the evidence suggests otherwise. The scene was staged, and the murder weapon—a typewriter—was deliberately placed."

All eyes turned to Agatha, who paled. "I didn't do it," she blurted out, her voice cracking. "Why would I use my own typewriter? It makes no sense!"

"An excellent question," Khumalo said, his expression neutral. "And one I intend to answer. But for now, I urge everyone to remain cooperative and avoid pointing fingers prematurely."

Victor Reynolds, the suave biographer, raised an eyebrow and adjusted his cufflinks. "Surely, Inspector, you don't expect us to stay locked up indefinitely? Some of us have reputations to maintain."

Lorraine, perched dramatically on the arm of a worn leather chair, let out a theatrical sigh. "Oh, mon Dieu! Such drama over a little confinement. I, for one, am thrilled. It's like living in a real-life mystery novel! Perhaps I shall even write my memoirs when this is over."

"Hopefully they'll be better than your fake French accent," Oliver White muttered from the corner, earning an indignant scowl from Lorraine.

Khulamo's sharp whistle silenced the brewing argument. "There will be no more disruptions. Each of you will be questioned individually, and I advise against withholding information. Lies have a way of unraveling under scrutiny."

Mike, barked once, as if in agreement, drawing a ripple of uneasy laughter from the group.

"Inspector," Scarlett said, her tone suddenly sweet. "If I might suggest, perhaps starting with those who had..." She paused, choosing her words carefully. "...less-than-pleasant interactions with Eleanor?" Her gaze lingered on Nigel.

Nigel bristled. "Oh, don't play coy, Scarlett. We all know Eleanor's acid tongue didn't spare anyone here. Including you."

"And yet," Scarlett said with a sly smile, "I'm not the one who stormed off after a particularly heated breakfast debate yesterday."

Khulamo's raised hand stopped Nigel's retort. "Thank you for your input, Ms. Beaumont. Rest assured, everyone's interactions with Ms. Price will be thoroughly examined."

Victor cleared his throat. "If this interrogation is going to take all night, perhaps we could be allowed a drink while we wait?"

The Inspector's lips twitched, almost forming a smile. "You're free to use the bar. But stay within sight of the common area. And no one, I repeat, no one leaves the lodge."

As the group began to disperse in subdued murmurs, Lorraine leaned toward Agatha and whispered loudly enough for everyone to hear, "I don't know about you, but my money's on Oliver. He's got that whole 'brooding murderer' vibe."

Oliver rolled his eyes. "Thank you, Lorraine. I'll be sure to add that to my author bio."

Agatha managed a weak smile, but her mind was racing. Someone in the room had killed Eleanor and was trying to frame her. Clearing her name would require unraveling the secrets hidden among these eccentric characters—before the killer struck again.

7

THREE FRIENDS AND A MURDER

"I was thinking," Agatha blurted out as they sat in her cabin later that afternoon.

Emma and Lorraine shifted their gaze to her almost in unison.

"Whoever did this had to have been around us last night when you gave me the typewriter," Agatha continued, pacing the small space. "How else would they know about its existence, let alone where to find it?"

Lorraine, sprawled dramatically across an armchair, waved her hand. "Maybe they have a crystal ball, ma chérie. Like in that book I read where the murderer was actually a psychic who—"

"Lorraine," Emma interrupted, fighting a smile. "This is serious."

"I am being serious!" Lorraine protested. "Are they even sure Eleanor is actually dead? Because I read this fascinating mystery where they used this special herb that made someone appear dead for days. Très dramatique! He woke up in his own grave!"

Agatha and Emma exchanged looks, wondering if the stress had finally gotten to their friend.

"What?" Lorraine demanded. "It could happen! Though I suppose Eleanor didn't look very... herbed. More like... typed to death." She winced. "Désolée, Agatha. Too soon?"

"You should write your own mysteries, Lorraine," Emma said, shaking her head. "You've certainly got the imagination for it."

"Non, non. I'll leave the writing to our dear Agatha. I prefer to be the comic relief in her stories." Lorraine paused. "Speaking of which, when you write about this, make sure you describe my hair as 'luxuriously styled' and not 'stress-frizzed' like it is now."

"Can we focus?" Agatha reached into her suitcase and pulled out a notepad and several colored pens. "Let's make a list of everyone who was at the fire pit last night when you gave me the typewriter."

She uncapped a blue pen and wrote at the top of the page: "SUSPECTS - Present at Typewriter Reveal."

"Okay," Emma said, leaning forward. "Obviously Nigel Thompson was there. He was the one going on about his publishing success."

"Oui," Lorraine added. "And making Eleanor's face turn that interesting shade of purple when he mentioned his bestseller lists."

Agatha wrote down their names. "Victor Reynolds was there too, sitting quietly in the corner as usual."

"Don't forget Naomi Ndlovu," Emma contributed. "She was the one who kept checking her phone and giving Eleanor strange looks."

"And Oliver White," Lorraine chimed in. "Though he barely said two words. Very suspicious, if you ask me. The quiet ones are always hiding something." She gasped suddenly. "Like a crystal ball!"

"Lorraine!" Emma and Agatha exclaimed together.

"What about Scarlett Beaumont?" Emma asked. "She

showed up partway through, making that grand entrance about her helicopter being delayed."

"Ah yes, Madame Diva," Lorraine rolled her eyes. "She certainly seemed interested in everyone's business."

"So that's six people who knew about the typewriter. Six potential suspects," Agatha said, studying her list.

"Well, nine if you count us," Lorraine added brightly. "Though I must say, if I were to commit murder, I would choose something more elegant than a typewriter. Perhaps poisoned macarons or a very sharp baguette."

"Lorraine!" Emma exclaimed, fighting back a smile.

"I think we can safely eliminate ourselves from the suspect list," Agatha said dryly. "Unless you two are hiding some very dark secrets behind all those French pastries."

"The only thing I'm hiding is an extra croissant in my purse," Lorraine admitted. "For emergencies, you understand. Oh! And don't forget the ghost of that troll doll. Very suspicious character."

"We're not counting the troll doll," Emma said firmly.

Agatha tapped her pen against the paper. "What we need to figure out is who had the opportunity to take the typewriter from my cabin, and more importantly, why they'd want to frame me for Eleanor's murder."

"Perhaps we should make a list of who hated Eleanor," Lorraine suggested. "Though we might need more paper."

"Lorraine!" Emma scolded, but Agatha was already flipping to a new page.

"Actually, that's not a bad idea," she said. "We know Eleanor had... strong opinions about everyone's work. Maybe someone finally took offense."

"In that case," Lorraine said, reaching for a pink pen, "let me add some of those delightful comments she made about every-one's writing. I have quite the memory for insults, especially when they're delivered with such... how do you say... snobby flair?"

As they began their list, Agatha couldn't help but wonder: was the answer hidden somewhere in Eleanor's caustic critiques, or was there something deeper, something they were all missing?

"Look at this," Emma said suddenly, pointing at Agatha's list. "Almost everyone here had some kind of confrontation with Eleanor yesterday." She started counting off on her fingers. "Nigel during breakfast, Naomi at lunch, and even Scarlett right after her dramatic helicopter entrance."

"Oui, but none of them had access to Agatha's precious type-writer," Lorraine pointed out, then paused thoughtfully. "Unless... mon Dieu! What if they all worked together? Like in that Agatha Christie book where—"

"Not everyone is a secret criminal mastermind, Lorraine," Emma interrupted gently.

"Though she does have a point about access," Agatha mused, tapping her pen against the notepad. "Someone either had a key to my cabin or..."

"Or what?" Emma and Lorraine asked simultaneously.

"Or they never left the lodge after the firepit gathering." Agatha's eyes widened. "Think about it. What if someone waited until we all went to our rooms, then slipped in while I was in the bathroom getting ready for bed?"

"But wouldn't Mike have barked?" Emma asked.

"Not if it was someone he knows," Agatha replied slowly. "Someone he's friendly with."

Lorraine gasped dramatically. "Are you suggesting one of us is the killer?"

"Of course not!" Agatha shook her head. "But Mike has gotten quite comfortable with several people here. He absolutely adores Victor, for instance. And Naomi's been sneaking him treats."

"Speaking of Victor," Emma said, "did anyone else notice how calm he was when Eleanor was criticizing everyone? Almost too calm?"

"And he does have that whole 'quiet observer' thing going on," Lorraine added. "Very suspicious. Like a cat waiting to pounce. Or a troll doll plotting revenge."

"Lorraine, please stop with the troll doll," Emma sighed, massaging her temples. "We have bigger concerns right now."

"But—" Lorraine started to protest, then froze at the sharp knock on the door. They all jumped, and Mike let out a low growl.

Agatha approached cautiously and peered through the peephole, her heart pounding. "It's Inspector Khumalo," she whispered, quickly hiding their list under a magazine. Her hands trembled slightly as she opened the door.

The inspector's face was granite, his eyes sharp and assessing as they swept over the three women. "Ladies," he nodded, stepping into the room. The evening light cast long shadows across his features, making his expression even more ominous. "We've completed our preliminary forensics report."

He reached into his jacket and withdrew an evidence bag, holding it up so the harsh overhead light caught the white residue inside. "Can any of you explain why we found sleeping pill residue on the typewriter keys?"

Inspector Khumalo's gaze sharpened. "Forensics confirmed Eleanor was poisoned. We believe someone mixed the sleeping pills into her drink shortly before her death."

Lorraine's face drained of color. "Oh là là... this is not good." She sank onto the edge of the bed, her usual dramatic flair replaced by genuine fear.

"I... I never even checked on the typewriter this morning,"

Agatha admitted, her voice barely above a whisper. "I was running late for breakfast and planned to look at it later. I wasn't even certain it was mine at the crime scene until..." Her voice trailed off as the implications hit her.

Inspector Khumalo's expression remained unchanged. "So you're saying someone could have taken it without your knowledge?"

"Yes! I mean, I suppose..." Agatha ran her hands through her hair in frustration. "I was going to write this morning, but I saw the time and rushed out to meet Emma and Lorraine for breakfast. I didn't even open the case."

"The case?" The inspector's eyes sharpened. "Was the typewriter stored in a case?"

"Yes," Emma jumped in. "A seafoam green case, very distinctive. It's vintage, made of molded plastic with rounded edges and a metal latch at the front."

"Quite unique," Lorraine added, warming to the subject. "C'est très chic, actually. Not like those boring boxy cases you usually see. This one has a certain... how do you say... elegance?"

Inspector Khumalo's pen paused over his notebook. "Yet at the crime scene, the typewriter was removed from this distinctive case. Was the case found?" He directed this question to one of the officers hovering near the door.

"No sir," the officer replied. "No sign of any seafoam green case."

"Interesting," the inspector murmured, making another note. "So our perpetrator took the time to remove the typewriter from its case and bring only the typewriter to the crime scene. That suggests either knowledge of the typewriter's value or..." He left the thought hanging.

"Or what?" Agatha asked, her throat dry.

"Or they specifically wanted the typewriter to be found at

the scene," he finished, his eyes studying Agatha's reaction carefully.

The implications of his words hung heavy in the air. Someone had deliberately placed her typewriter at the crime scene—but why? And more importantly, who knew about the gift in the first place?

"Inspecteur," Lorraine leaned forward, her voice uncharacteristically serious, "only a few people even knew about the typewriter. Emma and I brought it as a surprise for Agatha. We kept it hidden in my vintage luggage until last night."

"And who else knew about this gift?" Inspector Khumalo asked, his pen poised over his notebook.

Agatha's brow furrowed in concentration. "Well, we were all excited when they gave it to me... I remember one of the lodge staff, a young woman whose name I can't recall, came by to deliver fresh towels, and she saw us unpacking it."

"Oui, and that pretentious publisher, Nigel Thompson, was lurking about," Lorraine added, wrinkling her nose. "He made some condescending comment about vintage typewriters being 'charmingly obsolete.'"

"Eleanor was there too," Emma said quietly. The name fell like a stone in the room. "She was passing by my cabin when we were carrying it to Agatha's room. She seemed... particularly interested in it."

Inspector Khumalo's pen scratched across his notebook. "And what exactly did Ms. Price say about the typewriter?"

"She asked if it was a Hermes 3000," Agatha recalled, her voice distant. "She mentioned something about how they were favored by many famous mystery writers. Then she gave me this strange look and said, 'I hope you're planning to write something worthwhile with it.'"

"Mon Dieu!" Lorraine exclaimed. "I had forgotten about that! She was quite... how do you say... intense about it."

The inspector's eyes narrowed. "And this conversation happened just hours before her death?"

A heavy silence fell over the room. Mike whined softly and pressed against Agatha's leg.

"There's something else," Emma said hesitantly, a slight flush of embarrassment coloring her cheeks. "Earlier at dinner, I was... well, I was eavesdropping, to be honest. Eleanor was on the phone in the corner, and I overheard her saying something about 'exposing the truth' and 'fraudulent claims.' I couldn't hear who she was talking to, but she seemed very upset."

"Why didn't you mention this before?" Inspector Khumalo asked sharply.

"I... I didn't think it was relevant until now," Emma admitted, wringing her hands. "Everything happened so fast with finding her, and then the typewriter..."

"Anything else any of you would like to share?" The inspector's tone suggested this wasn't really a question. "Any other conversations or suspicious behavior you've 'forgotten' to mention?"

Lorraine opened her mouth, probably to mention the troll doll again, but Emma quickly cut her off. "No, Inspector. That's everything we can think of."

"Very well." Inspector Khumalo closed his notebook with a decisive snap. "Ms. Royale, I'll need you to come to the station tomorrow morning to make a formal statement about your typewriter. Eight AM sharp." He turned to Emma and Lorraine. "You two as well. And ladies... don't discuss this case among yourselves anymore. We wouldn't want any other... memory lapses."

After he left, Agatha sank onto the bed, her head in her hands. "How did this happen? Yesterday I was just a bookstore owner on a writing retreat, and now I'm a suspect in a murder investigation."

"Non, non," Lorraine said firmly, sitting beside her. "You are not a suspect. You are... how do you say... a person of interest?"

"Not helping, Lorraine," Emma muttered.

"What I mean is," Lorraine continued, undeterred, "someone is clearly trying to frame you, ma chérie. But why? And why use your beautiful typewriter?"

Agatha lifted her head, a determined glint in her eye. "Those are exactly the questions we need to answer. Eleanor was arguing with someone about 'exposing the truth.' What truth? And who would want to silence her?"

"Agatha," Emma warned, "the inspector just told us not to discuss the case."

"Non," Lorraine said, surprising them both with her forceful tone. "The inspector told us not to discuss it amongst ourselves. He said nothing about conducting our own... how do you say... investigation?"

8

MIDNIGHT MUSINGS AND MORNING MYSTERIES

Later that night, Agatha lay in her bed tossing and turning, the weight of being a murder suspect in a foreign country pressing heavily on her mind.

Mike, who had been sleeping peacefully at the foot of the bed, lifted his head at her restlessness, his dark eyes reflecting concern in the dim light.

"Sorry, little guy," she whispered, reaching over to stroke his soft fur. "Didn't mean to wake you." Her eyes drifted to the digital clock, its harsh red numbers showing 3:15 a.m. "What's going to happen to you if I go to prison?"

Mike held her gaze for a moment before laying his head back down, his gentle snoring resuming within minutes.

Agatha smiled despite herself, finding comfort in her faithful companion's uncomplicated response. She settled back against her pillow, closing her eyes as the wild symphony of the savannah drifted through her window. "Tomorrow we'll start figuring this out, buddy," she murmured. "Soon we'll be back home in Bristol Lake, where the only midnight chorus is the neighborhood dogs."

THE NEXT MORNING FOUND AGATHA, Emma, and Lorraine gathered at what had quickly become their regular breakfast table. Lorraine was engaged in her typical morning ritual of analyzing the breakfast offerings while simultaneously stuffing pastries into her purse, wrapped carefully in paper napkins.

"I barely slept a wink last night," Agatha confessed, stirring her coffee absently.

Emma yawned. "I was the opposite—collapsed the moment I got back to my cabin and didn't move until my alarm went off."

"Mon amies," Lorraine interjected, pausing her pastry-pilfering operation, "I had the most intriguing thought before I dozed off over my novel last night. Perhaps whoever is trying to frame you, Agatha, is the same person who invited you to this retreat?" She glanced around conspiratorially before continuing, "After all—no offense, ma chérie—but have you noticed that all the other guests are successful authors?"

Emma gasped. "Lorraine!"

"No, she has a point," Agatha said thoughtfully. "Why would they invite a small-town bookshop owner to a prestigious writers' retreat?"

"But how would they even know about you?" Emma mused, taking a bite of her pastry. "Unless... the murder was planned before anyone arrived here."

"Mon Dieu! Emma, you're brilliant!" Lorraine exclaimed. "What if the killer attended one of your Mystery Book Club meetings? Or perhaps visited the bookstore during an author tour?"

Lorraine's excitement suddenly deflated, and she let out a theatrical sigh. But unlike her usual flair, this one lingered with something heavier. Her shoulders drooped, and her eyes drifted into the distance, unfocused. For a rare moment, Lorraine fell silent—her lips slightly parted, as if caught off guard by a memory she hadn't meant to find. The sparkle that usually danced in her expression flickered out, just for a moment.

"What's wrong?" Emma and Agatha asked in unison.

"I brought some of Eliza's pastries with me," Lorraine admitted sheepishly. "But when I went to indulge last night, I found them half-eaten by some mysterious creature! Only tiny bites remained of my precious scones and éclairs!" She clutched her chest dramatically. "How can I survive such trauma?"

Agatha and Emma exchanged amused glances. "I think being accused of murder might be slightly more traumatic," Agatha noted dryly.

"Oui, oui, you're right," Lorraine conceded. "But these were meant to be our comfort food during this crisis!"

Their conversation was interrupted by Mike's sudden departure from their table. The three women watched in surprise as he bounded across the room to greet a young housekeeper, his tail wagging with familiar enthusiasm.

"Who is she?" Emma asked, setting down her coffee cup.

"I have no idea," Agatha replied, watching Mike's enthusiastic greeting with growing curiosity.

"Neither do I," Lorraine chimed in, momentarily forgetting about her ruined pastries.

They exchanged puzzled looks.

Agatha continued to observe their interaction, her detective instincts fully awakened. The young housekeeper, who couldn't have been more than twenty-five, bent down gracefully to pet Mike's head. Her uniform was crisp and neat, her long brown hair neatly braided, suggesting she had just started her shift. With practiced subtlety, she slipped Mike what appeared to be a treat from her pocket.

"She certainly came prepared to see him," Emma whispered,

her keen sense for detail picking up on the deliberate nature of the interaction.

Lorraine leaned forward, nearly knocking over her coffee cup in her eagerness to get a better view. "Oui, this is most suspicious. Look how familiar they are!"

The housekeeper then turned and moved toward the doorway with an air of purpose that caught Agatha's attention. She stopped abruptly, her posture changing as she began speaking with someone just outside their line of sight. Though Agatha couldn't see the person directly, a masculine shadow stretched across the hallway leading to the bathrooms. The shadow's height and broad shoulders suggested someone of considerable size.

"Can either of you see who she's talking to?" Agatha asked, trying to shift in her seat for a better angle.

Emma shook her head. "No, but whoever it is, she seems... nervous." She nodded toward the housekeeper's hands, which were fidgeting with her apron.

"The plot thickens," Lorraine murmured, her eyes sparkling with intrigue. "First Mike knows her, and now this clandestine meeting in the shadows? C'est très mystérieux!"

They exchanged puzzled looks. "Now how exactly does Mike know her?" Agatha wondered aloud, her detective instincts starting to tingle.

Agatha shifted her gaze as Lorraine suddenly rose from her chair. "Excusez-moi, but the ladies room is calling," she announced with her typical dramatic flair.

Agatha and Emma watched as Lorraine made her way toward the bathroom, her heels clicking rapidly against the tile floor. As she passed the young housekeeper, Lorraine's steps faltered. Her hand flew to her mouth, eyes widening in apparent shock at whoever the maid was speaking with. She quickened her pace, practically running the final few steps before disappearing into the bathroom, the door slamming behind her.

Agatha glanced down at Mike, who had returned to sit contentedly by her chair. "Just how do you know that young woman, boy?" she asked, scratching behind his ears. Mike simply licked her hand in response, his tail wagging happily, oblivious to her concern.

"Emma," Agatha whispered urgently, leaning across the table, "that woman's a housekeeper. She would have access to every cabin in the lodge." The implications suddenly hit her. "What if she was in my cabin?"

Emma's eyes widened. "You don't think..." she paused, lowering her voice, "she could have taken your typewriter?"

Before Agatha could respond, a blood-curdling scream erupted from the bathroom, followed by what sounded like Lorraine's voice crying out, "Mon Dieu! Au secours!"

The dining room erupted into chaos. Hotel staff rushed toward the bathroom, guests abandoned their breakfasts, and curious onlookers began gathering in the hallway.

Agatha and Emma exchanged alarmed looks before jumping to their feet, Mike at their heels as they hurried to join the growing crowd outside the bathroom.

As they pushed through the bathroom door, they found Lorraine perched precariously on top of a toilet, her safari outfit hiked up around her knees, both hands pressed against the stall walls for balance. In the corner, an enormous rat sat on its haunches, looking more annoyed than threatening as it stared up at her. The creature was the size of a small housecat, its whiskers twitching with what could only be described as disdain.

"Mon Dieu! C'est un rat mutant!" Lorraine shrieked, her French accent growing thicker with each passing second. "It's going to eat me alive!" She caught sight of Agatha and Emma in

the doorway and her voice took on a theatrical tone of martyr-
dom. "My darlings, please tell Maurice, my beloved goat, that I
love him. Take care of him for me—he only eats organic lettuce
and requires classical music at bedtime!"

As Lorraine began frantically crossing herself and muttering
rapid-fire French prayers, a distinguished-looking man hurried
into the bathroom. Mr. Rajesh Patel, the hotel manager, cut an
elegant figure in his perfectly tailored charcoal suit, his salt-and-
pepper hair swept back in dignified waves. His warm brown eyes
crinkled with embarrassment as he surveyed the scene.

"My sincerest apologies, madame," he said, his British-
Indian accent carrying a note of practiced calm. To everyone's
astonishment, he bent down and scooped up the enormous rat
with practiced ease. "I see you've met Frank. He's quite the
escape artist."

"Frank?" Emma echoed incredulously.

"Yes, my pet rat," Mr. Patel explained, stroking the creature's
head affectionately. "He's actually quite sweet. Would you like to
pet him?" He took a step toward Lorraine, holding Frank out like
a furry peace offering.

"Non! Non! Non!" Lorraine scrambled higher on her precar-
ious perch, nearly losing her balance. "Keep that monster away
from me! I don't care if his name is Frank or Fred or François—
it's still a rat the size of a small lion!"

"Actually, he's a Gambian pouched rat," Mr. Patel offered
helpfully. "They're quite intelligent and—"

"I don't need his curriculum vitae!" Lorraine interrupted,
still refusing to climb down. "Just... just take him away. S'il vous
plaît," she added, remembering her manners even in crisis.

As the manager retreated with his unusual pet, Lorraine
finally allowed Emma and Agatha to help her down from her
porcelain throne. Her legs were shaking, but her dignity
remained surprisingly intact.

"Not a word of this to anyone," she warned, straightening her outfit. "Especially about Maurice the goat."

As they filed out of the bathroom, still stifling their laughter at Lorraine's dramatics, Agatha caught sight of the mysterious housekeeper. The young woman stood at the far end of the hallway, her attention fixed on someone in the distance. Following her gaze, Agatha's amusement evaporated as she recognized the figure—Nigel Thompson. The two exchanged a silent nod, a gesture so subtle it might have gone unnoticed by anyone not looking for it.

But Agatha was looking. And suddenly, the morning's comedy seemed far less amusing.

9

SUSPICIONS AND SETTING THE STAKES

The next morning, a staff member from the lodge pulled Agatha aside and told her that Inspector Khumalo wanted to speak with her. Reluctantly, she made her way to the dimly lit lodge office, nerves building with every step. Agatha sat stiffly in the dimly lit lodge office, the wooden beams above her head creaking slightly as if the room itself were judging her. Inspector Khumalo stood by the window, his posture rigid as he flipped through a notepad. His sharp brown eyes flicked up to meet hers, and she felt her stomach churn.

"Miss Royale," he began, his voice calm but laced with authority, "you mentioned you were taking a walk around the lodge grounds near the time of the incident. Can you name anyone who might have seen you or can confirm your whereabouts?"

Agatha's hands clenched the hem of her cardigan. "No," she admitted. "I was alone. Lorraine and Emma knew I planned to take a walk, but they didn't actually see me out there."

Khumalo nodded slowly, making a note. "Your typewriter

was used in the attack. Care to explain how something from your locked cabin ended up beside the victim?"

"I... I can't," Agatha stammered. "It was secured in my room. I have no idea how anyone accessed it."

He tilted his head, his expression unreadable. "No signs of forced entry, yet your typewriter is at the center of a murder. That's a hard coincidence to ignore."

"Inspector, you have to believe me. I didn't kill Eleanor." "No one said you did, Miss Royale..." he paused deliberately, "at least not yet." Agatha's heart sank.

He sighed, closing his notepad. "For now, Miss Royale, you are a person of interest. I advise you to stay within the lodge grounds and refrain from interfering with the investigation."

Agatha nodded, though her mind was already racing. "Of course, Inspector," she murmured.

BACK IN THE MAIN LODGE, the atmosphere was tense. Conversations hushed as Agatha entered the dining area for breakfast. She could feel the weight of their stares, the whispered speculations prickling at her back.

"Oh, look who's here," Scarlett Beaumont drawled, her red lips curving into a smirk. She leaned back in her chair, twirling a strand of her perfectly styled hair. "Agatha Royale, our resident murder suspect."

Naomi Ndlovu, seated beside Scarlett, avoided Agatha's gaze, her hands trembling slightly as she poured tea. Nigel Thompson, ever the provocateur, chuckled darkly. "If you ask me, it's always the quiet ones. Isn't that right, Agatha?"

Agatha squared her shoulders, refusing to let their words rattle her. "If you have something to say, Nigel, say it outright. Or do you prefer hiding behind insinuations?"

Nigel's smile faltered, but before he could retort, Emma appeared at Agatha's side, her presence a reassuring anchor. "Ignore them," Emma whispered. "Let's sit over there."

They found a quiet corner, and Lorraine soon joined them, her dramatic entrance punctuated by the clinking of her bracelets. "Mon dieu, the tension in this room! I've seen more warmth at a funeral." She leaned in, her voice lowering to a conspiratorial whisper. "Don't let them get to you, Agatha. We'll figure out who really did this."

Agatha offered a small, grateful smile. "Thank you, both of you. I just... I need to clear my name before this gets any worse."

Emma nodded. "Let's start by figuring out who had the opportunity to take your typewriter."

LATER THAT MORNING, Agatha and Emma sat in their cabin, a makeshift detective's board taking shape on the small desk. Pieces of paper with hastily scribbled notes were scattered across the surface.

"Eleanor had plenty of enemies," Emma said, tapping a pen against her chin. "But who had access to your cabin?"

Agatha's thoughts drifted to the housekeeper from the previous day. "The staff have keys," she mused. "The housekeeper was in here yesterday morning. She seemed... peculiar."

"Peculiar how?" Emma asked, her green eyes narrowing.

"She lingered near my desk longer than necessary," Agatha said, frowning. "At the time, I thought I was imagining things, but now..."

Their conversation was interrupted by a faint knock at the door. Agatha exchanged a glance with Emma before rising to answer it. The housekeeper stood there, her shy smile in place, carrying a cleaning caddy.

"Good morning, madam," she said. "I've come to tidy up your room."

Agatha hesitated, then stepped aside. "Of course. Come in."

The woman moved with quiet efficiency, but Agatha's eyes were sharp, watching every movement. The housekeeper lingered by the desk again, her fingers brushing lightly against the papers stacked beside the laptop.

"Do you always work alone?" Agatha asked, her tone casual.

The housekeeper glanced up, her expression carefully neutral. "Yes, madam. I prefer it that way. Less noise."

Agatha nodded, her mind racing. As the housekeeper gathered her things and left, Emma joined her at the window. They watched silently as the woman walked briskly down the path, hesitating briefly before turning left toward Nigel's cabin.

"That's odd," Agatha muttered, motioning for Emma to follow. They stepped outside to get a clearer view, confirming where she was heading

Lorraine joined them, her bracelets jingling. "Mon amie, it looks like Nigel's cabin also needed cleaning."

"Yes, it does," Agatha observed, a puzzled look on her face. She gestured to the other cabins around them, including Emma and Lorraine's. "But why would she skip all these cabins and head straight to his?"

Emma nodded. "Good question."

"Oui, and my cabin needs cleaning for sure," Lorraine said, crossing her arms. "I was reading in bed last night, drinking some warm milk, and I spilled it during a very anxious part of the book." She rummaged in her purse and produced the book, showing the cover to Agatha and Emma.

Agatha smiled. "I read this one. It's excellent. I love how—"

Lorraine interrupted with a finger to her lips. "Shhhhh... no spoilers, please. Don't ruin it for me."

"Sorry, Lorraine." Agatha pretended to lock her lips with invisible keys.

"Let's focus on the real problem here," Emma whispered, pointing toward Nigel's cabin.

Agatha and Lorraine shifted their gaze in the direction Emma indicated. They observed as Nigel stepped out of his cabin with the housekeeper. The two seemed intimate, their conversation punctuated with flirtatious laughter.

"Hmmm, they look like they know each other very well, don't they?" Agatha said.

Emma and Lorraine nodded.

"We need to talk to the housekeeper and find out what she knows," Agatha said. She paused, her mind racing. "She's the one who's been cleaning my cabin." Another pause. "What if she stole the typewriter and gave it to Nigel to plant at the crime scene to set me up?"

"Mon Dieu," Lorraine exclaimed. "That makes sense." She shook her head. "She did it for sure. The housekeeper is almost always guilty in my books."

"Lorraine, this is not a book. And besides, how many books have you read in which the housekeeper is guilty?"

Lorraine shrugged. "I don't know, can't remember, but I'm sure I've seen that before in a book."

"How can we get closer to her without making her suspicious?" Agatha asked. "We need to make her feel comfortable enough to accidentally reveal something."

"Wouldn't it be great if we could just ask Nigel directly?" Lorraine said, raising an eyebrow.

Emma snorted. "Yeah, if we had a death wish."

Agatha nodded gravely. "Exactly. If he did kill Eleanor and finds out we're onto him, we might be next."

Lorraine shivered dramatically. "That gave me the chills,"

she said, crossing herself and muttering something in French under her breath.

The tension hung thick in the room as they mulled over their options. They spent the rest of the evening brainstorming ideas, throwing out wild theories and discarding most of them. Finally, they decided their best approach was to get to know the housekeeper better during her next visit to Agatha's cabin—without raising her suspicions.

AGATHA WOKE to the sound of a knock on her cabin door. Before she could fully sit up, Emma's urgent voice came through the wood. "Agatha, wake up! Lorraine's gone!"

Groggily, Agatha got out of bed and opened the door, rubbing the sleep from her eyes. The early morning light filtered through the thin curtains behind her. Mike stirred at her feet, tilting his head curiously at Emma.

"What do you mean, she's gone?" Agatha asked, her voice still raspy with sleep.

"I checked her cabin," Emma explained, pacing the small porch. "It's empty. Her shoes, her purse—everything is gone. I thought she might be out for an early morning walk, but I've already checked outside."

A sense of unease crept over Agatha. Lorraine wasn't exactly the type to go anywhere quietly. She was usually a whirlwind of dramatic proclamations and French phrases, even when fetching her morning coffee.

"Alright, let's find her," Agatha said, throwing on a light-weight jacket over her pajamas. She grabbed Mike's leash, and he jumped off the bed, tail wagging. "Maybe she's just exploring. You know how she loves to be dramatic."

The two women and Mike ventured out into the lodge's

grounds. The sun was just beginning to rise, casting a golden glow over the rustic setting. Birds chirped merrily in the distance, and the smell of dew and earth filled the air. Yet, despite the picturesque morning, worry gnawed at Agatha.

They checked the communal areas first. The small dining area was empty, save for a few sleepy guests sipping coffee. The veranda overlooking the savanna was equally devoid of Lorraine's flamboyant presence. Just as Agatha was about to suggest checking the walking trails, the enticing aroma of something sweet and fried caught her attention.

"Do you smell that?" Agatha asked, sniffing the air.

Emma nodded, her brow furrowing. "It's coming from the kitchen."

The two women hurried toward the lodge's kitchen, Mike trotting happily beside them. As they pushed open the swinging door, they were greeted by an unexpected sight.

Lorraine stood at the center of the bustling kitchen, flour dusting her hair and apron like a halo. She was expertly flipping beignets in a cast-iron pan, her face aglow with determination. Around her, the lodge's kitchen staff watched in awe, some taking notes as she gestured dramatically with her spatula.

"Lorraine!" Emma exclaimed, half-relieved, half-exasperated. "What on earth are you doing?"

Lorraine turned to them, a triumphant grin spreading across her face. "Ah, mes amies! I could not sleep, and then I thought, why not bring a bit of Paris to this retreat? The guests deserve something magnifique for breakfast, do they not?"

Agatha exchanged a lock with Emma. "Lorraine, you're supposed to be on vacation. Not commandeering the kitchen."

Agatha leaned toward Emma and whispered, "Does she mean bringing a little of New Orleans to this retreat?"

They laughed quietly, trying not to draw Lorraine's attention.

Lorraine waved a flour-covered hand dismissively. "Nonsense! Cooking is my therapy. Besides, look at their faces!" She gestured to the staff, who nodded enthusiastically.

"She's amazing," one of the chefs said. "We've never seen beignets made like this."

Agatha couldn't suppress a smile as she watched Lorraine's flair for the dramatic extend even to her impromptu cooking demonstration. "Alright, Lorraine. But if you're going to do this, at least let us help."

"Mais oui!" Lorraine said, handing Emma a bowl of powdered sugar. "You, dust the beignets. And Agatha, you can plate them with a touch of elegance. Presentation is everything!"

Mike barked eagerly, and Lorraine chuckled. "Ah, and for you, mon petit chien, perhaps a special treat later, oui?"

By the time breakfast was served, the lodge's dining area buzzed with delighted chatter. The guests raved about the beignets, their golden-brown exteriors giving way to soft, airy centers, perfectly dusted with powdered sugar. Even the most reserved among them couldn't resist going back for seconds.

As Agatha sat back with her own plate of the delectable pastries, she couldn't help but laugh. "Only Lorraine could turn a writers' retreat into a culinary spectacle."

Emma nodded, a smile tugging at her lips. "She has a way of making everything more colorful."

Lorraine approached their table, a satisfied look on her face. "Well, ladies? Am I not a genius?"

"You're something, alright," Agatha said with a smirk.

The three friends clinked their coffee cups together, their laughter filling the room. For a moment, all thoughts of murder and mystery faded away, replaced by the simple joy of friendship and the perfect beignet.

Unbeknownst to Agatha and Emma, Lorraine had a hidden motive for her culinary spectacle. As the last of the guests savored their beignets, the lodge's housekeeper arrived, drawn by the enticing aroma. She approached Lorraine with a warm smile, her demeanor unusually friendly. "These smell divine. May I try one?" she asked, her tone almost conspiratorial.

Lorraine beamed and offered her a plate. "Mais bien sûr! Please, tell me what you think."

As the housekeeper took a bite, her expression lit up. "Absolutely delicious," she said, nodding appreciatively. She leaned closer, adding in a low voice, "You'll have to show me how you make these. Perhaps we can trade recipes sometime?"

Agatha and Emma exchanged surprised looks, realization dawning on their faces. Lorraine's plan had worked perfectly—this entire endeavor had been orchestrated to get close to the housekeeper. Agatha smirked, shaking her head in admiration. "She always has an angle, doesn't she?" she murmured to Emma, who chuckled softly in agreement.

10

SHADOWS OF SUSPICION

Agatha woke the next morning, the accusations against her weighing heavily on her mind. The throbbing in her temples reminded her of the turbulent events of the last few days. "This headache could rival the mysteries we're caught in," she muttered, rubbing her forehead.

She shuffled to the couch, where her purse sat, and rummaged through it. "I know I had some acetaminophen in here... Oh, for goodness' sake, where is it?" Her watch told her it was just past 6 a.m. She debated heading to Emma or Lorraine's cabin but felt guilty about waking them so early. After a restless fifteen minutes of tossing and turning, she gave up on sleep, dressed, and grabbed Mike's leash.

"Let's go, Mike," she said. His tail wagged enthusiastically as they stepped outside.

The morning air was cool, and the lodge paths were silent, except for the faint rustle of leaves and the distant call of a bird. As Agatha locked her cabin door, she glanced down the road and froze. Two figures emerged from a cabin a few doors down —Nigel Thompson and the housekeeper. They stood on the porch, speaking in hushed tones. Agatha ducked behind the cover of her porch, her heart racing.

"Why would they be meeting so early?" she whispered, peering cautiously around the edge of the cabin. She watched as the housekeeper walked briskly toward the lodge's main facilities, her posture tense. Nigel lingered on the porch, lighting a cigarette, his face etched with worry.

"Today's the day I find out what you're hiding, Ms. Housekeeper," Agatha murmured before turning her attention back to her original plan. She knocked on Emma's door, and to her surprise, it was Lorraine who answered.

Lorraine looked utterly disheveled—dark circles under her eyes, hair tousled, and her pajamas wrinkled.

"Good morning," Agatha said cautiously. "Where's Emma?"

Lorraine waved a hand toward the couch, where Emma lay snoring softly. "Come in," she said, her voice subdued but tinged with her usual dramatic flair.

"You stayed here last night?" Agatha raised an eyebrow, stepping inside.

Lorraine's face clouded. "I didn't have much of a choice," she replied. "It was a terrifying night."

Emma stirred and sat up groggily. "She showed up at 3:15 a.m. banging on the door like the police were after her," she mumbled, rubbing her eyes. "What happened, Lorraine?"

Lorraine's hands flew up in an exaggerated gesture. "Mon Dieu, it was horrible! I heard someone at my door, trying to get in! The handle was turning, and then I heard a key—yes, a key —trying to unlock it!" Her voice rose with each word, her accent becoming more pronounced.

"What did you do?" Agatha asked, frowning.

"I grabbed the first thing I could—my precious books—and threw them at the door. That must have scared them off because they ran away."

"That's terrifying," Emma said, now fully awake. "We need to report this to Mr. Patel or Inspector Khumalo."

Lorraine nodded but then added, "Can we eat breakfast first? The stress of the night has made me ravenous."

Emma and Agatha exchanged smiles. "Of course," Agatha said. "But first, let's stop by your cabin. I want to see if there are any signs of a break-in."

AFTER AGREEING to eat breakfast first, the trio made their way to Lorraine's cabin. Agatha couldn't shake the image of Nigel and the housekeeper from her mind. Something about their early-morning meeting felt wrong, but she pushed the thought aside for the moment. Lorraine's cabin came into view, its curtains still drawn and door shut tight.

"Did you lock your cabin before you came to Emma's?" Agatha asked.

Lorraine nodded vigorously. "Of course! But I was too scared to stay there alone."

As they stepped inside, Agatha scanned the room. The cabin looked undisturbed at first glance, but Lorraine's collection of books—her prized possessions—were scattered across the floor near the front door.

"This is where I threw them," Lorraine explained, gesturing dramatically. "I didn't even care which ones I grabbed. Poor Victor Hugo was a casualty of the night!" She lifted a battered copy of *Les Misérables* with a mournful sigh.

Agatha bent down to examine the area near the door. The lock appeared intact, but faint scratches on the doorknob caught her attention. She pointed them out. "Look at this. Could these be from someone trying to pick the lock?"

Emma leaned in. "Possibly, but why would anyone target Lorraine's cabin? What could they have been after?"

Lorraine folded her arms, looking indignant. "It must be my books. Perhaps this is a murderer with a literary grudge!"

Agatha stifled a smile but didn't dismiss Lorraine's theory outright. "It could also be someone looking for something they think you have," she said thoughtfully. "Lorraine, did you overhear or see anything unusual before this happened?"

Lorraine tilted her head, considering the question. "Well... now that you mention it, I did hear someone walking past my cabin late last night. Heavy footsteps, not dainty like mine."

Agatha frowned. "Which direction were they headed?"

Lorraine pointed toward the cabins farther down the road—the direction of Nigel's cabin. Agatha's pulse quickened. Could there be a connection between Lorraine's intruder and Nigel's early-morning visitor?

"I think we should take this to Inspector Khumalo sooner rather than later," Agatha said. "The scratches on the lock might be evidence of an attempted break-in."

Lorraine hesitated. "Before breakfast?"

"Yes, before breakfast," Emma interjected, exasperated. "We can't just ignore this, Lorraine."

Reluctantly, Lorraine agreed, and they headed to the main lodge to find Khumalo.

INSPECTOR KHUMALO WAS in the lodge's dining area, sipping coffee and scanning a notebook when they approached. He looked up, his sharp gaze narrowing on the trio.

"Ms. Royale," he greeted, his tone neutral but laced with suspicion. "And company. What brings you here so early?"

Agatha wasted no time recounting Lorraine's ordeal, including the scratches on the lock. Khumalo listened intently, jotting down notes.

"This is concerning," he admitted. "Especially given the circumstances surrounding Ms. Price's murder. But why would someone target your cabin, Ms. Dubois?"

Lorraine opened her mouth, likely to repeat her literary-murderer theory, but Agatha cut in. "We're not sure. It could have been a random attempt, or it could be connected to the larger case. Nigel was acting suspiciously this morning, too."

Khumalo's brow furrowed. "Suspiciously how?"

Agatha described what she had seen earlier—Nigel and the housekeeper meeting outside his cabin before dawn. "It might mean nothing," she said, "but it's worth noting."

Khumalo stood, slipping his notebook into his pocket. "I'll investigate both matters. In the meantime, I'd advise all of you to stay vigilant. Report anything unusual to me immediately."

As they left the lodge, Lorraine whispered to Agatha, "What if the killer thinks I know something? What if I'm next?"

Agatha placed a reassuring hand on her friend's arm. "We'll figure this out, Lorraine. You're not alone."

As the trio sat down for breakfast, Nigel entered the dining area, his expression unreadable. Agatha watched him closely, noting the tension in his movements and the way his gaze darted around the room. When their eyes met, he quickly looked away.

"I wonder what secrets you're hiding, Mr. Thompson," Agatha thought, her mind already spinning with possibilities. And then she noticed something strange: the housekeeper, who had been so lively earlier, was nowhere to be seen.

～

TWO DAYS AFTER THE INCIDENT, Inspector Khumalo called Agatha and Lorraine to the lodge office. Lorraine looked apprehensive, clutching her vintage handbag as though it might offer her protection.

"Have you found the culprit, Inspector?" she asked, her French accent thick with nerves. "Am I safe now?"

Khumalo gave a small smile. "Yes, Ms. Dubois. You're safe. The person who attempted to enter your cabin was not a murderer."

Agatha leaned forward. "Who was it, then?"

Khumalo pulled out a small notebook. "A guest staying in the cabin next to yours. He'd had a rather heated argument with his partner and, in his frustration, mistook your cabin for his own. When he couldn't get in, he pounded on the door—until, apparently, your... unique response startled him enough to retreat."

Lorraine gasped. "He ran off because I threw books at the door?"

Khumalo nodded, dry amusement in his tone. "He told me he heard loud thuds from inside and panicked, thinking someone was about to attack him. His words were: 'I didn't know what she was throwing, but it sounded dangerous.'"

Lorraine sniffed, still offended. "My books were not weapons! Though... I suppose they served their purpose."

Agatha smirked. "You may have created a new home defense system."

Khumalo closed his notebook. "The guest was too embarrassed to come forward until I questioned him. He didn't realize he had the wrong door until later."

"Well," Lorraine said, straightening her shoulders, "at least it wasn't a murderer. But I still think he owes Victor Hugo an apology."

All three shared a relieved chuckle. But as the laughter faded, Agatha's thoughts drifted back to Eleanor's murder. With this mystery resolved, she was left with the one that still loomed largest—and Nigel Thompson remained front and center in her mind.

11

THE TRAP TIGHTENS

The following morning, Agatha sat at her desk, attempting to write. Despite her efforts, the page before her remained stubbornly blank as her mind wandered. A sudden knock at the door startled her. She stood, setting her pen aside and pacing towards the door, her voice cautious. "Who is it?"

"Housekeeping," came the reply, a soft, accented voice.

Agatha opened the door quickly, almost too eager for a distraction. A young woman in a crisp uniform stood there, holding a basket of cleaning supplies. "Good morning," she said with a polite smile. "May I clean your room?"

"Of course," Agatha said, stepping aside. She glanced at the woman's name tag: "Marie Leclaire."

Marie entered and surveyed the space. "It looks very clean here," she remarked, her gaze drifting towards the adjacent room. "Your bed is already made? Didn't you sleep here?"

Agatha smiled. "I did. I can't start my day without making my bed. It's a habit I can't seem to shake."

Marie returned the smile. "I'm the same way."

Agatha studied her for a moment, noting her graceful movements and the slight, unplaceable accent. "Where are you from, Marie? Your accent's unique."

"I'm from Belgium, but I've lived in Botswana for the past ten years," Marie replied, her tone matter-of-fact.

"That's wonderful," Agatha said. "What brought you here initially?"

Marie's response was interrupted by Mike bounding into the room, his tail wagging furiously. The schnauzer barked happily and jumped up on Marie as though greeting an old friend.

"He seems to like you," Agatha remarked, raising an eyebrow.

Marie chuckled, bending down to scratch behind Mike's ears. "Yes, madame. Every time I clean your room, he keeps me company."

"I see," Agatha said, masking her surprise. She was about to press further when Marie rose and grabbed her supplies. "Excuse me, I'll get started in the bathroom."

Agatha's curiosity was piqued. She sent a quick message to Emma and Lorraine, and within minutes, the two women arrived. Lorraine burst into the room, as dramatic as ever.

"Oh mon chère, my room needs cleaning desperately," Lorraine declared, throwing her hands in the air. "It's so full of crumbs from all the treats..." She trailed off, realizing her mistake. "I mean, it's terribly dusty."

Emma stifled a laugh. "Sounds like someone's been indulging in midnight snacks."

"And who would that someone be?" Lorraine retorted with mock indignation. "We all know how disciplined I am with my diet. Absolutely not me."

Agatha shook her head, turning her attention back to Marie as she emerged from the bathroom. "Marie, you mentioned you've been here for ten years. That's quite a long time. Have you seen many changes at the lodge?"

Marie hesitated, arranging towels on the bed. "It's always been quiet here. I came as a volunteer for animal protection, but I needed a job to support my visa. The lodge has been good to me."

"And the guests?" Agatha pressed gently. "Have you known many of them over the years?"

Marie's movements slowed. "Some," she said carefully. "Mr. Thompson, for example, is a regular. He's visited many times."

Lorraine's eyebrows shot up. "Oh? How interesting. Tell us, Marie, what's your opinion of Nigel?"

"Lorraine, behave," Emma muttered.

"What?" Lorraine said, feigning innocence. "There's nothing wrong with a little curiosity." She turned back to Marie with an exaggerated wink. "You must know him quite well."

Marie's cheeks flushed. "Not as well as you think," she said sharply. "He stays here often, but that's none of my business."

Agatha caught the flicker of unease in Marie's expression. "It must be difficult to keep things to yourself when you work so closely with the guests," she said, trying a softer approach. "Nigel seems... complicated."

Marie's jaw tightened, and she busied herself with straightening a lamp. "I don't involve myself in their lives, madame. If you'll excuse me, I have other rooms to clean."

She gathered her supplies quickly, avoiding their gazes. As she passed Lorraine, she added, "Including your dusty room."

Lorraine's mouth fell open in mock offense. "Dusty! How dare you?" she called after Marie, but the housekeeper was already gone.

Agatha watched her retreating figure, her mind spinning. Marie knew more than she was letting on. And if Nigel was as involved in this as Agatha suspected, Marie might hold the key to unraveling the mystery.

THE FOLLOWING morning Agatha sat on the porch of her cabin; her notebook open to a half-filled page of fragmented ideas. The accusations swirling around her, the tension among the retreat's attendees, and her gnawing fear for her own freedom had made focusing on writing impossible. Instead, her thoughts circled back to Nigel Thompson—his evasiveness, his sudden shifts from bravado to nervous energy, and the strange tension between him and Eleanor before her murder.

A sharp knock on her door startled her from her thoughts. Agatha's heart raced as she got up, half-expecting Inspector Khumalo's stern face to greet her. Instead, it was the young housekeeper, Marie Leclaire, holding a basket of clean linens.

"Good morning, madame," Marie said, her soft Belgian accent tinged with hesitancy. "May I clean your room?"

Agatha opened the door wider and stepped aside. "Of course. Come in."

Marie set down the basket and began her tasks with practiced efficiency. Agatha watched her, noting the subtle grace in her movements. Something about Marie seemed unusually poised for a housekeeper, as if she carried an invisible weight of knowledge.

"Marie," Agatha said casually, leaning against the wall, "I'm don't mean to pry, but I saw you and Nigel together and you honestly don't seem like don't know each other well. It actually seemed like you were very close."

Marie smiled faintly. "What are you talking about?" She seemed embarrassed.

Agatha folded her arms, her hazel eyes narrowing slightly. "You seem familiar with the guests, but you seem especially close to Mr. Thompson. It's odd—you say you don't know him well, but I've seen you two chatting more than once."

Marie froze, her fingers brushing against the edge of the counter as if searching for something to hold onto. A flicker of something—guilt? hesitation?—crossed her face. "Mr. Thompson is..." She exhaled slowly, avoiding Agatha's gaze. "He's close to the lodge."

Agatha tilted her head, unconvinced. "Go on."

"He's my godfather," Marie admitted, the words tumbling out in a rush. Her shoulders sagged as if a weight she'd been carrying had finally shifted. "My parents worked for his publishing house before they... before they passed away. He took me under his wing after that."

The room seemed to grow quieter, and Marie's voice softened, tinged with weariness. "I don't talk about it because..." She let out a dry laugh, shaking her head. "Well, people like to talk. They'd think I got this job because of him, not because I earned it. And with him being a guest here..." Her voice trailed off, her fingers fidgeting with the hem of her apron. "It's complicated."

Agatha's pulse quickened, but she kept her tone neutral. "That's kind of him. It must be comforting to have someone like family nearby."

Marie paused mid-swipe, her rag hovering over the counter. Her expression flickered—something unreadable but undeniably heavy—before her eyes dropped to the cloth in her hands. "He's not like family," she said quietly. Her voice had lost its earlier edge, replaced by something softer, almost resigned. "He's more like... an obligation."

Agatha blinked, caught off guard. "An obligation?"

Marie gave a faint, humorless laugh. "He helps, yes. But it always comes with expectations." She resumed her cleaning, her movements sharper now, as though scrubbing away more than just the surface of the counter. "And those expectations... they can feel heavier than the help sometimes."

Before Agatha could probe further, Marie straightened abruptly and resumed her work, her movements brisk.

"I'm sorry if I'm prying," Agatha said, softening her tone. "It's just that things have been so tense since Eleanor's death. Everyone seems to be carrying secrets."

Marie froze for a fraction of a second before continuing to fold a towel. "Secrets are part of life, madame. But some secrets can cost too much."

She hesitated, then added, almost to herself, "Nigel knew that... after all, he still owed Eleanor—" Marie's eyes widened. "I mean—he *would* have owed her something, if... you know, if things had been different."

The cryptic remark hung in the air. Agatha waited, but Marie didn't elaborate. Instead, she finished tidying and gathered her supplies.

"If you'll excuse me," Marie said, bowing her head slightly. "I have many rooms to clean."

Agatha followed her to the door. "Thank you, Marie. And... if you ever need someone to talk to, I'm a good listener."

Marie's lips twitched into a faint smile. "You're kind, madame. Be careful who you trust here."

LATER THAT AFTERNOON, Agatha couldn't shake the feeling that Marie's words carried deeper meaning. Determined to piece together the puzzle, she sought out Emma and Lorraine. They were lounging in the lodge's common area, Lorraine dramatically fanning herself with a travel brochure.

"Ladies," Agatha began, pulling up a chair, "I have a theory."

Lorraine perked up immediately. "Mon Dieu, tell us everything. Is it about that troll doll? Because I swear it's been moved again."

"No, Lorraine," Agatha said with a faint smile. "It's about Nigel. I think he's hiding more than his usual flair for theatrics."

Emma leaned forward. "Did you discover anything new?"

Agatha recounted her conversation with Marie, omitting the more personal details out of respect. "Marie let slip that Nigel might have owed Eleanor something. She seemed startled when she realized what she'd said, but if Eleanor had threatened to expose him, it could have ruined his already shaky reputation."

Lorraine's eyes widened. "A financial motive! Classic crime novel fodder."

Emma frowned. "But Nigel wouldn't kill Eleanor, would he? It's one thing to argue, but murder?"

"Desperation makes people do unthinkable things," Agatha said. "And Nigel's been acting more paranoid by the day. I think it's time I confront him—alone. He'll be less defensive that way."

"Alone?" Lorraine gasped, alarmed. "Darling, that's dangerous! What if he's guilty?"

"Then I'll know," Agatha said firmly.

AFTER SOME TIME spent gathering her thoughts, Agatha found Nigel in the lodge's small library, hunched over his laptop. He looked up sharply when she entered, his expression a mixture of wariness and irritation.

"Agatha," he said, forcing a smile. "To what do I owe the pleasure?"

She closed the door behind her and sat across from him. "I think we need to talk about Eleanor."

His smile faltered. "What about her?"

"I heard that you might have owed Eleanor something," Agatha said, her voice steady. "And that your career isn't as stable as you'd like everyone to think."

Nigel's face darkened. "How dare you?"

"I dare because I'm innocent," Agatha replied. "And I'm not going to sit back while someone frames me for murder."

Nigel's hands clenched into fists. "You have no idea what you're talking about. Eleanor was a parasite. She leeched off others' talent and tore them down when it suited her. If she's dead, she brought it on herself."

Agatha's heart raced at his vehemence, but she kept her tone calm. "Did she threaten you, Nigel? Is that why you killed her?"

He shot to his feet, his face flushed with anger. "I didn't kill anyone! And if you keep spreading these lies, you'll regret it."

Their argument had drawn the attention of a passing guest, who peeked into the library before hurrying away. Agatha stood her ground, meeting Nigel's glare.

"If you didn't kill her, prove it," she said. "Tell me what you're so afraid of."

Nigel stared at her for a long moment, his jaw tightening, but he offered no response. Instead, he grabbed his laptop and stormed out, leaving Agatha alone with her suspicions.

THE CONFRONTATION with Nigel haunted Agatha as she lay in bed that night, staring at the cracked ceiling of her cabin. She replayed every word they had exchanged in the library. Had she pushed him too hard? Had her accusations made him desperate enough to take drastic measures? Or had she unknowingly triggered someone else to act?

Mike stirred at her feet, letting out a low whine as if sensing her unease. She reached down to scratch behind his ears, whispering, "Sorry, buddy. I'm just overthinking everything again."

The savannah outside was alive with its nocturnal symphony —the chirping of cicadas, distant howls, and rustling underbrush. But to Agatha, it all felt like an oppressive reminder of how isolated they were from the safety of Bristol Lake. She rolled onto her side, willing herself to sleep.

Her exhaustion finally caught up with her, and her mind slipped into restless dreams filled with shadowy figures and poisoned glasses. A knock on the door jolted her awake. She blinked in the pale dawn light filtering through the curtains, heart pounding as she registered the sound again.

Rap. Rap. Rap.

Agatha scrambled out of bed and stumbled to the door. When she opened it, Emma stood there, pale and wide-eyed. Her red hair was disheveled, and her hands trembled slightly as she clasped them together.

"Agatha," she whispered, her voice barely audible. "Nigel's dead. They found him in his room this morning."

Agatha's breath hitched. "Nigel's... dead?" The words felt foreign, like someone else was speaking them. Her mind raced, grasping for clarity, for a reason—any reason—this could be happening.

Emma nodded, swallowing hard. "Inspector Khumalo is already there. It looks bad. They're saying..."

"Saying what?" Agatha demanded, stepping out onto the porch. The crisp morning air stung her skin, but she barely noticed.

Emma hesitated, her green eyes dark with worry. "They're saying it might be poison. Like Eleanor."

A chill raced down Agatha's spine. She clutched the door-frame to steady herself. "Another murder. Another suspect eliminated. And once again, the trail leads right back to me."

"We have to find Lorraine," Emma said, tugging at Agatha's arm. "She'll want to know. And we need to stick together. This is getting too dangerous."

Agatha nodded numbly. Together, they hurried down the

path toward Lorraine's cabin, their footsteps crunching against the dirt. The morning sun had barely begun to rise, casting long shadows across the lodge grounds. Agatha's thoughts raced ahead of her. She knew one thing for certain—whoever had killed Nigel was still out there, and she had to uncover the truth before it was too late.

12

THE SHADOWS DEEPEN

Lorraine flung the door open just as Agatha and Emma arrived at her cabin. She was wearing an oversized nightgown and had a sleep mask pushed up on her forehead. "What in heaven's name are you doing here so early? And why do you both look like you've seen a ghost?"

Emma took a deep breath and stepped forward. "It's Nigel. He's dead."

The color drained from Lorraine's face. She froze, gripping the doorframe. "Dead? Nigel? How... how do you know?"

"Emma heard it straight from the staff," Agatha explained quietly. "Inspector Khumalo is already at the scene. They're saying it might be poison. Just like with Eleanor."

Lorraine's eyes widened in shock. "Mon Dieu... Not again. This place is cursed. We're trapped with a killer!"

"We need to stay calm," Agatha said, trying to steady her own nerves. "Let's get dressed and head to Nigel's cabin. We need to figure out what's going on before rumors start flying."

Lorraine hesitated, then nodded, her usual dramatic flair momentarily subdued. "Give me five minutes. I need to put on something more presentable. If I'm going to be part of this horror show, I'm not doing it in my nightgown."

Emma managed a faint smile, but the tension didn't lift. Within minutes, the trio was on their way, their footsteps echoing in the early morning stillness. The weight of what awaited them pressed heavily on their minds.

They hurried along the dusty paths, Mike trotting anxiously beside them. The murmur of voices grew louder as they neared Nigel's cabin. Guests had gathered, forming tense clusters of murmuring onlookers. Eyes darted toward Agatha, some filled with fear, others suspicion.

"Move back! Everyone, keep your distance," Inspector Khumalo ordered, his voice sharp and commanding. His tall frame was silhouetted against the doorway, a barrier between the growing crowd and the scene of death.

Agatha strained to hear the conversation between two officers standing near the cabin entrance.

"Poisoning, maybe," one officer muttered. "Symptoms were consistent. Possible sleeping pills found."

"He must have been drugged first," the other replied. "There's no sign of struggle."

Agatha's stomach twisted. She tightened her grip on Lorraine's arm. "Poison. Just like Eleanor was incapacitated before she was..."

Lorraine's eyes widened in horror. "Mon Dieu... How many more people are going to die on this retreat?"

Emma crossed her arms and shook her head. "This can't be random. Someone here is systematically targeting people."

Agatha swallowed hard, her thoughts racing. It was only a matter of time before someone connected the dots and pointed fingers in her direction.

Agatha's eyes scanned the gathered guests. Victor Reynolds stood apart from the others, his face expressionless but his gaze focused on the cabin. Scarlett Beaumont appeared visibly shaken, her usual poise cracked. Naomi Ndlovu clutched a small notebook, scribbling furiously as if the act of writing might shield her from the reality unfolding around her.

Victor caught Agatha's eye and held her gaze. There was a question in his eyes—or perhaps a warning.

"They're all afraid," Emma whispered beside her. "Afraid and suspicious. You can feel it."

"We need answers," Agatha replied. "And soon."

AN HOUR after leaving Nigel's cabin, Inspector Khumalo's glare was as sharp as the questions he fired at Agatha. They stood inside the lodge's office, the air heavy with tension.

"You were seen arguing with Mr. Thompson yesterday," Khumalo said, flipping open his notepad. "One witness said you were confrontational. Care to explain?"

Agatha took a deep breath. "We had a conversation. Yes, it was heated, but I wasn't threatening him. We were discussing... personal matters."

"Personal matters?" Khumalo's eyebrows lifted. "Interesting choice of words. And now he's dead. Quite a coincidence, don't you think?"

"Inspector, I'm being framed," Agatha said firmly. "Someone is orchestrating this and using me as a scapegoat."

Khumalo leaned forward, his voice low. "Coincidence or not, two people have died with you at the center of it. Stay out of my investigation, Ms. Royale. You're under close watch."

Agatha clenched her fists but nodded curtly. "Understood."

LATER THAT EVENING, unable to shake the feeling they were missing a crucial detail, Agatha, Emma, and Lorraine crouched behind a cluster of shrubs near Nigel's cabin. The air was cool and still, the scent of damp earth and crushed grass lingering after the afternoon heat had faded. A faint glow spilled from the cabin windows, flickering across the uneven ground.

A rustle of movement made Lorraine flinch. Crickets chirped nervously as though sensing the tension. A twig snapped beneath Emma's knee, and Agatha shot her a warning look.

"Shh," Agatha mouthed.

From inside the cabin, the low murmur of voices drifted through the thin walls. The women strained to hear.

"The sleeping pills... definitely used to knock him out first," one officer said, his voice low but clear.

Agatha's pulse quickened. Sleeping pills?

"But the notebook... It's odd. Looks like there were pages torn out."

"Maybe the killer took something important," the other officer replied, a note of intrigue creeping into his tone.

Agatha's mind raced. Torn pages could mean evidence. Evidence someone didn't want anyone else to see. Her stomach tightened. What could Nigel have written that was dangerous enough to kill for?

Lorraine leaned in, her breath warm against Agatha's ear. "A torn notebook?" she whispered theatrically. "This is straight out of a murder mystery novel. Maybe it was a confession or a list of suspects."

Agatha shot her a sharp look, but Lorraine only widened her eyes innocently.

"Or a record of something incriminating," Emma added softly. Her eyes gleamed in the dim light, her voice steady despite the unease in her posture. "Something that connects the dots between Nigel and Eleanor."

Agatha's gaze shifted back to the cabin, her mind churning. Could the missing pages have contained the answers they needed? Her heart thudded against her ribs.

Just then, a shadow shifted at the edge of the clearing. Agatha's breath hitched as she spotted Victor Reynolds standing at a distance, partially concealed by a tree. His tall frame was outlined against the dark backdrop of the woods, his posture tense, his hands shoved deep into the pockets of his jacket. His gaze was locked on the cabin entrance, unmoving.

He didn't look like someone casually observing—he looked like a man with secrets to guard.

"Look over there," Agatha whispered, nudging Emma.

Emma's eyes narrowed. "Victor's here. He's watching them too."

Victor's expression was hard to read. His shoulders were rigid, and the crease between his brows deepened when the officers moved closer to the door. He was standing unnaturally still, as though trying not to be seen.

"What's he doing?" Lorraine murmured.

"I don't know," Agatha replied, her mind buzzing with possibilities. "But he's definitely nervous about something."

Lorraine sighed quietly. "Well, darling, if he's hiding something, I hope it's worth all the secrecy. Suspicious men in these situations often have a flair for dramatic revelations."

Agatha stifled a smile. Despite Lorraine's flair for drama, she wasn't wrong. Victor's presence was too pointed to ignore.

Victor's eyes flicked toward the woods, as though he sensed he was being watched. A moment later, he turned and melted into the shadows.

Agatha's breath caught. "He's leaving," she whispered.

Emma's gaze sharpened. "He knows something."

Agatha's eyes stayed fixed on the dark path where Victor had disappeared. He was hiding something—something connected to Nigel's death.

It was time to find out what.

THE NEXT DAY, Agatha spotted Marie near the staff quarters, her slight figure half-hidden behind a line of drying linens fluttering in the breeze. Marie's head was down as she folded a stack of towels, her movements brisk but tense, like someone trying to stay busy to avoid thinking.

Agatha approached carefully, the dry grass crunching under her feet. "Marie?"

Marie's shoulders jerked, and she nearly dropped the towels. She turned, her wide eyes dark with hesitation. "Ms. Royale."

Agatha lowered her voice. "We need to talk."

Marie's gaze darted past Agatha, scanning the narrow path that wound between the staff cabins. A bead of sweat rolled down her temple despite the cool morning air.

"You saw Nigel yesterday morning," Agatha said, stepping closer. "He was scared, wasn't he?"

Marie's fingers tightened around the edge of the towel. "I—I already told the police everything."

Agatha's gaze sharpened. "Marie."

Marie swallowed, her throat bobbing. "He... he said something about a deal gone wrong," she admitted, her voice barely above a whisper. "He thought someone was after him. That's all I know."

Agatha studied her, watching the tension gathering in the lines of her face. "Did he mention any names?"

Marie's eyes flicked toward the path again, her hands trembling as she tucked the folded towels into a basket. "No." Her breath hitched slightly. "Please—I told the inspector everything."

Agatha hesitated, noting the slight shake in Marie's hands and the way her shoulders hunched inward, as if trying to make herself smaller. A nervous tic—or guilt?

Marie's gaze slid toward the far end of the staff path. Agatha followed her line of sight and spotted Victor walking toward the main lodge. His eyes were downcast, but his posture was as rigid as a steel rod.

Marie's lips parted as though she were about to say something more—but then she clamped them shut and shook her head quickly. "I—I have to get back to work."

Agatha reached out, lightly touching her arm. "Marie."

Marie stiffened but didn't pull away.

"If you remember anything else—anything at all—come to me," Agatha said gently. "It might be important."

Marie's eyes flicked to Agatha's face, then toward Victor's retreating figure. A flash of conflict crossed her features before she offered a weak smile. "Alright."

She gathered her basket and hurried down the path, disappearing between the laundry lines.

Agatha remained where she stood, the soft sound of rustling sheets blending with the distant chatter of birds. A chill settled over her despite the sun breaking through the early morning mist.

Marie was hiding something. And Nigel's paranoia—his fear—wasn't just in his head.

Someone was after him.

And if Marie knew more than she was admitting, that someone might still be watching

～

AGATHA RETURNED to her cabin to find Mike growling at the door. A folded piece of paper lay on the desk inside. Her heart pounded as she opened it.

Please be careful. It would be better for you to stay out of this. Terrible things could happen... A friend.

She stared at the note, her mind racing. Someone was either warning her—or playing a dangerous game.

13

THE SHADOW LURKING

gatha couldn't shake the image of Victor Reynolds watching Nigel's cabin from a distance. His stance had been rigid, his gaze unrelenting. What had he been looking for—or hiding? The thought plagued her as she lay awake that night, listening to the unfamiliar symphony of nocturnal animals outside her window. The low grunts of distant lions, the rustle of unseen creatures, and the occasional eerie call of a hyena created a tension-filled backdrop to her thoughts. Mike stirred at her feet, sensing her restlessness.

"I need to know what you were doing there, Victor," she murmured into the darkness.

Morning came slowly, the soft orange hues of the sunrise casting long shadows across the lodge. Agatha rose with a renewed sense of determination. Emma and Lorraine were already waiting for her in the dining area, their faces reflecting the tension that had permeated the lodge since Nigel's death. Conversations around them were hushed, the other guests casting furtive glances at Victor Reynolds, who sat alone in a corner, methodically stirring his coffee. His usual composed demeanor seemed intact, but there was a stiffness to his movements, as if he were carrying an invisible burden.

"Look at him," Lorraine whispered, leaning toward Agatha. "The picture of a guilty man if I've ever seen one. What do you suppose he's thinking about?"

Agatha kept her eyes on Victor. His gaze was distant, unfocused, like a man haunted by something only he could see. "I'm going to find out."

Emma raised an eyebrow. "What's your plan? March over there and confront him?"

"Something like that," Agatha replied, pushing back her chair. "Stay here. If things get heated, I'll need you two to intervene."

As she crossed the room, Victor's eyes slowly lifted to meet hers. His hand stilled, the spoon clinking softly against the porcelain cup. For a moment, an unreadable expression flashed across his face before he composed himself, his features settling into polite detachment.

"Good morning, Ms. Royale," he greeted, his voice measured. "What brings you to my table?"

Agatha didn't bother with pleasantries. "I saw you near Nigel's cabin last night. Care to explain what you were doing there?"

Victor leaned back in his chair, folding his arms across his chest. "You've been watching me. That's interesting. Should I be worried?"

"I think that's a question you should answer," Agatha shot back. "You've been acting suspicious ever since Nigel's death. People are starting to notice."

Victor sighed, his gaze drifting to the window where sunlight filtered through the lodge's dusty curtains. "Suspicious... That's a convenient word in times like these. Everyone's looking for someone to blame, aren't they? As a matter of fact, Ms. Royale, there are witnesses to an argument you had with Nigel the day before his death. And let's not forget the lingering suspicion surrounding your role in Eleanor's demise. Perhaps the scrutiny should be on you instead."

Agatha's eyes flashed in defiance, though her heart pounded at his accusation. She leaned forward slightly, narrowing the space between them. "I'm not the one lurking around in the shadows, Victor. Suspicion cuts both ways," she countered.

"Nigel and Eleanor both ended up dead," she continued. "And you've been hovering around both crime scenes. Forgive me if that raises questions."

Victor tapped a finger thoughtfully against the table. After a long pause, he leaned forward, his eyes narrowing slightly. "You're not with the police, and I'm not a suspect. But because I have nothing to hide, I'll tell you this much: I was there because Nigel had something that could ruin me. I needed to get it back."

Agatha's eyes narrowed. "What kind of something?"

"A manuscript," Victor admitted. "He had a draft of my latest novel, and Eleanor knew about it. She was planning to write a scathing review. I couldn't let that happen."

Agatha frowned, trying to piece it together. "How did Nigel get your manuscript?"

Victor sighed, rubbing his temples. "I'm a bit paranoid about early drafts getting out. We had exchanged notes on writing once, and he took a copy of my manuscript under the pretense of giving feedback. Then he refused to return it, claiming there were issues with it—including allegations of plagiarism—and that I'd copied ideas from him."

"Plagiarism?" Agatha's frown deepened. "Did he have any proof?"

"Not that I'm aware of," Victor replied, shaking his head. "It was all part of his power game. He wanted to use my manuscript to control me, leveraging the threat of exposure to demand money. If that draft was leaked, especially with false claims like that, it would have damaged my career beyond repair."

"You expect me to believe you were just there to retrieve papers?"

Victor's jaw tightened. "Believe what you want, Ms. Royale. I didn't kill Nigel. I was trying to protect my reputation, not take his life."

Agatha studied him for a moment. His words rang true, but she couldn't ignore the tension in his voice. There was more he wasn't saying. "Do you have an alibi for the time Nigel died?" she asked.

Victor hesitated. "I was... walking near the staff quarters. Maybe one of the staff saw me, but I can't be certain. I don't recall the exact time."

"I know you don't have to tell me anything, and I appreciate you being honest with me. I just want to understand what really happened. If you do remember anything else, I'd be grateful if you let me know. Thank you, Victor."

Victor nodded curtly and returned to his coffee. Agatha walked back to her table, where Emma and Lorraine awaited her with curious expressions.

"Well?" Emma prompted.

"He says Nigel was blackmailing him with a manuscript," Agatha explained. "He claims he didn't kill him but admits to sneaking around to get it back."

"Classic motive," Lorraine muttered, nibbling on a croissant. "But is he telling the truth?"

"That's what we need to find out," Agatha replied. "I'll talk to Marie. If she saw Victor, it might clear him—at least for now."

∾

LATER THAT MORNING, Agatha found Marie in the laundry room, folding sheets with the careful precision of someone who finds comfort in routine. Sunlight streamed through the small window, highlighting the swirling dust motes and casting a warm glow across the neatly stacked linens. When Marie spotted Agatha, her eyes brightened momentarily before a shadow of sadness dimmed them again.

"Ms. Royale," Marie greeted, her voice soft as the sheets she handled. A sigh escaped her lips as she set down her folding. "It doesn't seem real about Mr. Thompson, does it? The lodge feels... different without him bustling about, complaining about everything."

"I imagine it's especially hard for you," Agatha said, leaning against the doorframe. She noticed how Marie's fingers trembled slightly as they smoothed a wrinkle from the sheet. "You mentioned he was like family to you."

Marie nodded, a small, sad smile playing at her lips. "He had his thorny side—goodness knows he could be demanding—but he remembered my birthday every year. Brought me a chocolate croissant from town." She straightened her shoulders, as if the memory itself provided strength. "Most people never saw that side of him."

"The best parts of people are often hidden beneath the surface," Agatha agreed, her voice gentle as a summer breeze. "Like treasures waiting to be discovered."

Marie's eyes glistened. "Exactly so, Ms. Royale."

Agatha hated to disturb the moment, but questions needed asking. "Marie, I wonder if you might have been near the staff quarters last night? Around the time when..." She let the words trail off delicately.

"When Mr. Thompson was killed?" Marie finished, folding her arms across her chest like a shield. "Yes, I was cleaning the corridor that leads to the storage rooms. I always do the evening shift on Thursdays." She smoothed her apron. "It helps to stay busy when the world feels topsy-turvy."

"I completely understand," Agatha said, thinking of how she'd reorganized her entire bookshop after her divorce. "Did you happen to notice Victor Reynolds in that area?"

Marie twisted the corner of a pillowcase, her brow furrowing. "Actually, yes. He walked by, looking like he had the weight of the world on his shoulders. I asked if I could help—that's my job, after all—but he just shook his head and hurried past."

"Thank you, Marie," Agatha said warmly. "That's quite helpful."

Marie stepped closer, lowering her voice to a whisper that rustled like leaves. "Please be careful, Ms. Royale. People get strange when they're frightened. They'll believe almost anything if it makes them feel safe again." Her eyes held genuine concern.

"I appreciate your worry," Agatha replied with a reassuring smile. "But sometimes the truth is what helps us feel safe again."

Marie nodded, returning to her folding with renewed purpose. "Mr. Thompson used to say he could spot a person with backbone a mile away." Her smile grew more genuine. "I think he would have liked you, Ms. Royale. You remind me of the detectives in those mystery novels he pretended not to enjoy."

As Agatha left the laundry room, the scent of fresh linens following her like a comforting ghost, she couldn't help but wonder what other secrets were hidden in the folds of this mystery—waiting, like Marie's carefully pressed sheets, to be smoothed out into the light.

THAT AFTERNOON, Agatha gathered Emma and Lorraine in her

cabin. She recounted her conversation with Victor and the confirmation from Marie.

"So Victor has an alibi," Emma summarized, tucking a strand of hair behind her ear. "But it still doesn't explain the missing pages from the notebook."

"Or who poisoned Nigel," Lorraine added, absently arranging the colorful bracelets on her wrist. "What if there's more than one person involved?"

Agatha tapped a pen against her notepad. "It's possible. If Nigel was blackmailing multiple people, anyone could have had a reason to silence him."

Emma leaned forward, her eyes bright with curiosity. "What's our next step?"

"We keep digging," Agatha said, determination warming her voice. "Someone here knows more than they're letting on. And we're going to find out who."

Mike barked in agreement, his tail wagging furiously against the wooden floor.

Lorraine chuckled softly. "At least Mike's on board."

The three women shared a moment of levity before settling into their investigation plans. But as they did, a loud crash echoed from the direction of the main lodge, followed by raised voices. Agatha's eyes widened as she sprang to her feet.

"What now?" she muttered.

They hurried to the window just in time to see Elias backing away from a toppled serving cart, china and silverware scattered across the veranda. Naomi stood nearby, arms crossed, while Scarlett gesticulated wildly, her voice carrying across the grounds though her words remained indistinct. The lodge manager hurried over with a broom, his soothing gestures doing little to calm the agitated guests.

"Just another day in paradise," Emma sighed, turning away from the window.

"At least it's not another body," Lorraine whispered, crossing herself quickly.

Agatha lingered at the window a moment longer, watching the scene unfold. The shadow of suspicion loomed larger than ever over the safari lodge, and she knew the answers they sought might be closer—and more dangerous—than they had imagined

14

LAYERS OF DECEPTION

Agatha sat on the edge of her bed, her thoughts swirling after the morning's revelations. Victor's guarded responses lingered in her mind. Could he really be innocent? Or was he simply a master manipulator?

A knock on the door broke her train of thought. When she opened it, Inspector Khumalo stood there, his expression serious but measured.

"Ms. Royale, I'm afraid I need to speak with you about Nigel Thompson's death," he said. "Could we talk in the lodge office?"

Agatha's heart sank, but she nodded. "Of course."

THE WALK to the office stretched in an uncomfortable silence, though the lodge hallway was anything but quiet. A ceiling fan clicked rhythmically overhead, while outside the open windows, afternoon birds called to one another across the savanna. Shadows danced on the wooden walls as sunlight filtered through swaying palms.

Agatha stole glances at Inspector Khumalo, whose stoic

expression reminded her of Gladys when she was hiding a royal flush during their weekly poker nights back home.

"Inspector, may I ask what exactly you're looking for?" Agatha ventured as they passed a charming display of local handcrafts.

Khumalo's steps didn't falter, but he responded in a measured tone that carried just a hint of warmth. "Answers, Ms. Royale. The truth has a way of hiding in plain sight, like a cookie jar that everyone pretends not to notice." The corner of his mouth twitched. "The question is whether you're hiding it."

Agatha's stomach churned, though the comparison to a cookie jar momentarily distracted her.

They reached the office, where a small desk fan battled valiantly against the afternoon heat. Khumalo held the door open for her, gesturing to the chair across from the desk before positioning himself near the window. His silhouette cut a commanding figure against the golden light of the afternoon sun.

"Please, sit," he said, flipping open his notepad with a practiced motion. "There are witnesses who saw you and Mr. Thompson arguing the day before his death. Would you care to explain what that was about?"

Agatha inhaled deeply, her fingers finding a loose thread on the armrest of the chair. "Nigel and I had a heated argument. He... he had a way of getting under people's skin, like sand in your bathing suit at the beach." She smiled apologetically at the casual comparison. "He accused me of being out of place here— that I didn't belong among the other writers. He mocked my work, saying I was just 'playing detective.' I lost my temper, but that was it. Words were exchanged, nothing more. I would never hurt him."

Khumalo's gaze didn't waver. "Ms. Royale, you were also a key witness when Eleanor Price was found dead. Now, with another murder at the retreat, the evidence is starting to paint a troubling picture."

"Inspector," Agatha said suddenly, leaning forward, "have you actually tried lifting that Hermes 3000 typewriter you found at Eleanor's crime scene?"

Khumalo paused, his pen hovering above his notebook. "I examined it, yes."

"Then you must have noticed how heavy it is," Agatha said, spreading her hands to indicate the size. "Nearly thirty pounds —about the weight of a Thanksgiving turkey. Someone my size could barely lift it with both hands, let alone swing it with enough force to..." She paused, swallowing hard at the mental image.

"Well, you understand. I couldn't possibly have used it as a weapon, especially not without leaving evidence of strain or injury on myself."

Khumalo regarded her thoughtfully. "An interesting point, Ms. Royale. Our technicians did mention its unusual weight when collecting it from the scene." He made a note in his pad. "Though this doesn't explain why it was there, or why you were seen near Nigel's cabin the night he died."

"Inspector, I know how this looks," Agatha said earnestly. "But someone is framing me. Nigel and Eleanor had plenty of enemies here, like bears around a honeypot. I'm not the only one they had conflicts with."

Just as Khumalo opened his mouth to respond, a firm, clear voice from the doorway interrupted them.

"She's telling the truth," Victor Reynolds said as he stepped into the room, the scent of his sandalwood cologne briefly over-whelming the musty office air.

Khumalo raised an eyebrow but didn't stop him. "And what makes you so certain, Mr. Reynolds?" Khumalo asked, his pen poised above his notepad.

"Because I was also near Nigel's cabin that night," Victor admitted, his usually perfect hair slightly disheveled. "I was retrieving a manuscript he'd stolen from me. I'd thought he might try to use it against me."

Khumalo's eyes narrowed. "And you didn't think to report this sooner?"

"I didn't want to implicate myself," Victor replied, straightening his collar with a nervous gesture that seemed out of character for the normally composed author. "But after seeing how Agatha is being treated, I realized staying silent wasn't right."

Agatha blinked in surprise. For the first time, she saw a hint of vulnerability in Victor's eyes, like catching a glimpse of a normally aloof cat playing with yarn. "Thank you," she murmured.

Khumalo sighed, leaning back in his chair that creaked like Emma's porch swing after a rainstorm. "This doesn't clear either of you, but it does give me more to consider." He closed his notebook with a gentle snap. "The typewriter weight argument is compelling, Ms. Royale. Not many women—or men, for that matter—could wield such a heavy object with the force needed. Our team will factor that into their assessment."

As he escorted them out, Khumalo added, "We'll be conducting further interviews. In the meantime, please stay within the lodge grounds. Bristol Lake's book club would be quite disappointed if their favorite shop owner didn't return home safely."

Agatha couldn't help but smile at the unexpected reference to her hometown. Perhaps Inspector Khumalo was more observant—and more personable—than she'd initially given him credit for.

❧

LATER THAT AFTERNOON, Agatha and Victor strolled slowly through the lodge's sprawling gardens. The scent of wildflowers mixed with the earthy aroma of the savanna, and a warm breeze rustled the tall grass nearby. The tension between them had eased, though the weight of unanswered questions lingered in the air like the sweet perfume of distant acacia trees.

"You really didn't have to do that," Agatha said quietly, glancing at him.

Victor slipped his hands into his pockets, his gaze distant toward the golden horizon. "I know. But I'm tired of the lies and suspicion. I'm not perfect, Agatha, but I'm not a murderer either. Nigel... he wasn't a saint, but I didn't want him dead."

A staff member, a young man named Elias, approached with a polite nod, his khaki uniform crisp despite the afternoon heat. "Mr. Reynolds, Ms. Royale, everything alright?"

"We're fine, thank you," Agatha replied, offering a small smile.

Elias hesitated, shifting his weight from one foot to the other. "Actually, I meant to speak with you both earlier but... I was embarrassed. I overheard your conversation the other day, and I wasn't sure if it was my place to say anything. But I did see Mr. Reynolds near the staff quarters last night. He was pacing, deep in thought."

Agatha's eyes widened. "That's very helpful, Elias. Thank you. And you're not the only one who believes they saw him— Marie also thought she caught a glimpse of Victor that night."

As Elias walked away, Victor exhaled, rubbing the back of his neck. "Well, that certainly helps. Looks like I've got an alibi after all."

Agatha chuckled softly. "For now. But something tells me this mystery is far from over."

They walked in silence for a moment before Victor slowed his pace. "There's something else you should know. I overheard

Naomi having a private argument with Nigel yesterday evening. Just hours before..."

"Before he died," Agatha finished for him, her voice dropping to just above a whisper. "What were they arguing about?"

Victor hesitated, his eyes scanning the grounds to ensure no one was within earshot. "I couldn't hear everything, but she was furious. Accused him of threatening to expose something about her. Said he was going to ruin everything."

Agatha's mind raced. "Expose what?"

"I don't know," Victor admitted, his forehead creasing with concern. "But what troubles me is what I saw later that night, at dinner. Naomi was seated at the table behind Nigel, and when he stepped away briefly to speak with the server, I saw her lean over and slip something into his drink."

Agatha's breath hitched. "You're saying she poisoned him?"

"I don't know for certain it was poison," Victor said quickly. "But I heard the police found sleeping pills in Nigel's system. The timing seems suspicious, doesn't it? He looked uneasy after he returned and drank from his glass. Left the table early, saying he felt unwell."

A flicker of doubt crept into Agatha's mind. Naomi had been one of the quieter attendees, staying mostly in the background, her nose often buried in a notebook. But what if she wasn't as innocent as she seemed?

She and Victor continued their walk, the sun beginning to dip below the horizon. The golden light cast long shadows across the savanna, stretching far and wide, much like the questions now circling in Agatha's mind. What could Nigel have had on Naomi?

∾

THE LATE AFTERNOON sun cast long shadows across the lodge's veranda as Agatha approached, the dusty path crunching pleasantly beneath her shoes. Emma and Lorraine were already settled in the woven rattan chairs, teacups balanced on saucers in their laps. Upon noticing her, Lorraine's face lit up with her characteristic dramatic flair.

"Mon dieu, Agatha!" Lorraine exclaimed, gesturing with her free hand while carefully balancing her teacup with the other. "You look like you've seen the ghost of Agatha Christie herself! What has happened now?"

Agatha sank into the empty chair beside them, the cushion exhaling softly beneath her weight. A gentle breeze carried the scent of brewing coffee from the lodge kitchen and rustled the leaves of the potted aloe plants decorating the veranda.

"I just had the most interesting conversation with Victor," she explained, gratefully accepting the cup of tea Emma poured for her. The familiar warmth of the porcelain against her fingers was comforting. "He's gone to Inspector Khumalo to provide me with an alibi for the night Nigel was killed."

Emma nearly spilled her tea. "An alibi? How?"

"He told Khumalo he was by Nigel's cabin that evening," Agatha said, her voice tinged with relief. "Said he didn't see me. The time he mentioned would have been right when..." She trailed off, not needing to finish the sentence.

"When poor Nigel was meeting his untimely end," Lorraine whispered, her eyes wide with intrigue. "How fortunate! I knew Victor was one of the good ones. Such distinguished salt-and-pepper hair couldn't possibly belong to a villain."

Agatha smiled despite herself. "He also mentioned overhearing a rather heated exchange between Naomi and Nigel before his death. Apparently, Nigel was threatening to expose something about her."

Emma's eyebrows rose with interest as she set the sturdy earthenware teapot back on the tray. "Expose what exactly?"

"That's just it—he wasn't specific," Agatha replied, stirring a spoonful of honey into her tea. The tiny silver spoon clinked rhythmically against the cup. "But Victor also noticed her slipping something into Nigel's drink that evening at dinner. Said he left the table looking rather unwell shortly after."

Lorraine's eyes widened to saucers. She leaned forward conspiratorially, her voice dropping to a stage whisper that was probably audible three cabins away. "Poison? How deliciously old-fashioned! Just like in 'The Mysterious Affair at Styles.' Though I do hope she was more creative than arsenic—it's been done to death, if you'll pardon the expression."

"Lorraine," Emma scolded gently, though the corners of her mouth twitched upward. "This isn't one of Agatha's mystery novels come to life. This is serious."

"Thank goodness for Victor," Agatha said with genuine relief, watching a lilac-breasted roller perch on the branch of a nearby acacia tree. "Not only has he cleared my name with Inspector Khumalo, but he's given us a solid lead about Naomi." She adjusted the napkin in her lap, smoothing out invisible wrinkles. "I was beginning to think we'd never find an ally in this place."

She took a sip of her tea, savoring its warmth. "We need to discover what Nigel had on Naomi," she continued, setting her cup back in its saucer with a delicate clink. "The motive is hiding there, I'm certain of it. And something tells me we're not the only ones digging for answers."

Just then, a startled cry pierced the peaceful afternoon, sending the roller flapping away in a flash of brilliant blue. The three friends exchanged worried glances before setting their teacups down with synchronized clinks.

"That came from the front garden," Emma said, already rising from her chair.

They hurried along the veranda and around the corner of the lodge, their footsteps falling into a synchronized rhythm on the wooden boards. The garden appeared serene at first glance —hardy desert roses and spiky grasses swayed gently in beds of red earth, and yellow butterflies danced between the sparse blossoms—but then they spotted Scarlett.

She stood frozen beside a small stone water feature, her normally perfect posture crumpled, arms wrapped tightly around herself as though she were cold despite the warm afternoon. Her face had drained to the shade of the bleached animal skull that served as an artistic centerpiece in one of the garden beds.

"Scarlett, what on earth happened?" Agatha asked, her voice gentle as she approached, the way one might address a startled springbok.

Scarlett's gaze darted toward the scrubby tree line before returning to them, her breathing still uneven. "I—I was just enjoying a walk when I sensed I wasn't alone." Her manicured fingers clutched at the silk scarf around her neck. "Someone was watching me from behind those umbrella thorn trees. When I turned, they darted away, but I caught a glimpse of them."

Emma glanced toward the scattered acacias, shielding her eyes against the slanting sunlight. "Could you make out who it was?"

"No, it was too shadowy," Scarlett replied, making a visible effort to compose herself. "But they were small—petite, really. Shorter than most people here. A woman, I think. They moved with such quickness, like a meerkat startled from its burrow." She swallowed hard. "I only saw them for a moment before they vanished between the trees."

"A small person," Agatha repeated softly, her mind spinning like the ceiling fan in her cabin. "You're absolutely certain?"

Scarlett nodded, the color slowly returning to her cheeks. "Absolutely. And they were definitely watching me. I could feel their eyes boring into my back before I turned." She shivered slightly. "It was rather unnerving."

The four women stood in silence for a moment, the only sound the distant call of a fish eagle and the gentle rustling of dry grass. The peaceful setting suddenly seemed to hold unseen dangers, like a beautiful baobab fruit concealing a bitter taste— seemingly innocent, yet potentially deadly.

15

A TASTE OF AFRICA

The morning sun streamed through the lodge's open windows, casting warm rectangles of light across the large communal kitchen. The space—normally off-limits to guests—had been transformed for the day's special activity. Wooden tables formed a large U-shape, each station equipped with cutting boards, knives, and colorful ceramic bowls. The air carried the aromatic blend of unfamiliar spices that made Agatha's nose tingle pleasantly.

"A cooking class?" Emma whispered as they entered. "After everything that's happened, we're supposed to just... cook?"

Lorraine, who had been dragging her feet about attending any lodge activities since Eleanor's death, suddenly perked up. "Mais oui! This is exactly what we need. Food brings people together, even in the darkest times." She inhaled deeply, her eyes closing in appreciation. "Those spices... I detect cardamom, coriander, perhaps a touch of harissa?"

Despite her reservations, Agatha felt a small smile tug at her lips. After days of tension, suspicion, and fear, perhaps a few hours of normalcy was exactly what they needed. Besides, observing the other guests in a more relaxed setting might reveal something they'd missed.

Chef Mandla, a stout man with an infectious smile and hands that moved with practiced precision, clapped to gain everyone's attention. "Welcome, welcome! Today, we journey through Botswana's flavors. You will learn to prepare three traditional dishes: seswaa, our national dish of pounded beef; pap, a maize porridge; and chakalaka, a spicy vegetable relish that will wake up your taste buds!"

He assigned them to stations, deliberately mixing up the retreat guests. Agatha found herself alongside Victor and Naomi, while Emma was placed with Scarlett and a quiet older man she hadn't spoken with yet. Lorraine, to everyone's amusement, was partnered with Inspector Khumalo, who had apparently been invited to join as a courtesy.

"I didn't realize you'd be joining us, Inspector," Agatha remarked as he rolled up his sleeves.

"Even investigators must eat, Ms. Royale," he replied with the barest hint of humor. "Besides, I find people are more forthcoming when their hands are busy."

Lorraine immediately took charge of her station, tying an apron around her waist with a dramatic flourish. "Now, Inspector, you must let me show you the proper way to chop these onions. It's all in the wrist, you see." She demonstrated with surprising skill, her knife a blur as she reduced an onion to perfect, uniform pieces.

Khumalo raised an eyebrow, clearly impressed. "You've done this before."

"Cooking is like breathing to me, monsieur," Lorraine replied with a wink. "Essential and automatic."

At Agatha's station, the atmosphere was considerably more tense. Victor methodically chopped vegetables while maintaining a steady stream of pleasant, seemingly innocent conversation. Naomi, meanwhile, barely spoke, her movements jerky and uncertain as she struggled with the unfamiliar ingredients.

"Have you ever cooked African cuisine before, Agatha?" Victor asked, his tone friendly.

"No, but I enjoy experimenting with new recipes," she replied, watching him carefully. Despite his pleasant demeanor, she couldn't shake the feeling that something was off about him. "What about you?"

"I spent some time in North Africa researching a book. The spices are different here, but there are similarities." He handled his knife with practiced ease, his movements confident and precise.

Naomi dropped her knife with a clatter, muttering an apology as she bent to retrieve it.

"Are you alright?" Agatha asked her quietly.

Naomi glanced up, her eyes darting nervously to Victor and back. "Fine. Just... clumsy today."

Chef Mandla moved around the room, offering guidance and encouragement. When he reached their station, he beamed at Agatha's perfectly diced tomatoes. "Excellent technique! You have done this before, yes?"

"Just lots of practice making stew for book club meetings," she replied, warming to his enthusiasm.

"Ah, books and cooking—both feed the soul!" He moved on to help Naomi, gently correcting her grip on the knife.

Across the room, Emma was engaged in an animated conversation with the older man at her station, their laughter carrying across the kitchen.

Scarlett appeared to be making an effort to join in, though her smile seemed forced.

As they progressed to cooking the meat for the seswaa, the

room filled with the rich aroma of slow-simmering beef. Chef Mandla demonstrated the traditional technique of pounding the meat once it was tender.

"In Botswana households, this is often done by the men of the family," he explained, rhythmically crushing the meat with a wooden tool. "It requires strength and patience."

"Perhaps you would like to try, Inspector?" Lorraine suggested, offering Khumalo the pounding tool with an exaggerated curtsy.

To everyone's surprise, Khumalo accepted, rolling up his sleeves further and approaching the task with the same careful attention he gave to his investigations. His methodical pounding soon gave way to a more natural rhythm, and a subtle transformation came over him—his shoulders relaxed, and the perpetual furrow in his brow smoothed.

"You're a natural, Inspector!" Chef Mandla praised. "You would make a fine Botswanan husband."

Lorraine clapped her hands in delight. "Oh, what a compliment! And well-deserved. The Inspector has many hidden talents, it seems." She shot Khumalo a look that made the stoic man actually blush.

The lesson continued, and slowly, the tensions that had defined the retreat began to ease, if only temporarily. The simple act of creating something together—of measuring, chopping, stirring, and tasting—provided a welcome respite from the shadow of death that had hung over them.

As they prepared the chakalaka, Agatha noticed Naomi gradually becoming more engaged, her initial nervousness giving way to concentration.

"I've never been much of a cook," Naomi admitted quietly when they found themselves momentarily alone. "My mother tried to teach me, but I was always too busy reading to pay attention."

"It's never too late to learn," Agatha replied, surprised by this small confidence. "Books will keep, but a good meal brings immediate joy."

Naomi offered a hesitant smile. "I suppose that's true." She glanced across the room at Scarlett, her expression darkening slightly. "Some things are worth the wait, though."

Before Agatha could probe further, Chef Mandla called for everyone's attention. "Now, we combine our creations for the feast! Bring your dishes to the center table."

The group gathered around the large harvest table on the lodge's covered patio, their completed dishes arranged buffet-style. Morning had given way to early afternoon, and a gentle breeze carried the scent of wild sage from the savanna. The retreat participants—who had been avoiding each other for days —now sat together, united by the simple pleasure of a meal they had created themselves.

"Before we eat," Chef Mandla announced, "it is our custom to thank those who came before us and to recognize that food is a blessing to be shared." He spoke a few words in Setswana, his voice melodic and reverent, before translating: "We are stronger together than apart, and what nourishes one nourishes all."

Lorraine, moved by the sentiment, raised her water glass. "A toast, then! To strength in community, even when far from home."

Glasses clinked, and the atmosphere shifted subtly. For the first time since Eleanor's death, conversation flowed naturally. Emma discussed photography with the older man from her cooking station, who turned out to be a wildlife photographer contributing to the retreat's promotional materials. Victor charmed a group of staff members with questions about their families and traditions. Even Scarlett seemed to relax slightly, laughing at something Lorraine said.

Agatha found herself seated beside Inspector Khumalo, who was savoring the seswaa with evident appreciation.

"This reminds me of my grandmother's cooking," he remarked. "She believed you could tell a person's character by how they approach a meal."

"And what does my approach tell you?" Agatha asked, curious.

Khumalo considered her for a moment. "That you pay attention to details others might miss, and you're not afraid to try new things." His gaze sharpened slightly. "Both useful qualities in your current... hobby."

Agatha smiled. "I'm not sure 'hobby' is the right word for being accidentally involved in a murder investigation."

"Perhaps not," he conceded. "Though you seem to have a talent for it."

Across the table, Lorraine was regaling a group with tales of her culinary adventures in Paris, her accent growing more pronounced with each anecdote. "...and the chef, he was furious! 'Madame,' he says to me, 'one does not simply add truffle oil to a classic béchamel! It is sacrilege!' But I tell him, 'Monsieur, with all due respect, your sauce needs that little something extra.' We argued for ten minutes before he tasted it himself and—voilà!— he had to admit I was right." She beamed triumphantly. "His restaurant now serves 'Béchamel à la Lorraine' as their signature dish."

Emma caught Agatha's eye and shook her head fondly, mouthing "completely made up... the woman has never even been to Paris" with a grin.

Agatha leaned closer so only Emma could hear and whispered, "Hey, this is a literary retreat, so it's a good place to make up stories."

As the meal progressed, Agatha observed the shifting

dynamics around her. Despite the momentary harmony, under-currents remained. Naomi kept her distance from Scarlett, though she occasionally cast longing glances in her direction. Victor maintained his charming facade, but Agatha noticed his eyes constantly scanning the room, assessing, calculating.

Yet for all the complexities and dangers that surrounded them, this moment—sharing food, listening to stories, experiencing another culture—felt like a precious gift. A reminder that even in the midst of darkness, community could still be found.

As the gathering began to disperse, Chef Mandla approached Agatha with a small, cloth-wrapped package.

"A gift," he said, presenting it to her. "Traditional spices for your home kitchen. To remember Botswana when you have returned to your own community."

Touched by the gesture, Agatha accepted the package, the rich aromas reminding her that some memories of this place would be worth preserving.

"Thank you," she said sincerely. "I'll treasure this." As she joined Emma and Lorraine to walk back to their cabins, Agatha felt more centered than she had in days. The mystery wasn't solved, the danger hadn't passed, but for a few hours, they had been reminded of the simple pleasures that made life worth protecting—good food, shared stories, and the connections that bind people together, even when far from home.

Mike greeted her at the cabin door, his tail wagging enthusiastically as he picked up the unfamiliar scents on her clothing.

"Yes, I brought you something," she laughed, pulling a small piece of beef from a napkin in her pocket. "Don't tell Chef Mandla I broke the rules."

As Mike happily accepted the treat, Agatha's mind returned to the investigation. Surprisingly, the brief respite had cleared her thinking rather than distracting her. Sometimes, she reflected, you needed to step back from a problem to see its shape more clearly.

And now, with renewed focus, she was ready to continue unraveling the deadly mystery that had unexpectedly ensnared them in this beautiful, dangerous place.

16

NAOMI'S SECRET

The distant calls of the savanna's nocturnal creatures echoed in the night, blending with the rhythmic chirping of insects. Agatha sat on the back porch of her cabin, a warm cup of tea cradled in her hands as she watched the moonlight cast long shadows over the dry grass. Mike dug enthusiastically in a corner of the porch, his small paws kicking up dust. The image of Scarlett's terror-stricken face kept flashing through Agatha's mind. Someone had been watching. Someone had been lurking in the shadows. "A small person. Quick-footed. Someone who had reason to fear being caught." Agatha whispered the thought to herself, barely audible over the rustling leaves. "Naomi."

The thought settled in Agatha's mind like a weight. Naomi had been one of the quieter guests, blending into the background, often overlooked. But was that deliberate? Had she been hiding in plain sight all along? Agatha turned onto her side, trying to push the thoughts away, but the pieces were falling into place. It was time to investigate.

～

By MORNING, the lodge was buzzing with hushed conversations. Nigel's death had cast a shadow over the retreat, and guests whispered among themselves, exchanging glances filled with fear and suspicion. Scarlett sat stiffly at breakfast, her eyes darting toward the windows as though she expected someone to be lurking just beyond the glass.

Agatha spotted Naomi sitting at a corner table, alone, stirring her tea absentmindedly. Her fingers trembled slightly as she lifted the cup to her lips.

"Perfect." Agatha approached with a neutral smile. "Mind if I join you?" Naomi glanced up, her eyes wary, but she nodded. "Of course."

Agatha sat, placing her hands on the table. "How are you holding up?" she asked, keeping her voice gentle.

Naomi exhaled a shaky breath. "Honestly? Not well. I can't believe all this is happening. First Eleanor, and now Nigel."

"I know," Agatha agreed. "It's unsettling." She paused, pretending to hesitate before adding, "But Scarlett's scare last night... that was the most unnerving part. Someone was watching her."

Naomi blinked, her expression unreadable. "What? I—what are you talking about?" Her voice wavered slightly, but she quickly composed herself, shaking her head. "I don't understand."

Agatha leaned in, keeping her voice level. "Scarlett saw someone watching her last night. A small figure, quick, moving through the trees. She was terrified."

Naomi's eyes widened, and she let out a short, breathy laugh. "That's... shocking. Who would do something like that?"

"That's what I'd like to find out," Agatha said, watching her closely.

Naomi hesitated, then picked up her tea, taking a slow sip before lowering it back to the table. "That's... awful."

"Whoever it was, they were small," Agatha continued casually, watching Naomi's reaction closely. "Scarlett thought it might've been a woman."

Naomi scoffed, shaking her head. "That could be anyone. The staff, a guest—people get paranoid in situations like this."

Before she could press further, a shadow loomed over their table. Elias, one of the lodge staff, cleared his throat. "Ms. Ndlovu, I saw you walking toward the guest cabins pretty late last night. I hope everything was alright?"

Naomi's face remained composed, though her grip on her teacup tightened. "I stepped out for some air. The walls of the cabin felt like they were closing in."

Elias nodded, seemingly unaware of the tension that had thickened around the table. "Of course. Just thought I'd mention it. Strange times we're in." With that, he walked away.

Naomi set her cup down, her fingers steady as she met Agatha's gaze. "Are you questioning me?"

Agatha leaned in slightly. "I just want to understand, Naomi. If there's something you're hiding—"

"I'm not hiding anything," Naomi interrupted sharply. "Why are you even asking me this?"

Agatha kept her tone even. "Because you argued with Nigel. People heard you."

Naomi let out a strained laugh. "Everyone argued with Nigel... including you. Are you interrogating all of them, or just me?"

Agatha studied her, sensing the defensiveness was more than just grief. Naomi was trying to divert the attention away. But why?

Naomi pushed back her chair abruptly. "I don't have to sit here and be interrogated by you," she said, grabbing her teacup and rising to her feet.

"Naomi, I—"

"I have nothing to explain," she snapped. "People like Nigel make enemies. Maybe you should look at the others instead of wasting time on me."

Without waiting for a response, she turned sharply and walked away, her steps brisk and controlled, but her shoulders slightly hunched. Agatha watched her retreat, the air between them thick with unspoken words. Naomi was hiding something. Now, she just had to find out what.

LORRAINE WAS ALREADY WAITING for Agatha outside the lodge when she stepped out. "Ma chérie, I have news."

"What is it?" Agatha asked.

Lorraine lowered her voice. "I overheard the staff talking about a missing toxin bottle from the supply room while I was in the kitchen making beignets. They didn't notice me, too busy whispering about how it had disappeared overnight. They seemed really nervous about it."

Agatha's heart skipped a beat. "What kind of toxin? And why would a lodge even have toxins in storage?"

Lorraine furrowed her brow. "Apparently, they hosted a conference on local poisonous plants a few months ago. Some of the samples were kept in storage for reference, but now one is missing."

She paused, lowering her voice as she glanced around. "And you know who has been asking around about poisonous plants?" She leaned in slightly, her voice taking on a conspiratorial tone. "Naomi. She told people it was research for the thriller she's writing. But if you ask me, that sounds like a very convenient excuse."

Agatha narrowed her eyes. "You think she was looking for something specific?"

Lorraine shrugged. "It certainly makes her look more suspicious, doesn't it?"

Agatha exhaled sharply. "That can't be a coincidence."

"No, it can't."

THAT EVENING, Agatha returned to her cabin, determined to dig deeper. She retrieved her laptop and settled onto the bed, Mike curling up beside her. "Let's see what we can find out about our mysterious Naomi," she murmured, pulling up social media.

She started with the basics—searching for Naomi's profiles across different platforms. The author maintained a professional presence with carefully curated posts about writing and publishing, but nothing particularly revealing. Agatha scrolled back through Naomi's timeline, searching for any mention of Nigel. At first, nothing stood out—just standard industry interactions and a few polite comments on his publishing announcements. Then she saw it. Three days before Nigel's death, Naomi had shared an article about predatory publishing practices with a comment that made Agatha's breath catch: "Some people destroy careers and call it 'business.' One day, karma will collect its debt. #JusticeIsComing" In the comments, someone had asked, "Is this about anyone in particular?" Naomi's reply was simple but chilling: "Ask Nigel Thompson. While you still can."

The post was deleted shortly after, but someone had taken a screenshot that continued to circulate in writing groups, with commenters speculating about the "publishing drama." Agatha sat back, her heart racing. This wasn't just vague suspicion anymore—this was digital evidence of Naomi threatening Nigel days before his murder.

She reached for her phone to call Emma and Lorraine.

Naomi was hiding something significant—and Agatha was getting closer to uncovering exactly what it was.

17

A CHANGE OF PACE

The chatter of birds filled the morning air, blending with the earthy scent of damp ground and wildflowers. It promised the start of what was meant to be a lighter day.

Agatha was sipping her tea on the back porch of her cabin when she heard an enthusiastic knock at the door. Before she could even stand, the door swung open, and Lorraine and Emma strolled in, grinning like schoolgirls up to mischief.

"Rise and shine, ma chérie!" Lorraine sang, tossing a colorful scarf over her shoulder as she examined Agatha's outfit. "Tell me you are not planning to wear that on our grand adventure."

Agatha raised a brow. "It's a perfectly respectable outfit."

Emma snorted, setting a bag down on the small table. "Respectable? Yes. Safari-chic? Not so much."

Agatha sighed, setting her teacup down. "I take it you two are overly prepared for today?"

"Absolutely!" Lorraine clapped her hands together. "A morning tour of downtown and an afternoon trip to see lions and giraffes? This is the best distraction from—" She hesitated, casting a quick glance at Emma. "Well, you know."

Agatha appreciated the effort. After days of tension and suspicion, a bit of normalcy was much needed. "Alright," she relented. "But if you try to put me in a ridiculous hat, I'm staying behind."

Emma waved a hand. "No promises."

AFTER DRESSING IN AN OUTFIT DEEMED "ACCEPTABLE" by Lorraine, the trio made their way to the lodge's dining area. The scent of freshly baked bread and strong coffee filled the air, making Agatha's stomach rumble.

As they settled into a table near the window, their light-hearted chatter was interrupted when Agatha spotted Naomi sitting across the room, speaking in hushed tones with Elias. Naomi's hand slipped something small and folded into Elias' palm before he pocketed it discreetly.

Lorraine nudged Agatha under the table. "Did you see that?"

Agatha nodded, narrowing her eyes. "That looked like money."

Emma took a sip of her coffee, glancing between them. "She could be tipping him for something innocent."

"Or," Lorraine whispered conspiratorially, "she could be paying him for information or keeping him quiet about something."

Agatha let out a breath. "It's suspicious, but we'll have to keep an eye on her without making it obvious."

Lorraine waved a hand. "We are masters of subtlety."

Emma nearly choked on her coffee laughing. "You? Subtle?"

Agatha smirked, shaking her head. "Let's focus on enjoying today. We can worry about Naomi later."

THE DOWNTOWN TOUR was a lively affair, with sandy streets lined by small, colorful buildings, bustling open-air markets, and vendors under thatched canopies selling handcrafted goods. The air carried the rich aroma of grilled meat and roasted maize, mingling with the scent of fresh fruit from nearby stalls. The cacophony of voices haggling in multiple languages, punctuated by occasional bursts of laughter and the distant rhythm of drums, created a symphony of everyday life.

The energy of the market immediately captivated Lorraine. Every few steps, she gasped dramatically at a vibrant kente cloth, a delicately woven basket, or a wooden carving of an elephant, marveling at the craftsmanship. "I need this," she announced at nearly every stall, her fingers trailing over the intricate beadwork of a necklace.

Emma, ever practical, rolled her eyes. "You don't need it. You just want it."

"What's the difference?" Lorraine shot back, clutching an intricately beaded necklace to her chest as though it was a priceless artifact. She turned to an elderly vendor whose weathered face crinkled with amusement at her enthusiasm. "C'est magnifique! How long does it take to create something so beautiful?"

The woman smiled, gesturing with her hands as she explained through a combination of broken English and expressive gestures that each piece took several days.

Lorraine nodded with exaggerated understanding, already reaching for her wallet.

Agatha chuckled, enjoying the lightness of the moment—a welcome respite from murder and suspicion. For the first time since arriving in Botswana, her shoulders relaxed, tension melting away with each step through the vibrant marketplace. She found herself drawn to a beautifully bound leather notebook from a small bookshop tucked between stalls selling hand-made beadwork and painted pottery.

"Perhaps for your next mystery?" Emma suggested, noticing Agatha's interest in the notebook.

"Or just for recording happier memories," Agatha replied, running her fingers over the soft leather cover.

They paused at a food stall where a young man was grilling meat on skewers, the savory aroma too tempting to resist. Emma bravely ordered for all three of them, and they found a small table beneath a colorful umbrella to savor their impromptu lunch.

"To normality," Lorraine proposed, raising her paper cup of freshly squeezed fruit juice. "However brief it may be."

Agatha and Emma clinked their cups against hers, grateful for this pocket of joy amid the chaos they'd been thrust into.

BY MIDDAY, they were heading toward the jeeps waiting to take them into the savanna. As they approached, Agatha's heart quickened at the sight of Naomi stepping into one of the vehicles, a pair of dark sunglasses hiding her eyes.

"She's coming with us," Emma whispered.

Lorraine let out an exaggerated sigh. "Well, that should make things interesting."

Agatha nodded, slipping into her seat. "Indeed."

As the jeep rumbled forward, heading into the golden expanse of the wild, the vast savanna stretched endlessly before them, golden grasses swaying beneath the brilliant blue sky. Herds of giraffes moved gracefully in the distance, their long necks swaying like rhythmic dancers, while a pride of lions lazed beneath the shade of an acacia tree, their golden coats blending seamlessly with the landscape.

Lorraine, overwhelmed with excitement, gripped the side of the jeep as they bounced over a rough patch of terrain. "Mon dieu! Did you see that? That lion just yawned, and I swear, I saw every single one of his teeth! He could swallow me whole!"

Emma laughed. "Well, let's make sure you stay inside the jeep then. I don't think we'd make a good case for rescuing you from a lion's lunch."

Just as Lorraine was about to protest, the jeep hit another bump, sending her tilting dangerously to the side. Agatha barely managed to grab her arm in time. "You're going to end up as part of the food chain if you're not careful."

Lorraine clutched her chest dramatically. "I was nearly lost to the wilderness! My obituary would have been fabulous, though."

As they settled from their laughter, Agatha caught sight of Naomi a few seats away, her posture stiff as she jotted something into her notebook.

Curiosity piqued, Emma leaned slightly to get a better look, catching glimpses of hurried scribbles. Her breath hitched as she swore she saw the names Nigel, Eleanor, and—was that DIE?

Emma pulled back quickly, her heart pounding. She met Agatha's gaze and whispered, "We need to talk later."

Agatha nodded, her eyes narrowing at Naomi. Today was proving to be more than just a scenic adventure. Tension coiled in her chest.

After a long and entertaining day downtown and on safari, the trio returned to the lodge, dusty but exhilarated from their excursion. The setting sun cast an amber glow over the landscape as they freshened up before heading to dinner.

As they gathered in the dining room, Emma leaned in and whispered, "I need to tell you both what I saw in Naomi's notebook today."

Lorraine, mid-sip of her wine, perked up. "Do tell."

Emma's voice dropped to a near whisper. "I saw the names Nigel and Eleanor... and what I could swear said 'DIE'."

Agatha's fork clattered against her plate. "Are you sure?"

Emma hesitated. "It was quick, but yes. She was taking notes, and I'm almost certain that's what I saw."

The air between them thickened as they exchanged glances. Naomi sat across the room, dining alone, occasionally glancing in their direction. After a while, Victor approached her table and leaned in, speaking in hushed tones. Naomi's expression remained unreadable.

When she finally rose from her seat and left the dining room, Agatha wasted no time.

She waved Victor over. "Victor, could we speak for a moment?"

Victor approached with a raised brow. "Of course, what's on your mind?"

Agatha kept her tone light. "The other day, you mentioned seeing Naomi the night Nigel was killed. Could you tell me a little more about that?"

Victor's expression turned to confusion. "I'm not sure what you mean. I never said anything about seeing Naomi that night."

Agatha blinked. "That's not what I recall."

He shook his head. "I think you must be mistaken. I don't remember saying anything like that."

Agatha's stomach tightened. He was lying. But why?

She leaned back, masking her surprise. "Right. My mistake."

As Victor returned to his table, Agatha turned back to Emma and Lorraine. "He's covering for something. I know what I heard before. And now, Naomi's suspicious behavior, the notebook, and Elias—it's all connected."

Lorraine took a sip of wine and smirked. "Then, my dear, I'd say we have a mystery to solve."

AFTER DINNER, Agatha made her way to the lodge's dog daycare, where Mike had spent the day while they were out on their tour. As soon as she stepped inside, Mike's tail wagged furiously, and he let out an excited bark, bounding toward her.

"There's my good boy!" Agatha cooed, crouching down to ruffle his scruffy fur. "Did you have a fun day?"

Mike responded by licking her cheek enthusiastically, causing her to laugh. "Alright, alright. I missed you too!"

She clipped his leash on and led him outside, enjoying the cool night air as they strolled back toward her cabin. As they rounded a corner, Agatha spotted Naomi walking a short distance ahead, her steps hurried. Before she could decide whether to call out, Mike suddenly stopped, his ears perked up, and a low growl rumbled from his throat.

Agatha stiffened. Mike was an excellent judge of character, and he rarely reacted this way to people. As Naomi glanced over her shoulder and caught sight of them, she visibly tensed before picking up her pace and disappearing down the path.

Agatha narrowed her eyes. "Well, well, Mike. It seems like you don't trust Naomi either. And I've learned to always trust you."

She gave him a reassuring scratch behind the ears before heading inside, her mind racing with even more questions. Naomi was hiding something—now, Agatha was sure of it.

18

DIGGING INTO NAOMI'S PAST

The morning air was crisp as Agatha sipped her coffee on the lodge's veranda, the distant hum of the waking savanna filling the air. The previous day's events still lingered in her mind, particularly Naomi's strange behavior and Victor's sudden denial of seeing her the night of Nigel's murder. Something wasn't adding up.

Emma and Lorraine joined her, both looking equally pensive. "Alright," Emma said, setting down her plate of fruit and toast. "I couldn't sleep last night thinking about Naomi. I say we keep digging into her past and see what else we can find."

"I actually started looking into her last night," Agatha said, reaching for her phone. "I found something disturbing on social media—a post Naomi made about Nigel just days before his death. She wrote that karma would collect its debt and when someone asked if she was referring to anyone specific, she replied "Ask Nigel Thompson. While you still can.""

Lorraine gasped dramatically. "Mon Dieu! That's practically a written confession!"

"It's certainly suspicious," Emma agreed, leaning closer. "What else did you find?"

"The post was deleted shortly after, but someone had screen-shot it. It was being discussed in writing forums," Agatha explained. "But I think we should dig deeper into her professional history too. Let's look at her books and see if Eleanor had written a review about Naomi. That might give us more insight into their relationship."

Lorraine nodded, her eyes sparkling with excitement. "I do love a good literary scandal. If she has more skeletons in her closet, we must unveil them with flair!"

Agatha opened a search engine on her phone. "Let's see what else our mysterious author has been hiding."

A few keystrokes later, Emma let out a small gasp. "Got something." She turned her screen toward Agatha and Lorraine. The headline read: *A Merciless Review from Eleanor Price: 'Derivative, Dull, and Dead on Arrival'.*

"Ouch," Lorraine winced, taking a sip of her tea. "That's harsher than I expected."

Agatha skimmed the article. "Looks like Eleanor's review absolutely ruined Naomi's debut book. Sales tanked, her publisher dropped her, and she basically disappeared from the literary world for years."

Emma scrolled further. "And it gets worse. Naomi finally landed another publishing deal—guess who her editor was?"

Lorraine gasped. "Nigel?"

Emma nodded. "And apparently, he was awful to her. Belittled her writing, made her do endless rewrites, then ultimately pulled her contract."

Agatha leaned back in her chair, exhaling. "So Eleanor crushed her career, and Nigel destroyed her second chance. That's motive if I've ever heard one."

Lorraine waggled her brows. "She had every reason to want them both gone."

Agatha chewed her lip. "But was it enough to kill?"

Before anyone could answer, they noticed Naomi slipping out of the dining hall. Agatha nudged Emma. "She's leaving. Let's follow."

THE TRIO discreetly tailed Naomi through the lodge, keeping their distance as she made her way toward the market stalls just outside the lodge's gates. The dirt path was lined with vendors displaying colorful wares, their stands shaded by makeshift canopies. The scent of roasting maize and grilled meat mixed with the rich aroma of spices, creating a heady blend that made Agatha's stomach grumble. But they had more pressing matters.

Naomi stopped at one of the vendors and exchanged words with a man selling dried herbs. Her body language was tense, her head shifting from side to side as if making sure no one was watching.

Emma tensed. "That's the same vendor Scarlett bought from the other day."

Agatha narrowed her eyes, watching as Naomi handed the man some cash in exchange for a small, wrapped package. She leaned in closer to whisper, "We need to find out what she's buying."

Lorraine adjusted her sunglasses and sauntered forward, her movements exaggerated. "Leave that to me, mes chéries."

Emma sighed. "This is going to be ridiculous, isn't it?"

Agatha smirked. "Most likely."

Lorraine strutted up to the vendor, her accent thickening. "Bonjour, monsieur! What delightful wonders are you selling today?"

The vendor, an older man with deep-set wrinkles and shrewd eyes, gave her an amused look. "You look for something special, madame?"

"Oh, always," Lorraine said, pretending to examine a bundle of dried roots. She tilted her head, lowering her voice. "That woman—Naomi—she just bought something from you. I must know! Is it for beauty? Healing? Something more... exotic?"

The vendor chuckled, shaking his head. "Ah, no, no. She bought medicinal herbs. Good for digestion, headaches. But also, in the wrong amount... very bad." He gave Lorraine a knowing look. "You understand?"

Lorraine gasped dramatically. "Ah! A woman must be careful with such things, non?"

He nodded sagely. "Very careful."

Lorraine returned, looking immensely pleased with herself. "She bought dried herbs used for medicinal purposes," she relayed. "But in the wrong dosage? They're poisonous."

Emma sucked in a breath. "Could that be what was in Nigel's drink?"

Agatha's stomach twisted. "We need to find out what Naomi was really doing that night—and why she's still acting so suspicious."

Just then, Naomi turned the corner, walking briskly past them with the small package clutched in her hand. She didn't notice them, her head down, eyes scanning the ground as if lost in thought.

They decided to follow her further, careful not to draw attention. Naomi led them through a winding path between the market stalls, stopping occasionally to glance behind her, almost as if she sensed she was being watched.

Agatha whispered, "She's nervous. She knows something."

Naomi turned sharply and entered a small café at the edge of the market. The trio hesitated before slipping inside. The cozy interior was dimly lit, the scent of strong coffee and fresh pastries filling the air. Naomi sat at a corner table, hunched over a notebook, scribbling furiously.

Emma, pretending to browse a nearby shelf of souvenirs, tried to catch a glimpse of Naomi's notes, but couldn't see clearly from her position. "Agatha," she murmured, "I can tell she's writing frantically, but I can't make out what it says from here."

Agatha's heart pounded. "We need to get closer."

Lorraine, ever dramatic, hatched a plan. She 'accidentally' tripped near Naomi's table, knocking over a nearby chair.

As Naomi looked up in surprise, Agatha took the chance to glance at the notebook. It wasn't just notes about Nigel and Eleanor. There were numbers, lists of names, and phrases scribbled in the margins—'it wasn't supposed to happen like this.'

Naomi snapped the notebook shut, eyes locking onto Agatha. "Why are you watching me?"

Agatha kept her face neutral. "We were just getting coffee."

Naomi's jaw clenched. She stuffed the notebook into her bag and quickly stood up. "I have to go."

They watched as she hurried out of the café.

Emma turned to Agatha. "She's hiding something. And whatever it is, it's big."

Agatha nodded, determination flaring in her chest. Naomi's secrets were unraveling faster than expected. Now, it was only a matter of figuring out how deep they went.

19

STARLIGHT STORIES

"Whthe on earth are you wearing?" Emma asked, staring at Lorraine's elaborate outfit as they met outside Agatha's cabin.

Lorraine twirled, showing off her flowing caftan adorned with what appeared to be hand-sewn sequins arranged in constellation patterns. A matching turban wrapped around her head was topped with a small silver star. "My stargazing ensemble, of course!" Lorraine declared, as if it were perfectly obvious. "One must dress for the celestial occasion."

Agatha bit back a laugh. "I didn't realize stargazing had a dress code."

"Everything has a dress code, ma chérie," Lorraine insisted. "Would you wear a bikini to a funeral? A ball gown to feed chickens?"

"Do I look like someone who owns chickens?" Emma muttered.

The lodge had announced a special stargazing event for the evening. After days of tension, suspicion, and seemingly endless questioning, the chance to do something normal—even touristy —held undeniable appeal.

"I need a break from murder," Agatha admitted as they walked along the path toward the designated viewing area. "Just a few hours without thinking about typewriters, poisons, or suspicious stationery."

"And what better distraction than the cosmos?" Lorraine agreed, nearly tripping over her flowing garment. "Though I must warn you both, I tend to gasp dramatically at celestial wonders. It's entirely involuntary."

Emma rolled her eyes. "Like your 'involuntary' shriek when you saw that gecko in the bathroom?"

"That was different," Lorraine sniffed. "That gecko was giving me judgmental looks."

The viewing area was a small clearing a short distance from the lodge, where light pollution was minimal. Several blankets had been spread on the ground in a semicircle, and a man was setting up a professional-grade telescope in the center.

To Agatha's surprise, Detective Khumalo stood off to one side, looking surprisingly casual in khaki pants and a navy sweater.

"Didn't expect to see you here, Detective," Agatha remarked as they approached.

Khumalo's usually stern expression relaxed slightly. "Even detectives appreciate the stars, Ms. Royale."

"Do you solve many cases by starlight?" Lorraine asked, adjusting her turban.

"Sadly, no. Though it would add a certain drama to police work." His eyes twinkled with unexpected humor as he took in Lorraine's outfit. "I see you've dressed for the occasion."

"One must honor the heavens appropriately," Lorraine replied with dignity, though the effect was somewhat ruined when she immediately tripped over the hem of her caftan.

The astronomer, introduced as Motsamai, called everyone to gather around. He was a cheerful man with an infectious enthusiasm for his subject. "The skies above Botswana are among the clearest in the world," he explained. "Tonight, you will see stars that are entirely invisible from Europe or North America."

"Invisible stars?" Lorraine gasped, right on cue. "How thrilling!"

As they found places on one of the blankets, Agatha noticed Victor approaching. He carried a small notebook and wore an expression of polite interest.

"Mind if I join you?" he asked.

Before Agatha could respond, Mike, who had been quietly padding alongside her, let out a low growl.

"Mike!" Agatha scolded gently, though she found his reaction interesting. "Sorry, Victor. He's been oddly protective lately."

"No offense taken," Victor assured her, choosing a spot at a respectful distance. "Dogs have excellent instincts."

"Better than some humans," Emma murmured, just loud enough for Agatha to hear.

Motsamai began his presentation, pointing out constellations and sharing both scientific facts and local folklore. "That grouping there," he said, indicating a bright cluster, "is known to Western astronomers as part of Scorpius. But to the San people, those stars tell the story of a young woman who threw ashes into the sky to create a path home."

"How romantic!" Lorraine sighed, loudly enough to make several people turn. "I mean, not the ashes part—that sounds messy—but creating a pathway home through the stars!"

When it was their turn to look through the telescope, Lorraine approached with such ceremony that one might have thought she was about to be knighted. "Prepare me for the cosmic wonders," she announced to no one in particular.

"It's a telescope, not a time machine," Emma said dryly.

Lorraine peered through the eyepiece and immediately let

out such a dramatic gasp that a nearby couple actually jumped. "Mon Dieu! The majesty! The splendor! The—oh wait, that's my eyelash. False alarm."

Motsamai, to his credit, took Lorraine's theatrics in stride. "Perhaps try closing one eye, madam."

"Ah! Much better!" Lorraine exclaimed after adjusting. "Now I can truly see the pathway of ashes! Though it could use a good vacuuming."

Emma caught Agatha's eye and they both struggled not to laugh out loud.

As the evening progressed, the formal presentation gave way to a more relaxed atmosphere. People drifted between blankets, sharing snacks and swapping stories. Tau, one of the older lodge staff members, entertained a small group with traditional Tswana folklore about the stars.

"My grandfather taught me that the stars are the campfires of those who have gone before us," he explained. "They watch over us and guide us when we lose our way."

"That's beautiful," Emma said. "Much nicer than just balls of burning gas."

"Also less likely to give you heartburn," Lorraine added thoughtfully.

Agatha found herself relaxing despite everything. The vastness of the night sky provided much-needed perspective—whatever dangers lurked at the lodge seemed smaller when viewed against the backdrop of eternity.

Her peaceful contemplation was interrupted when Lorraine suddenly sat bolt upright. "Did anyone else see that? A shooting star! Quick, make a wish!"

"I'm pretty sure it was a satellite," Emma said.

"You're ruining the magic," Lorraine complained. "Now my wish won't come true."

"What did you wish for?" Agatha asked.

"I can't tell you or it definitely won't come true. Although I will say it involved a certain handsome detective and a moonlit tango lesson."

"Lorraine!" Emma hissed, glancing nervously toward where Khumalo sat.

"What? The cosmos respects romance." Lorraine adjusted her star-topped turban, which had begun to list precariously to one side.

The evening took an unexpected turn when Motsamai brought out a battery-powered projector and shone it onto a white sheet he'd hung between two trees.

"This will help us see some of the fainter constellations," he explained.

As the stars appeared on the makeshift screen, someone near the back called out, "This reminds me of that scene in 'Midnight in the Sahara'—you know, where the explorer gets lost and follows the North Star home?"

To everyone's surprise, it was Scarlett who had spoken. The normally reserved author seemed to relax slightly when discussing fiction.

"I loved that book!" another guest exclaimed.

Soon a lively discussion broke out about fictional uses of stars in literature. Even Khumalo joined in, mentioning a detective novel where an astronomer solved a murder using stellar positions.

"You see?" Lorraine whispered to Agatha. "Even hardened detectives enjoy a good star-crossed romance now and then."

"I think that was a detective story, not a romance," Agatha whispered back.

"Every story is a romance if you squint hard enough," Lorraine insisted.

As the hour grew late, Motsamai invited everyone to simply lie back and absorb the majesty of the night sky.

Agatha found herself between Emma and Lorraine, Mike curled contentedly against her side.

"I never realized how much we miss, living with all that light pollution back home," Emma said, yawning. "You can barely see a tenth of these stars from Bristol Lake."

"Speaking of home," Lorraine said, fiddling with a loose sequin on her blouse, "do you think Eliza's bakery will still be standing when we return? I had a nightmare that Juliette from the French boulangerie had returned and staged a croissant coup while we were away."

"A croissant coup?" Agatha repeated, unable to suppress her smile. "I wouldn't worry about that. As far as I know, Juliette is still enjoying her extended stay at a state prison."

"Oui! But in my dream, she escaped and built barricades made of baguettes and everything. Very dramatic."

"Your mind is a strange and wonderful place, Lorraine," Emma said, shaking her head with affection.

"Merci! I've always thought so." Lorraine beamed, completely unperturbed.

Despite the lighthearted conversation, Agatha found herself studying the other guests. Victor sat alone now, making occasional notes in his small book. Naomi had positioned herself as far from Scarlett as possible, though Agatha caught her stealing glances in the author's direction. And Khumalo, though seemingly relaxed, maintained the alert posture of someone who never truly stopped observing.

The peaceful interlude had been welcome, but Agatha's detective instincts wouldn't quite switch off. As they lay there under the infinite expanse of stars, she couldn't help but feel they were still missing something important—a crucial piece of the puzzle that would make everything clear.

"There's Orion," Emma pointed out, tracing the constellation with her finger. "See the three stars in a row? That's his belt."

"Is he the hunter?" Lorraine asked. "Or the one who turned into a bear? I always mix up my celestial men."

"The hunter," Agatha confirmed. "Always pursuing, never quite catching."

"Story of my love life," Lorraine sighed dramatically.

Eventually, Motsamai announced that the official stargazing session was concluding, though anyone was welcome to stay longer if they wished. Most of the group began gathering their belongings, voices low as if reluctant to break the peaceful atmosphere that had developed.

As they walked back toward their cabins, the pathway lit by soft solar lamps, Mike suddenly stopped short, his ears pricked forward. He let out a soft growl, staring intently at a dark space between two buildings.

"What is it, boy?" Agatha asked, squinting into the shadows.

For a moment, she thought she glimpsed a figure slipping away, but it was gone too quickly to identify.

"Probably just a mongoose or something," Emma suggested.

"Or a cosmic visitor," Lorraine whispered theatrically. "This would be the perfect setting for an alien abduction."

"Please don't get abducted," Agatha laughed. "The paperwork would be a nightmare."

"Besides," Emma added, "any self-respecting alien would take one look at your outfit and think Earth fashion was too advanced for contact."

Lorraine preened. "I'll take that as a compliment."

As they reached their cabins, Agatha found herself taking one last look at the star-filled sky. The evening had been a welcome diversion—a reminder that there was beauty and wonder in the world beyond the dark mystery they were trying to solve.

"Goodnight, stars," Lorraine called out, blowing a kiss skyward. "Thank you for the cosmic fashion inspiration!"

Mike nudged Agatha's leg gently, reminding her that the night air was growing colder.

"You're right," she told him, scratching behind his ears. "Time for bed. Tomorrow we see things more clearly."

But as she closed her cabin door, she couldn't help but wonder about that fleeting shadow she'd glimpsed. In a place where everyone had secrets, even the stars couldn't illuminate every dark corner

20

THE SEARCH FOR MARIE

Lorraine huffed as she kicked aside a crumpled towel near the bed. "Honestly, this place is a disaster. Where is Marie? She's usually tidying up by now."

Agatha glanced around the room, noting the unmade bed and the empty tray where breakfast should have been delivered. A knot tightened in her stomach.

"When's the last time anyone saw her?" Emma asked, her brow creasing.

Lorraine frowned. "Now that you mention it... I don't remember seeing her at breakfast."

"She didn't bring the morning tea either," Agatha said. "And she always does."

A tense silence settled over them. Agatha's mind raced through a dozen scenarios, none of them good.

"If Marie hasn't been seen since Nigel's death," Agatha said, setting her teacup down with a decisive clink, "then something is terribly wrong. She might have been the only one who knew something, and now she's missing?"

Emma ran a hand through her hair, exhaling sharply. "I

don't like this. If she disappeared right after his murder, that's not just bad timing—that's a red flag."

Lorraine, perched on the edge of the bed, pulled her shawl tightly around her shoulders. "Mon dieu. What if she didn't just leave? What if someone made sure she wouldn't talk?"

Agatha's jaw tightened. "That's exactly what I'm worried about. We need to find out where she is."

Emma stood, adjusting the sleeves of her blouse. "Let's start by asking the lodge staff. They might have seen her before she vanished."

Lorraine, ever the dramatist, flung her shawl over one shoulder and stood with an air of determination. "Then what are we waiting for, mes chéries? A mystery waits for no woman."

With that, they grabbed their bags and stepped out into the warm night air. The soft glow of lanterns illuminated the lodge's winding paths, casting flickering shadows against the wooden cabins. Crickets chirped in the distance, blending with the rustling leaves as a faint breeze swept through the trees. The quiet stillness of the surroundings only amplified the unease settling in Agatha's stomach.

THEY MADE their way to the front desk, where the lodge's receptionist, a kind-faced woman named Thandi, greeted them with a polite smile. "Good evening, ladies. How can I help you?"

Agatha hesitated for a moment before speaking, choosing her words carefully. "We were wondering if you've seen Marie lately. We just realized we haven't run into her since... well, since that night with Nigel."

Thandi's smile faded. "Marie?" She frowned and flipped through a logbook. "She called in sick the morning after that guest's death. We haven't heard from her since."

Emma exchanged glances with Agatha. "She never came back?"

Thandi shook her head. "No. We assumed she'd gone home to rest, but... now that you mention it, she hasn't checked in, and no one has seen her in days."

Lorraine put a hand to her chest. "Mon dieu. That's not normal, is it?"

Thandi hesitated, then leaned in slightly. "Between you and me, no. Marie never misses work. And I found it odd that she didn't pick up her last paycheck."

A chill ran down Agatha's spine. "Do you know where she lives?"

Thandi nodded slowly. "She stays in the staff quarters near the back of the lodge."

Agatha turned to Emma and Lorraine. "We need to check her room."

THEY FOUND the staff quarters tucked behind the main lodge, a row of small, neatly arranged cabins. Agatha knocked on the door labeled Marie and waited. Silence. She tried the handle. It turned easily.

"Unlocked?" Emma whispered.

Agatha pushed the door open, revealing a sparsely furnished room. The bed was unmade, and a thin layer of dust coated the nightstand. Drawers stood partially open, clothes missing. It looked as though someone had left in a hurry.

Lorraine stepped in, arms crossed. "Either Marie had a sudden urge to pack up and vanish, or someone was looking for something."

Emma scanned the small space and pointed toward the bed. "Look at that."

Agatha followed her gaze and spotted a crumpled sheet of paper on the floor, partially tucked under the mattress. She picked it up carefully and smoothed it out, revealing what appeared to be an incomplete letter. The handwriting was rushed, as if the writer had been interrupted.

Nigel,

I don't know how to say this, but I need to warn you. Something isn't right, and I think you're in danger. I overheard—

The letter ended abruptly, the ink trailing off in a jagged line. Agatha frowned. "She was trying to warn Nigel."

Lorraine gasped. "Warn him about what?"

Emma leaned closer, reading the unfinished letter again. "Whatever it was, she never got the chance to finish."

As they left Marie's room, discussing what they'd found, Naomi appeared at the end of the hall. She stopped in her tracks when she saw them, her posture stiffening.

"What are you three doing here?" Naomi's voice was clipped, her eyes darting between them.

Agatha, always quick to adapt, smiled casually. "Looking for Marie. Have you seen her?"

Naomi hesitated for just a fraction of a second before shaking her head. "No. I haven't."

Lorraine stepped forward. "Strange. Because she's been missing since Nigel's death."

Naomi's fingers curled into fists. "I don't know anything about that. Just because she cleans my room doesn't mean we're friends. I barely even know her."

Emma studied Naomi carefully. "You sure? Because you look like you do."

Naomi's jaw tightened. "I have nothing to say." She turned on her heel and walked away.

Agatha exhaled. "That was... suspicious."

Lorraine raised an eyebrow. "You think?"

THAT EVENING, after dinner, Agatha noticed something peculiar. Naomi and Scarlett stood near the back entrance of the lodge, engaged in a hushed conversation. Agatha, careful to remain unseen, watched as Naomi handed Scarlett something—a small bottle.

Scarlett nodded, slipped it into her pocket, and walked off toward the darkness of the savanna.

Emma appeared at Agatha's side. "What was that?"

Agatha's voice was barely above a whisper. "I don't know. But I intend to find out."

AS THEY FOLLOWED Scarlett at a safe distance, they watched her dig a small hole in the dirt and bury the bottle. Lorraine, barely able to contain herself, whispered, "Why would she hide something unless it was important?"

Emma frowned. "We need to get that bottle."

Agatha nodded. "Tonight. After she's gone."

Lorraine huffed. "Naomi and Scarlett are probably working together. I mean, look at them—whispering in the shadows, handing off secret bottles, burying things in the dead of night. It's like a terribly written crime novel."

Emma smirked. "Except we're in it."

Agatha sighed. "And we still don't know the ending."

A twig snapped behind them. They froze. A shadow loomed in the darkness. Someone was watching them.

21

A WEB OF DECEPTION

The shadow in the darkness moved closer, and Agatha's heart pounded in her chest. Lorraine stiffened beside her, gripping Emma's arm so tightly that Emma yelped. "Lorraine! That's my actual arm, not a loaf of bread!"

"Pardon, ma chérie, but I do not wish to be mauled in the wilderness alone. If something attacks us, I'd at least like the dignity of going down together." Lorraine hissed.

Emma rubbed her arm, shooting Lorraine a glare before turning back toward the figure approaching them. Agatha held her breath, ready to either flee or fight, when a familiar voice broke the tension.

"Don't scream," Marie whispered, stepping into the dim glow of the moonlight. She looked exhausted, her clothes dusty, her eyes wild with worry. "It's just me."

Agatha exhaled sharply, relief flooding her. "Marie! Where have you been?"

Marie cast a nervous glance over her shoulder before answering. "I had to leave. I didn't think I was safe."

Emma guided her toward Lorraine's cabin, where they could talk in private. Once inside, Marie collapsed onto the edge of the bed, rubbing her face with her hands. "I didn't mean to disappear like that, but I had no choice. Someone was watching me."

Lorraine crossed her arms. "Who?"

Marie hesitated. "I don't know. I think they believed I knew something, but I don't. I don't know anything more than what I've already told you and the police."

Agatha exchanged a glance with Emma before leaning in. "Marie, we found your letter. The one you were writing to Nigel. What were you trying to warn him about?"

Marie's lips parted in surprise, then she exhaled. "I overheard a conversation the night before he died. Naomi was arguing with him about something important. She was furious. I couldn't hear everything, but she said something like 'You have no idea what you're dealing with.'"

Emma frowned. "That doesn't look good for Naomi."

Marie nodded. "That's why I was afraid. I didn't know what it meant, but after he was killed, I panicked. I was sure Naomi saw me that night, and combined with the feeling that someone was watching me, I just ran."

Agatha's gaze sharpened. "Why did you decide to come back now? What changed?"

Marie hesitated, her eyes flicking toward the floor. "Nothing changed," she said softly. "I heard you were asking about me, and that motivated me to return."

Lorraine tapped a finger on her lips. "So, Naomi is looking even guiltier."

Agatha, however, wasn't so sure. Something about Naomi's outburst the previous night still nagged at her. "Maybe. But I don't think we should discount Scarlett just yet."

～

THE NEXT MORNING, Marie returned to her small room in the staff quarters, relieved but still shaken.

Meanwhile, Agatha and Emma made their way to breakfast. As they entered the lodge's dining area, Naomi was sitting in a corner, stirring her tea absently, a deep frown etched onto her face. She looked up at them, then quickly dropped her gaze, her fingers tightening around her cup.

Before Agatha could approach, a voice interrupted. "You're wasting your time with her."

Victor slid into the seat beside them, sipping his coffee with a knowing smirk. "Naomi's guilty. You can see it in her eyes."

Agatha studied him, trying to read between the lines of his too-casual demeanor. "You seem pretty sure of that."

Victor shrugged. "She's been acting strange since Nigel died. Always looking over her shoulder. Plus, I caught her sneaking around near the guest cabins two nights ago."

Lorraine raised an eyebrow. "And you didn't think to mention that earlier?"

Victor chuckled. "I wasn't sure what it meant. People are free to wander around—it's not a crime. But now, with everything else..." He let the implication hang in the air.

Agatha nodded thoughtfully. Victor seemed genuinely concerned, his tone steady and calm.

DETERMINED TO CONFRONT NAOMI, Agatha and Emma found her in her cabin later that day, frantically packing a suitcase. The moment she saw them, she let out an exasperated sigh. "Oh, what now?"

Agatha crossed her arms. "Going somewhere?"

Naomi's hands trembled as she shoved clothes into her bag. "I don't have to explain myself to you."

Emma stepped forward. "Marie told us she overheard you and Nigel arguing the night before he died."

Naomi's head snapped up, eyes blazing. "So what? We argued all the time! That doesn't mean I killed him."

Agatha's gaze drifted toward the half-packed suitcase sitting on the bed. She motioned toward it. "Then why are you running?"

Naomi's shoulders sagged, her expression turning tired. "Because I know how this looks. I know how you all see me. But I didn't kill him."

She reached into a drawer and pulled out a small notebook, tossing it onto the bed. "If you really think I did it, take that. It has all my notes about Nigel. All the times he humiliated me, tore my work apart, made my life miserable. But if I wanted him dead, don't you think I'd have done it sooner?"

Agatha picked up the notebook and flipped through it. The words were full of anger, frustration—but also... grief? It wasn't a record of revenge. It was the notebook of someone who had been broken by a cruel man but still wanted to prove herself.

Emma crossed her arms. "That's all well and good, Naomi, but we saw you. We know you bought herbs at the market and later handed something to Scarlett. What was that about?"

Naomi's eyes flashed with irritation. "You've been spying on me now?" She exhaled sharply, rubbing her temples before answering. "Scarlett asked me to pick up some herbs for her. She said it was for research for her next novel."

Agatha narrowed her eyes. "And you just went along with it?"

Naomi let out a humorless laugh. "It's not a crime to buy herbs. You're all treating me like some villain when all I did was help a fellow writer." Her voice cracked slightly, betraying the anger beneath the surface.

Emma shifted uncomfortably. "If not you... then who?"

Naomi's gaze darkened, her lips tightening. "Maybe you should be asking Scarlett. She was always around Nigel. And if you ask me, she's the one with secrets worth killing for."

Silence settled over the room like a heavy fog. Agatha studied Naomi's tense expression, searching for cracks beneath the anger. Naomi met her gaze, unflinching.

Lorraine's eyes widened. "So you think Scarlett—"

"I don't know what to think," Naomi cut in. "But you're wasting your time chasing me when Scarlett has been playing her own game this whole time."

Agatha's thoughts raced. Was Naomi deflecting or revealing a crucial piece of the puzzle?

THAT EVENING, Agatha and Emma returned to the spot where Scarlett had buried the bottle. But when they arrived, the ground had been disturbed.

The bottle was gone.

Agatha's stomach twisted. Someone had taken it.

A rustling sound came from the opposite side of the clearing. Agatha turned her head sharply, just in time to see a shadow dart behind the trees. She caught a glimpse of Naomi's silhouette disappearing into the night, her posture tense, as if she had just been caught doing something she shouldn't.

Then, just beyond the trees in the opposite direction, another shadow moved. Agatha turned again just in time to see Victor walking away, his hands in his pockets, whistling softly.

Lorraine stepped up beside her. "Tell me you saw that."

Agatha's eyes flickered between the two disappearing figures. "Oh, I saw it," she murmured, her mind spinning. "But which one of them took it?"

22

A SHIFT IN SUSPICION

The breakfast hall bustled with activity—the clink of cutlery, the murmur of polite conversation, and the occasional burst of laughter. Sunlight danced across the delicate china as Agatha, Emma, and Lorraine settled at a table by the window. The scent of warm pastries and freshly brewed tea wrapped around them, but their conversation remained hushed, their thoughts snagged on the lingering questions from the night before.

Lorraine nibbled at a piece of toast, then sighed dramatically. "I feel like we're playing detective in a play where everyone's suspicious, and I hate all my lines."

Emma smirked, but her expression quickly turned serious. "Victor was there. Naomi was there. Either one of them could have taken that bottle."

Agatha stirred her coffee, watching Victor from across the room. He sat near the window, laughing and chatting as he scrolled through his phone. His carefree demeanor didn't match that of someone hiding a dark secret. He even lifted his phone to his ear, speaking in an animated tone to someone, pausing only to chuckle at something they said. He didn't look like a man with something to hide.

Lorraine squinted at him. "A murderer wouldn't be that chipper before noon, would he?"

Emma shook her head. "He doesn't seem worried at all. If anything, it's Naomi who looks on edge."

As if on cue, Naomi entered the dining hall, her eyes darting around as if expecting an ambush. She spotted them and hesitated before making her way to the buffet. Agatha exchanged a look with Emma.

"I think it's time we get some answers," Agatha said, setting her napkin down.

They rose from the table, weaving through the other guests. Naomi was already loading her plate when Agatha approached her side.

"Naomi," Agatha said softly.

Naomi stiffened, her hand hovering over a platter of fruit. "Not now."

"We just need a minute," Emma added.

Naomi sighed, then shook her head. "Fine. Outside."

OUTSIDE, they found Naomi pacing near the lodge's entrance. When she saw them approaching, she exhaled sharply. "Oh, for the love of—what now?"

Agatha crossed her arms. "We need to talk about last night. We saw you near the trees when the bottle went missing."

Naomi's face twisted in frustration. "What are you talking about?" Naomi frowned. "Bottle? What bottle?" She shook her head. "I have no idea what you're referring to."

Emma narrowed her eyes. "The bottle we saw Scarlett burying."

Naomi exhaled sharply. 'I don't know anything about a bottle... I was taking a walk, and I felt like someone was watching me. Then I noticed someone in that area and went to check. When I got there, I saw that the ground had been disturbed. It gave me an eerie feeling, so I left. But I swear, I didn't see any bottle."

"What about the herbs you got for Scarlett, mon ami?" Lorraine asked. "I spoke to the man at the market, and he told me that, used in the right amount, they could be deadly."

Naomi threw up her hands. "It's not illegal to buy herbs! I'm aware of their poisonous properties, if that's what you're wondering... That's why Scarlett wanted them. She knew I was going to the market and asked me to get them for her." She glanced around nervously, as if to check if anyone was listening.

"Couldn't she research that online? Why would she need the actual herbs?" Agatha asked.

Naomi sighed. "Scarlett insists on hands-on research. She says she needs to see, touch, and smell things to describe them accurately." She rubbed her temples before throwing up her hands. "It's not illegal to buy herbs! Why are you all acting like I orchestrated some elaborate murder plot?"

She exhaled sharply, her frustration evident. "I don't know what Scarlett is up to, but maybe you should be asking her these questions instead of me." She hesitated, lowering her gaze. "I have nothing else to say... I swear, I had nothing to do with Nigel's or Eleanor's deaths." Her voice cracked as she covered her face with her hands, letting out a quiet sob. "I wasn't even there."

"But we know what Eleanor and Nigel did to you," Agatha said, exchanging a glance with Emma and Lorraine. "You had plenty of reasons to dislike them."

Naomi looked pensive, as if choosing her words carefully. "Yes, but I didn't want to harm them. My vengeance was going to be proving them wrong—showing them that I was better than they believed. My new release is set to be a huge success."

She grabbed her phone and held it out to Agatha, Emma, and Lorraine. "Look. My pen name made it to the New York Times Best Seller list on the very morning of Eleanor's fateful passing."

Agatha's eyes widened as she read the name on the book cover Naomi displayed. "I didn't realize you had a pen name."

Naomi hesitated, then sighed. "There's one more thing," she said, glancing away. Her fingers twisted nervously in her lap. "I used them as characters in my new book. I even used their first names — with different last names. Eleanor became Eleanor Pence, a cruel literary critic who meets an untimely end in chapter three. And Victor... well, he's Victor Reynolds in real life, but in my book, he's Victor Elridge, the seemingly charming but ultimately murderous biographer."

She looked up, a hint of defiance in her eyes. "That was my vengeance. I thought letting them die in fiction would be enough to satisfy me. Maybe if they'd read it, they would have recognized themselves and felt some shame. It's petty, I know, but writers have to channel our anger somewhere."

Agatha, Emma, and Lorraine exchanged glances before bursting into laughter.

"You mean to tell me," Lorraine managed between gasps, "that your big revenge plot was killing them off in your novel? Mon Dieu! That's the most writerly form of revenge I've ever heard!"

Emma wiped tears from her eyes. "While actual murders were happening around us, you were committing fictional ones?"

Naomi's cheeks flushed. "It sounds ridiculous now, doesn't it? Especially considering what really happened."

Agatha, still chuckling, reached over to pat Naomi's hand.

"Actually, I think it's perfectly sensible. Much better than the alternative." Her expression grew more serious. "And it certainly helps confirm your innocence. Someone planning actual murder wouldn't waste time on fictional revenge."

"My editor thought the characters were too obviously based on real people," Naomi admitted with a small smile. "She made me change Eleanor's death scene three times because it was 'too satisfying.' Said readers wouldn't believe someone could be that vindictive in real life."

"If only she knew," Emma murmured, shaking her head.

Lorraine leaned forward, eyes gleaming with interest. "I don't suppose you're still looking for beta readers, are you? I'm particularly good at critiquing revenge scenes."

Just then, Marie, who had been listening nearby, suddenly stepped forward. "Naomi didn't do it. She wasn't anywhere near Nigel when he died. I saw her in the kitchen at the time. She was making tea, and she stayed there most of the night. A few other authors were there too, and they were discussing their book ideas. She wasn't sneaking around—she was right in front of us the whole time."

Emma frowned. "Why didn't you tell us this before?"

Marie shrugged. "Because I already told Inspector Khumalo when he asked. That's what mattered."

Agatha and Emma exchanged a look. Naomi was telling the truth. The suspicion hanging over her evaporated, but that left them with an even bigger question.

"Then who?" Emma murmured.

Naomi's gaze darkened. "I don't know what Scarlett is up to, but if you ask me, she's the one with secrets worth killing for."

～

THAT EVENING, as Agatha and Emma made their way toward Scarlett's cabin, Victor appeared beside them. "I heard you're looking into Scarlett," he said, his voice low.

Agatha nodded warily. "You don't seem surprised." She hesitated, her brow furrowing. "News travels fast around here. I don't even remember mentioning that I was looking for her to anyone."

Victor shrugged. "Let's just say she's been acting strange for a while. I thought you might need an extra pair of eyes."

Agatha hesitated, but Emma gave a subtle nod. Victor was offering to help, and despite her reservations, Agatha wasn't about to turn down an opportunity to get closer to the truth.

They walked together toward Scarlett's cabin, the air tense with unspoken thoughts. Victor said nothing, his expression unreadable as they approached the door.

When they arrived, Scarlett's door was slightly ajar, and from inside, they could hear her voice—low and urgent. Agatha paused, signaling for the others to stay quiet.

"I told you, I handled it," Scarlett hissed.

A pause.

Then, a second voice, muffled but unmistakably nervous. "But what if they find out?"

Emma's eyes widened, and Lorraine grinned. "Well, well. Looks like we're about to get our answers."

Agatha took a deep breath, then pushed the door open. "Scarlett, we need to talk."

Scarlett froze, eyes darting between them and the shadowed figure across from her. The tension in the room was thick, and Agatha knew—whatever they were about to uncover, they were finally on the right track.

23

CLOSING IN

Agatha took a step inside Scarlett's cabin, her eyes darting between the two figures. Scarlett stood rigid, her expression blank, but the man sitting across from her, Elias—the lodge staff member—looked like a deer caught in headlights.

Elias quickly shot to his feet. "I was just leaving."

Scarlett's lips pressed into a thin line. "I think you should."

But Agatha stepped in his way. "Not so fast. We heard you say you 'handled it.' Care to explain?"

Scarlett scoffed. "Eavesdropping now? How very amateur sleuth of you."

Lorraine grinned. "Oh, chérie, we're far beyond amateur. Now spill."

Elias glanced anxiously at Scarlett. "I don't know anything about this. I just—" He shook his head. "I shouldn't even be here."

"But you are," Emma pointed out. "And if you don't start talking, it's going to look a lot worse for you."

Scarlett rolled her eyes. "For heaven's sake, Elias, they're not the police."

Agatha caught the flicker of irritation on Scarlett's face and knew they were onto something. "You're right, but I imagine Inspector Khumalo would be very interested in what's going on here."

That got a reaction. Elias swallowed hard, glancing toward Scarlett for guidance, but she remained silent, arms crossed. After a tense moment, he sighed. "Fine. Scarlett asked me to retrieve something from the storage room the night before Nigel died."

Emma tilted her head. "What kind of something?"

Elias hesitated. "A small vial. I don't know what was in it. She just said it was for research."

Agatha's pulse quickened. "And did she tell you what to do with it after?"

Scarlett cut in sharply. "Enough. Elias doesn't know anything. I told him to fetch the vial because I was writing about poisons in my novel. That's it."

Lorraine clapped her hands together dramatically. "Oh, Scarlett, you are positively dripping with guilt."

Scarlett shot her a glare. "Don't be ridiculous."

You're right to check for continuity with what Inspector Khumalo previously said. If you're not certain whether he mentioned finding records of blackmail in Nigel's cabin, we can modify the approach slightly to avoid creating a contradiction.

Here's a revised version that doesn't rely on specific information from Khumalo:

As Agatha studied Scarlett, the conversation naturally turned to Nigel.

"We've been thinking about Nigel's personality," Emma said

thoughtfully. "He seemed like the type to keep careful records, especially of things he could use against people."

Scarlett's composure faltered for just a fraction of a second— a slight widening of her eyes, a visible catch in her breath. Her fingers, which had been calmly resting on the armrest, suddenly gripped the fabric with such force that her knuckles turned white.

"What makes you say that?" Scarlett asked, her voice pitched slightly higher than normal.

"Just an observation," Agatha replied, watching closely. "People who blackmail others often keep detailed evidence to protect themselves."

Scarlett reached for her teacup, but her hand trembled so violently that tea sloshed over the rim. She quickly set it down, a flash of panic crossing her face before she masked it with a tight smile.

"I wouldn't know anything about that," Scarlett said, surreptitiously wiping her palm on her skirt. "Though I suppose it makes sense for someone like him. I just hope they don't find anything that might... complicate matters for innocent people caught in his schemes."

The tension in her voice and her specific concern about 'innocent people' told Agatha everything she needed to know. Scarlett was hiding something significant, and it had to do with whatever Nigel had on her.

Lorraine pressed a hand to her chest dramatically. 'If she grips that armrest any tighter, she'll need to pay for new upholstery,' she whispered, never taking her eyes off Scarlett's white knuckles.

"You seem awfully concerned about what Nigel might have documented," Agatha observed carefully.

"I'm simply making conversation," Scarlett replied, her voice tight.

Victor, who had been quietly observing from nearby, suddenly stepped forward. "If there's nothing to hide, Scarlett, why do you look so worried?" His tone was gentle but probing.

Scarlett's eyes darted between them, her composure cracking further. "I'm not worried. I just..." She swallowed hard. "This conversation is making me uncomfortable, that's all."

Emma crossed her arms. "Scarlett, you were seen talking to Nigel the night before he died. And now you're practically shaking at the mere suggestion he kept records of his blackmail activities. What exactly were you afraid he had documented?"

"This is absurd," Scarlett snapped, her jaw tightening. "I don't owe you any explanations."

Scarlett refused to talk and ordered them out.

Agatha knew she had something real now—a motive, a connection to Nigel's murder, and something Scarlett didn't want them to find.

As they left, Elias hesitated in the doorway, looking as if he wanted to say something—but Scarlett glared at him, and he stayed silent.

Lorraine let out a breath. "That woman is wound tighter than my favorite bottle of champagne."

Emma nudged Agatha. "So what now?"

Agatha glanced back at the cabin. "Now? We find proof. Scarlett's hiding something, and I intend to figure out what it is."

24

THE MEDICAL REPORT AND A HIDDEN IDENTITY

The morning sun peeked over the horizon, casting golden light across the lodge as Agatha stretched in her bed, trying to shake off the fog of a restless night. The events of the previous evening played over in her mind like an unsolved puzzle. Scarlett's trembling hands and panicked eyes when they'd mentioned Nigel's record-keeping had been telling—far too telling for someone claiming innocence. And then there was Naomi, acting cagey whenever their paths crossed, her demeanor shifting from nervous to defensive in an instant.

The two women were at the center of it all—Scarlett with her buried bottle and poorly concealed fear, Naomi with her evasive behavior and convenient absences during crucial moments. But which one was the killer, and which one was simply hiding something else?

Agatha sat up with a groan. Everyone had secrets, and at least one of them had killed Nigel.

A knock on the door interrupted her thoughts. Emma and Lorraine stood outside, looking just as sleep-deprived.

"Morning," Emma greeted, stifling a yawn. "Or should I say,

welcome to another day of figuring out which of our fellow guests is a murderer."

Lorraine clutched her silk robe dramatically. "I barely slept! I kept imagining Scarlett creeping around the lodge, plotting her next crime. Mon dieu, I even had a dream where she poisoned my breakfast croissant!"

Agatha smirked. "That would be a crime against humanity."

Lorraine sighed heavily. "Exactly! But in all seriousness, what's our plan today? Are we confronting Scarlett?"

Agatha thought for a moment. "Scarlett is definitely hiding something, but I want to talk to Inspector Khumalo first. We need to see if the forensic report tells us exactly how Nigel died."

Emma nodded. "And what about Scarlett? We still don't know what was in that bottle she buried, or why she's so tense."

"One thing at a time," Agatha said, tying her hair up. "Let's start with Khumalo. Then we deal with Scarlett."

As they headed to the main lodge, Agatha couldn't shake the feeling that they were running out of time to find the truth.

THEY FOUND Inspector Khumalo near the lodge entrance, speaking with one of his officers. When he spotted Agatha, he gestured for her to follow him to a quieter spot.

"Inspector," Agatha said once they were alone, "I need to know—how exactly did Nigel die?"

Khumalo studied her face for a moment, seeming to weigh how much to share. He hesitated, then flipped open his notepad with a resigned sigh.

"I suppose you've earned this information," he said, his voice low. "The forensic report just came in. Nigel Thompson was sedated before his death, but the actual cause of death was blunt force trauma."

Agatha inhaled sharply. "Sedated? With what?"

"Sleeping pills, likely slipped into his drink hours before he died," Khumalo confirmed. "And the murder weapon—the object that delivered the fatal blow—was found in Naomi Ndlovu's room."

Agatha's mind reeled. "Naomi?" She shook her head. "That doesn't make sense."

"She swears she had nothing to do with it," Khumalo said, studying Agatha's reaction. "She insists she's being framed."

A sharp bark interrupted them. Mike, who had been waiting patiently at Agatha's feet, stood at attention, his eyes darting between her and Khumalo.

Khumalo arched an eyebrow. "Does he always interrupt official investigations?"

Agatha smirked. "Only when he thinks someone's not being completely honest."

Mike gave a small "huff," his scruffy beard twitching, before turning his attention to Naomi, who stood a short distance away, watching them with wide, wary eyes.

"I need to talk to her," Agatha said.

Khumalo sighed. "You can, but tread carefully. I still haven't ruled you out."

Mike let out another small bark, as if offended on her behalf. Khumalo shot him a look before turning on his heel and heading back inside.

Agatha glanced at Emma and Lorraine. "Looks like Naomi is next on our suspect list."

THEY FOUND a table at the lodge's outdoor dining area, where breakfast was already being served. The scent of fresh pastries and coffee wafted through the air, but Agatha barely noticed.

Lorraine, however, had no such problem. She piled her plate high with buttery croissants and fresh fruit, humming to herself.

"How can you eat so much when someone tried to frame Naomi?" Emma asked, exasperated.

Lorraine waved a dismissive hand. "Ma chérie, an empty stomach is no help to an investigator. Besides, if someone *is* poisoning the food, I might as well go out happy."

Agatha rolled her eyes but smiled despite herself. Lorraine always knew how to lighten the mood.

Emma stirred her coffee. "So, Naomi was framed, but why? And why would someone leave the murder weapon in her room? It's too obvious."

Agatha nodded. "Exactly. Which means the real killer wants us to look at Naomi. That means we need to look elsewhere."

Just then, Scarlett strolled past their table, her head held high, a smug expression on her face.

Lorraine narrowed her eyes. "Look at her. She knows something."

Emma leaned forward. "She's the one who asked Naomi to buy the herbs. If those herbs match the poison in Nigel's system, then she might be our killer."

Agatha nodded. "Then let's make sure we find out."

LATER THAT MORNING, Agatha, Emma, and Lorraine joined a small group of retreat attendees for a guided nature walk. The lodge had arranged these morning excursions as a way to keep guests occupied and distracted from the grim events unfolding—a veneer of normalcy that fooled no one but was welcomed nonetheless.

Their guide, a young Botswanan man named Tau with an encyclopedic knowledge of local flora, led them along a winding path that skirted the edge of the savanna. The morning air was still cool, filled with the sweet scent of wild grasses and punctuated by distant birdsong.

"The relationship between plants and people in Botswana goes back thousands of years," Tau explained, his voice carrying easily to the small group. "Every plant you see has a purpose—medicine, food, tools, or spiritual significance."

Agatha positioned herself carefully, maintaining a casual demeanor while keeping both Scarlett and Naomi in her line of sight. Scarlett had dressed for the occasion in an expensive safari outfit that looked like it had never seen dirt, while Naomi hung back from the group, a small notebook clutched in her hand.

"This walk is absolutely magical," Lorraine declared, her voice rising with theatrical enthusiasm. "The primal connection to nature! The ancient wisdom of the land! I feel positively transformed!" She closed her eyes and spread her arms wide, nearly knocking Emma's hat off in the process.

Emma ducked, shooting Agatha an amused glance. "You said the same thing about hot yoga last winter," she reminded Lorraine. "Right before you declared it an instrument of torture designed by sadistic health nuts."

"That was mere physical discomfort," Lorraine replied with a dismissive wave. "This is spiritual awakening. I shall become a botanist and write a revolutionary guide to African plants."

Agatha smiled at her friend's predictable enthusiasm, but her attention kept returning to the quiet drama unfolding at the edge of their group.

Tau stopped beside a small shrub with distinctive jagged leaves. "This plant is particularly interesting," he said, carefully breaking off a tiny leaf to pass around. "It's called mokaikai in Setswana. For centuries, our healers have used it to treat insomnia and anxiety. But be warned—in large quantities, it can be dangerous."

When the leaf reached Naomi, Agatha noticed how her fingers trembled slightly. A flash of recognition crossed her face before she quickly passed the sample to the next person, wiping her hand against her pants as though the leaf had burned her.

With measured casualness, Agatha made her way to Naomi's side. "Fascinating plant, isn't it?" she remarked, her voice conversational but her eyes sharp.

Naomi flinched. "I suppose so."

"You seem familiar with it," Agatha pressed gently.

"No, I—" Naomi paused, catching herself. "I mean, I've just been researching local plants. For my writing."

Agatha nodded, keeping her expression neutral. "It looks a lot like the herbs you bought at the market. The ones you gave to Scarlett."

Naomi's face paled. "I don't know what you're talking about," she said, but her voice lacked conviction.

Across the path, Scarlett had wandered slightly away from the group, pretending to photograph a colorful bird while clearly straining to overhear their conversation. When she caught Agatha looking her way, she quickly averted her gaze, suddenly fascinated by the settings on her expensive camera.

Tau continued leading them deeper along the trail, pointing out medicinal plants, those used for dyes, and others prized for their wood.

The morning sun climbed higher, warming the air and bringing out rich earthy scents from the soil beneath their feet.

Emma had managed to extricate herself from Lorraine's botanical revelations and sidled up beside Agatha, speaking in a low voice. "Did you see that? When Tau mentioned the plant could be dangerous in large quantities, Scarlett nearly tripped over her own feet."

Agatha nodded slightly. "And Naomi recognized it immediately. If those are the same herbs she bought for Scarlett..."

"Then Scarlett's story about needing them for 'research' becomes even more suspect," Emma finished.

As the nature walk continued, with guests snapping photos and collecting small approved samples for pressed flower souvenirs, Agatha observed the increasingly telling behaviors of both women. Each time Tau mentioned a plant with dual purposes—beneficial in small amounts but toxic in larger ones—Naomi would tense, and Scarlett would find some reason to distance herself from the group.

The walk concluded near a small watering hole where zebras gathered in the distance, providing the perfect picturesque distraction for most of the guests. Agatha, however, couldn't tear her attention from the mystery unfolding before her—a mystery where every new piece of information seemed to deepen rather than resolve the puzzle.

THAT EVENING, Agatha took Mike for a walk around the lodge. The night was cool, and the stars stretched endlessly above. Mike suddenly stopped, ears pricked. A shadow darted between the trees. Agatha's heart pounded. She stepped forward, cautiously peering into the darkness. Then, she saw her. Marie.

The young housekeeper froze, her expression caught between fear and determination.

"Marie?" Agatha whispered.

Marie hesitated for a split second—then bolted.

Agatha ran after her. "Wait!"

Marie disappeared behind the cabins. Agatha stood there, breathing heavily. "Why in the world is she running?" She looked down at Mike, who tilted his head curiously. "I'm sure she saw me, didn't you see that, boy?"

Mike gave a soft woof in agreement, his ears perked forward in the direction Marie had fled.

Agatha tapped her finger against her chin, looking pensive. "Why was she avoiding me?" She knelt down beside Mike, scratching behind his ears. "What is she hiding, Mike? People don't run unless they have something to hide." *Or someone to protect,* she added silently to herself.

25

A WEASELLY MURDERER EMERGES

Agatha sat at the breakfast table with Emma and Lorraine, absently stirring her tea as her eyes tracked Elias. The young, weaselly-looking staff member lingered near the entrance to the dining room, his narrow shoulders hunched as if carrying an invisible weight. His gaze darted from conversation to conversation, lingering just long enough to catch snippets before moving on.

"Have you noticed how Elias always seems to be lurking around?" Agatha murmured, setting her spoon down with a quiet clink.

Lorraine gasped dramatically, nearly choking on her croissant. "Mon dieu! He does have the look of someone hiding something. That ferret-like face! Those nervous fingers constantly adjusting his collar." She dabbed her lips with a napkin. "And have you noticed how he avoids eye contact?"

Emma raised a brow. "I thought I saw him speaking with Victor earlier. But when I approached, Elias scurried off like he was afraid I'd heard something."

"What were they discussing?" Agatha asked, her voice low.

Emma shook her head. "I couldn't hear, but Victor looked tense. He kept checking to see if anyone was watching them."

"It's strange," Agatha mused, "how everyone at this retreat seems to have something to hide." She lowered her voice further. "Did you know Elias carries a small notebook everywhere? I've seen him scribbling in it after conversations with the guests."

Lorraine's eyes widened. "You think he's collecting information? Spying on the literary elite?" She waved her croissant dramatically. "Perhaps he's a struggling writer himself, stealing ideas for his masterpiece!"

"Or blackmail material," Emma said grimly. "In the publishing world, secrets can be worth a lot of money. Unpublished manuscripts, pending deals, ghostwriting arrangements..."

Agatha nodded thoughtfully. "Everyone here has a literary reputation to protect. Their careers depend on it."

"We need to figure out why he's so nervous," Agatha continued. "And what his connection to all this might be."

Lorraine leaned in with a conspiratorial whisper. "Shall we interrogate him? I have just the outfit for it." She tapped her chin thoughtfully. "A dramatic hat would add gravitas, non?"

Agatha rolled her eyes. "No interrogations. Not yet. Let's observe him first."

"Oh, spoil sport," Lorraine sighed, taking another bite of her croissant. "Though I suppose that's more subtle. Very Hercule Poirot of you."

"I'll take that as a compliment," Agatha replied with a small smile.

∾

LATER THAT AFTERNOON, Agatha positioned herself in the lodge's common area with a book, pretending to read while keeping Elias in her peripheral vision. He moved from table to table, refilling water glasses but clearly straining to overhear discussions. When he passed Victor and Naomi deep in conversation about publishing trends, he slowed noticeably, his head tilting slightly toward them.

When Elias disappeared down a corridor marked "Staff Only," Agatha waited a few moments before following. The hallway was empty when she entered, but she could hear voices coming from behind a partially open door at the end.

"—told you it wasn't my fault," Elias was saying, his voice trembling. "She was asking questions. What was I supposed to do?"

A muffled reply came, too quiet for Agatha to make out.

"I'm not stupid," Elias hissed. "I know what happens if I talk. But they're getting close. That Royale woman and her friends keep watching me."

"You're overreacting," came the reply, clearer now. "No one suspects anything."

"You don't understand," Elias insisted. "I've heard things. These people, these writers—they all have secrets. Plagiarism, ghostwriters, stolen ideas. I know what they're hiding."

Agatha pressed herself against the wall as footsteps approached the door. She ducked into a nearby utility closet just as Elias emerged, followed by—

Her breath caught. Scarlett Beaumont.

Scarlett looked pale, her usual confidence replaced by a haunted expression. "Just keep your mouth shut," she was saying. "And remember, if I go down, you do too."

Elias nodded jerkily. "I know where the bodies are buried in the publishing world. Literally and figuratively." He gave a nervous laugh that died quickly under Scarlett's glare.

They parted ways, neither noticing Agatha hiding in the shadows.

"SCARLETT AND ELIAS?" Emma repeated incredulously when Agatha recounted what she'd overheard. They'd gathered in Agatha's cabin, voices low despite the privacy. "What could connect those two?"

"Money, perhaps," Lorraine suggested, sprawled dramatically across the small loveseat. "Blackmail is always about money. Or sex. Or sometimes both."

"Or literary fraud," Agatha added. "Something about Scarlett's books, maybe? Remember what Elias said about ghostwriters and secrets in publishing."

Emma nodded slowly. "The publishing industry is ruthless. People have built careers on lies before."

"Think about it," Agatha continued, pacing the length of the cabin while Mike watched her with curious eyes from his spot on the bed. "Eleanor was a critic. She could have discovered something about Scarlett's writing. And Nigel was a publisher— he would know industry secrets."

"And Elias?" Lorraine asked. "Where does our little ferret fit in?"

"He's been working here for years," Emma pointed out. "Serving these writers, overhearing their conversations. If anyone knows their secrets, it would be him."

"Whatever it is, they're both scared," Agatha said. "And they know we're onto them."

"We need to confront one of them," Emma said decisively. "Elias seems the weaker link. If we push him, he might crack."

Lorraine sat up straight. "Oui! And I could wear my interrogation outfit after all!"

Before Agatha could respond, a sharp knock at the door made them all freeze. Mike let out a low growl, the fur along his spine rising.

"Who is it?" Agatha called, motioning for Emma and Lorraine to move away from the door.

"It's Scarlett," came the shaky reply. "Please, I need to talk to you."

Agatha exchanged looks with her friends before cautiously opening the door. Scarlett stood there, trembling, mascara smudged beneath red-rimmed eyes.

"I can't do this anymore," she whispered. "It's eating me alive."

Agatha stepped back to let her in. "Do what, Scarlett?"

Scarlett sank onto the nearest chair, her shoulders slumped in defeat. "Pretend I had nothing to do with this." She looked up, tears streaming down her face. "It's my fault Eleanor's dead. I agreed to meet her at that cabin. She was blackmailing me."

Agatha's heartbeat quickened as she sat across from Scarlett. "What did she know?"

"Everything," Scarlett whispered. "My secret. The reason I've been so successful." She drew a shuddering breath. "But I swear to you, when I arrived at the cabin, Eleanor was already dead. I panicked and ran."

"And Nigel?" Emma asked sharply.

Scarlett's head snapped up. "I had nothing to do with his death! But—" She hesitated, twisting her hands in her lap. "He knew my secret too. He started blackmailing me after Eleanor died."

"And now Elias is continuing the tradition?" Agatha guessed, her voice gentle but firm.

Scarlett nodded miserably. "I think... I think Elias killed them both. To keep them from talking."

"About your writing?" Lorraine pressed. "Your books aren't really yours, are they?"

Scarlett's eyes widened in shock. "How did you—"

"We didn't," Agatha said softly. "Until now."

Scarlett covered her face with her hands. "I can show you proof of everything. Will you come with me?"

Agatha glanced at Emma and Lorraine, who nodded encouragingly. "Lead the way."

As they left the cabin, Agatha couldn't shake the feeling that they were finally getting close to the truth—and that it might be more dangerous than any of them had imagined. In the literary world, some secrets were worth killing for.

26

SCARLETT'S CONFESSION

The African night enveloped them in velvet darkness as they followed Scarlett along the narrow path toward her cabin. A chorus of cicadas provided a relentless soundtrack, punctuated by distant animal calls that reminded Agatha how far they were from the cozy safety of Bristol Lake. The moon hung low and heavy, casting just enough silvery light to illuminate their way between the scattered cabins.

Mike padded alongside Agatha, his body tense and alert. Twice he stopped short, ears perked forward, a low rumble emanating from his chest as he stared into the darkness between the acacia trees. She'd learned to trust his instincts.

"Heel, boy," Agatha whispered, placing a reassuring hand on his head. His fur bristled beneath her fingers.

Lorraine hobbled behind them, her impractical sandals catching on every pebble and twig. She'd insisted on changing before their midnight excursion, and somehow that had translated to a flowing caftan and jeweled footwear that glinted treacherously in the moonlight.

"Mon Dieu," she hissed, stumbling for the third time. "If I

break an ankle chasing a murderer, I expect to be immortalized in your book, Agatha."

Emma shot her an exasperated look. "There won't be a book if we're caught sneaking around. Lower your voice."

Agatha glanced back at Scarlett, who seemed lost in her own thoughts, arms wrapped tightly around herself despite the lingering heat. The revelation that she'd been blackmailed had shocked Agatha, but something didn't quite add up—a discordant note in an otherwise plausible melody.

Emma suddenly gripped Agatha's arm, halting her mid-step. She nodded toward a cluster of shadows near the dining hall. Agatha squinted, making out a slim silhouette that disappeared as quickly as it had appeared.

"Was that—" Agatha began.

"Elias," Emma confirmed, her voice barely audible. "I'm sure of it."

Lorraine inched closer. "Are we walking into a trap? Because I'm dressed for intrigue, not mortal danger."

Agatha hesitated, watching Scarlett's retreating figure. "If it was a trap, why involve us at all? Scarlett could have simply gone to Khumalo."

"Unless she has more to hide than she's admitting," Emma murmured.

Mike nudged Agatha's leg, impatient to continue, his dark eyes reflecting the starlight. She nodded. "Let's hear her out. But stay alert."

Scarlett's cabin stood apart from the others, situated on a slight rise that offered a commanding view of the savanna. Unlike the rustic charm of their accommodations, hers exuded luxury—a concession to her bestselling status, no doubt. She unlocked the door with a shaking hand, ushering them inside before securing three separate locks behind them.

The interior was awash in earth tones and expensive textiles, the walls adorned with local artwork that probably cost more than a month's rent back home. A half-empty bottle of premium scotch sat on an intricately carved side table, alongside a crystal tumbler with lipstick traces on the rim.

"Please, sit," Scarlett said, gesturing to a seating area dominated by a plush leather sofa.

Lorraine immediately began a slow circuit of the room, examining Scarlett's possessions with undisguised curiosity. "Oh, I adore this," she cooed, stroking an ebony statuette. "Very chic."

"Lorraine," Agatha warned softly.

"What? I'm simply appreciating the decor." She winked at Agatha before continuing her inspection.

Emma, meanwhile, had noticed what Agatha had—the signs of Scarlett's actual work. Three laptops sat open at various stations around the cabin.

Manuscript pages were stacked in neat piles, some covered in red marks, others seemingly untouched. Post-it notes lined one wall in a rainbow of colors, forming what looked like a complex story outline.

Scarlett paced between the sofa and the window, repeatedly checking the locks and adjusting the blinds. Her fingers twisted an expensive-looking emerald ring, spinning it around and around her finger until Agatha thought the skin might chafe.

"Would anyone like a drink?" she finally asked, already moving toward the scotch.

"We're fine," Agatha said firmly. "Scarlett, you said Eleanor was blackmailing you. I think it's time you told us exactly what happened."

She poured herself a generous measure with trembling hands, the amber liquid sloshing dangerously close to the rim. After a long sip that emptied half the glass, she sank into an armchair opposite them, her shoulders slumping.

"I never meant for any of this to happen," she whispered. The polished Southern belle persona had vanished, leaving behind a woman who looked older and infinitely more fragile than the author who'd arrived by helicopter just days ago. "It all started so innocently."

"What did?" Emma prompted gently.

Scarlett stared into her glass. "My career. My success. It was real, at first. I wrote my first three books myself—romantic suspense with just enough literary flair to earn respect." Her mouth twisted in a bitter smile. "I won awards. Made the best-seller lists. It was everything I'd dreamed of since I was a little girl scribbling stories in Mississippi."

Mike had settled at Agatha's feet, but his eyes never left Scarlett. Animals have an instinct for truth, and Agatha found herself watching his reactions almost as closely as she watched Scarlett's.

"Then what happened?" Agatha asked.

Scarlett drained her glass. "Success happened. Suddenly everyone wanted a piece of me. My publisher pushed for two books a year instead of one. My agent scheduled appearances, book tours, lectures. The pressure was..." She trailed off, her gaze distant. "I developed writer's block. The worst kind—where I could still write, but everything I produced was garbage."

Emma nodded sympathetically. "And with expectations so high..."

"Exactly. I couldn't afford to disappoint. Not when my brand was built on delivering consistent quality." Scarlett laughed hollowly. "Brand. Listen to me. That's when I knew I'd lost myself—when I started thinking of my name as a brand instead of... well, my actual name."

Lorraine had completed her circuit of the room and settled on the arm of the sofa. "So you found a solution, non? A convenient literary shortcut?"

Scarlett's head snapped up, her eyes narrowing. "It wasn't like that. Not at first."

"Then what was it like?" Agatha asked quietly.

She closed her eyes. "Eleanor figured it out. I don't know how—maybe she recognized the style, maybe she heard something. But a few days ago, at breakfast, she cornered me." Scarlett's voice hardened. "She said she was going to expose me in her next review. Called me a fraud, a con artist. Said I'd built my career on deception."

Agatha tried to imagine the scene—Eleanor's cutting remarks delivered with surgical precision, Scarlett's growing panic as her carefully constructed world threatened to collapse.

"She wanted money, of course," Scarlett continued. "Critics don't make what authors do, especially not authors with film deals and merchandise lines." She gestured vaguely at a stack of papers on her desk. "I was supposed to meet her at the cabin, sign an agreement, arrange a transfer."

"But when you got there..." Emma prompted.

Scarlett's face crumpled. "She was already dead. Lying there, so still. I—I should have called for help, I know that. But I panicked. All I could think was that everyone would believe I killed her because of the blackmail."

A tear slid down her cheek. "So I ran. I've been living with that moment ever since, seeing it every time I close my eyes."

Mike whined softly, responding to the distress in her voice. Even he seemed confused by the conflicting signals—genuine emotion mixed with something else, something calculating.

"And then Nigel approached you," Agatha guessed, watching her reaction carefully.

Scarlett's breath hitched. "The very next day. He knew too—Eleanor had told him. His demands were bigger, his threats more explicit. He wanted a percentage of my future earnings, not just a one-time payment."

"Did you agree?" Emma asked.

"What choice did I have?" Scarlett pushed her hair back from her face. "But the night after I transferred the first payment, he was killed too."

Lorraine leaned forward. "And now Elias is blackmailing you as well?"

"Yes," Scarlett whispered. "It's like a nightmare I can't wake up from. Three people who knew my secret—two dead, one threatening me. And I'm terrified I'll be next... or worse, that I'll be blamed."

Agatha studied her face in the dim lamplight. Fear was evident in every line of Scarlett's body, but fear of what, exactly? Being exposed? Being arrested? Or something else entirely?

"Scarlett," Agatha said carefully, "you still haven't told us what your secret actually is. What did Eleanor discover?"

She looked up, her expression a mixture of shame and defiance. "I think you already know."

"We need to hear you say it," Emma insisted.

Scarlett drew a shuddering breath, her fingers twisting that emerald ring once more. "My books—the last seven of them—I didn't write them. Not a single word."

Agatha frowned. "I mean... I've always assumed ghostwriting happened more than people admit. I've seen those services offered, and I've heard of writers who make a full-time living doing it. I didn't think much of it—it just seemed like one of those behind-the-scenes things nobody talks about."

The woman across from her nodded grimly. "Exactly. Nobody talks about it. And yet I spent years—years—on panels, in interviews, slamming the idea. Calling it dishonest, unethical. How could I turn around and do the very thing I'd condemned?" She shook her head. "I suppose I deserved what I got."

Despite suspecting this very revelation, hearing her admit it sent a shock through them all. Seven books. Countless interviews. A reputation built on talent that wasn't hers.

"Who wrote your books?" Agatha asked gently, though she was already beginning to form a theory.

Before Scarlett could answer, the distinct sound of a twig snapping outside the window made them all freeze.

Mike was on his feet in an instant, a growl rising from deep in his chest as he faced the direction of the noise.

"Someone's out there," Agatha whispered, moving cautiously toward the window. Emma and Lorraine followed, peering out into the darkness. The three women scanned the area, but saw nothing but shadows and swaying branches in the evening breeze.

"I don't see anyone," Emma said quietly.

"They must have run off," Lorraine added, her voice uncharacteristically subdued.

Scarlett's eyes widened in terror. "He's here," she whispered. "He's been following me all along." After carefully checking that the area seemed clear, they agreed it was safest to retire to their own cabins for the night, with promises to reconnect in the morning.

27

THE GHOSTWRITING SECRET

The morning sun streamed through the windows of Agatha's cabin, illuminating dust motes that danced in the golden rays. Despite the cheerful light, a heavy atmosphere lingered from the previous night's interrupted revelations. She'd barely slept, her mind churning over Scarlett's partial confession and the ominous presence that had been lurking outside her window.

Emma sat at the small table, nursing a cup of coffee while reviewing her notes. Her red hair was pulled back in a practical ponytail, dark circles beneath her eyes suggesting she'd had no more rest than Agatha had.

"Do you believe her?" she asked without looking up.

Agatha sighed, pouring her own coffee. "Parts of it. Her fear seems genuine enough."

"But?" Emma raised an eyebrow.

"But there's something she's still hiding. The way she talked about her ghostwriter—there was resentment there. And why would Elias kill to protect her secret unless he had a stake in it?"

Lorraine burst through the door without knocking, a plate of pastries balanced precariously in one hand. Despite the early hour, she'd managed to apply a full face of makeup and dress in an outfit that would be more appropriate for lunch in Paris than a murder investigation in Botswana.

"Bonjour, mes amies! I come bearing sustenance for our detecting brains." She set the plate down with a flourish. "The kitchen staff are all buzzing about a secret meeting Elias had with Khumalo this morning. Very hush-hush."

Agatha straightened. "Elias spoke to Khumalo? About what?"

"That, my dear, is the mysterious part. They disappeared into the office for nearly an hour." Lorraine selected a croissant with surgical precision. "By the way, Marie says Scarlett hasn't left her cabin all morning. Had breakfast delivered. She's requested extra security locks for her windows."

Agatha and Emma exchanged glances. "We need to speak with her again," Agatha said. "Get the full story before Elias feeds his version to Khumalo."

"If that's what he's doing," Emma cautioned. "He could be reporting something else entirely."

Mike, who had been dozing in a patch of sunlight, suddenly lifted his head, ears perked toward the door. A moment later, a soft knock sounded.

Agatha opened it to find Marie, her usual composed demeanor replaced by evident anxiety. "Ms. Royale, Ms. Beaumont asks if you and your friends would join her for tea. She says it's urgent."

"Tell her we'll be there shortly," Agatha replied, noting the way Marie's eyes darted nervously around the room. "Is everything alright, Marie?"

She hesitated. "Be careful, please. There are... tensions in the lodge today. Inspector Khumalo has been questioning staff all morning."

After she left, Lorraine raised an eyebrow. "Tensions? Mon Dieu, what a delicate way of saying 'a killer is still among us."

"Let's not keep Scarlett waiting," Emma said, gathering her notebook. "I want to hear the rest of her story before anyone else disappears—or turns up dead."

SCARLETT'S CABIN looked dramatically different in daylight. What had seemed luxurious last night now appeared sterile, almost obsessively neat. Every surface gleamed, the manuscript pages had been tucked away, and even the scotch bottle had vanished. The transformation felt deliberate—an attempt to regain control through order.

Scarlett herself had undergone a similar metamorphosis. Gone was the disheveled, emotional woman of the previous night. In her place stood a composed, if pale, version of the best-selling author persona. Her hair was swept into an elegant updo, her casual clothing replaced by a silk blouse and tailored pants.

"Thank you for coming," she said, gesturing to a small table where an elaborate tea service awaited. Delicate china cups rested on saucers adorned with hand-painted roses, alongside a silver teapot that steamed gently. "I thought we might be more comfortable talking over something civilized."

"How British of you," Lorraine remarked, seating herself with a flourish.

Scarlett's smile didn't reach her eyes as she poured. "My grandmother was English. Tea was her solution to every crisis." She handed cups around with practiced grace. "I owe you the rest of my explanation. Last night was... interrupted."

"Someone was watching us," Agatha confirmed, accepting a cup. "Any idea who?"

"Elias, I assume. He's been following me." Her hand trembled slightly, causing the teacup to rattle against its saucer. "I've been afraid to speak openly, but time is running out. Khumalo's questioning everyone again, and I—I need you to understand what really happened."

Emma set her cup down without drinking. "You were about to tell us who really writes your books."

Scarlett took a steadying breath. "Yes. As I said, my early work was my own. But seven years ago, when the pressure became too much, I met a young writer at a conference in Chicago. She was talented but completely unknown—couldn't get published despite years of trying."

Agatha leaned forward. "Can you tell us her name?"

Scarlett hesitated, her fingers twisting nervously in her lap. "I'd rather not say. Our agreement includes strict confidentiality clauses that would financially ruin her if word got out." She glanced toward the window before continuing, her voice lower. "And frankly, naming her now could put both of us in even more danger than we already are."

"How so?" Emma prompted gently.

"This arrangement—it wasn't just a simple business transaction. It became..." Scarlett searched for the right words. "Complicated. Personal. There are people who would go to great lengths to keep this secret buried."

"Like Eleanor and Nigel?" Agatha suggested carefully.

"Exactly." Scarlett set her cup down and crossed to a bookshelf, retrieving a leather-bound journal. "A week after we met, she emailed me. She'd written a sample chapter in my style—perfectly in my voice, but... better. Fresher. She proposed an arrangement: she would ghostwrite, I would pay her generously, and we'd both get what we wanted."

"She needed money, you needed books," Lorraine summarized, helping herself to a small sandwich from the tea tray.

"Exactly." Scarlett's expression hardened slightly. "The first book was a massive success—better reviews than anything I'd written myself." A flicker of resentment crossed her face. "Soon we had a system. I'd provide a basic concept, she'd write the entire manuscript, I'd make minor edits and put my name on it."

"And no one knew?" Emma asked incredulously.

"No one. I paid her through an LLC registered as a 'research consultant' company. The contracts were ironclad, with confidentiality clauses that would—"

Suddenly, Scarlett's phone buzzed on the desk. She glanced at the screen and went pale.

"I—I'm sorry. I need to take this," she said quickly, grabbing the phone. She stared at the caller ID, her hand trembling. "Actually, you should go. I've already said too much."

"Scarlett, we can help you," Agatha offered, concerned by the sudden change.

"No, you can't," Scarlett insisted, her voice tense. "Please, for your own safety, forget we had this conversation. If certain people knew I was talking to you..."

The phone continued buzzing insistently in her hand.

"Go," she urged, already ushering them toward the door. "And be careful who you trust here."

As they reluctantly left, Agatha glanced back to see Scarlett answering the phone, her face a mask of carefully controlled fear.

Outside, the three friends exchanged troubled looks.

"Well," Emma said quietly as they moved away from the cabin, "that was abruptly terminated."

"Someone's got her terrified," Agatha murmured, her mind racing. "But who?"

"And what does her ghostwriter have to do with all this?" Lorraine wondered, for once without her dramatic flair.

28

THE BLACKMAIL PROOF

"I can't believe she clamped up like that," Emma said as they walked along the path back toward their cabins. The afternoon sun filtered through the acacia trees, casting dappled shadows across the dusty ground.

Lorraine suddenly stopped mid-stride, patting her pockets with increasing panic. "Mon Dieu," she exclaimed, her eyes widening dramatically. "My lucky charm! It's gone!"

"Your what?" Agatha asked, turning to her.

"My lucky elephant charm!" Lorraine explained, now frantically searching through her handbag. "The tiny carved wooden one I bought at the market yesterday. I had it in my hand while we were talking to Scarlett." She looked at them with genuine distress. "I must have set it down on her side table when I reached for that delicious little sandwich."

Emma sighed. "Lorraine, we can't just go barging back into Scarlett's cabin. She clearly wanted us to leave."

"But it's my lucky charm!" Lorraine insisted. "How am I supposed to survive in this den of murderers without my protection? It's practically a matter of life and death!"

Agatha exchanged a look with Emma, who rolled her eyes but nodded in resignation.

"Fine," Agatha said. "But we'll be quick—just ask for the charm and leave."

Mike trotted alongside them as they reversed course, heading back to Scarlett's cabin. The little schnauzer seemed almost pleased with the detour, his tail wagging as if he too was curious about what they might find.

"Remember," Emma cautioned as they approached the door, "we're only here for the elephant charm. No more questions about ghostwriters or publishing scandals."

"Scout's honor," Lorraine promised, making a gesture that looked nothing like any scout salute Agatha had ever seen.

When they reached Scarlett's cabin, Agatha knocked gently. After a moment, they heard footsteps approach, followed by a brief pause that suggested Scarlett was checking who it was before opening the door.

The door opened just enough for Scarlett to peer out, her expression a mixture of surprise and wariness. "You're back," she said, her voice tight with tension. "Is something wrong?"

"I am so sorry to disturb you again, ma chérie," Lorraine said, slipping effortlessly into her most charming persona. "But I seem to have left my little wooden elephant charm here. It's very precious to me—a good luck token, you understand."

"Yes, a precious good luck token that's precious to her," Agatha smiled, looking at Emma. "Never mind she just purchased it yesterday."

Scarlett hesitated, then opened the door wider with a sigh. "Come in, but please be quick. I'm... expecting someone soon."

They entered the cabin, which now felt different somehow—more tense, as if the very air had thickened since their earlier visit. Agatha noticed that Scarlett had swept her hair into an elegant updo since they'd last seen her just minutes ago, suggesting she was preparing for a visitor.

More notably, Scarlett was in the middle of gathering the blackmail notes they'd been examining earlier. As she hurriedly collected them from the table, her trembling hands betrayed her nervousness, causing several pages to flutter to the floor.

"I think I left it right there," Lorraine said, pointing to the small side table by the armchair she had occupied. "Next to that lovely silver coaster."

As Lorraine moved to retrieve her charm, Scarlett knelt to pick up the fallen papers, managing to gather most but missing a few that slid partially under the sofa. The evidence of blackmail remained scattered in plain sight despite her efforts.

"Is everything alright, Scarlett?" Agatha asked, unable to help herself despite Emma's warning glance.

"Yes, fine," Scarlett replied curtly, rising quickly to her feet with the papers clutched to her chest, her gaze darting to the window. "I just have some business to attend to."

The leather journal lay open on the coffee table, more incriminating notes clearly visible inside, as if their sudden return had interrupted her mid-task.

"Ah! Found it!" Lorraine exclaimed triumphantly, holding up a small wooden elephant no bigger than her thumbnail. "Thank goodness. I simply couldn't sleep without it."

"Good," Scarlett said, relief evident in her voice. "Now if you'll excuse me—"

A soft knock at the door made them all jump. Mike growled, positioning himself protectively in front of Agatha.

Scarlett checked the peephole, her face paling. "It's the lodge manager," she whispered. "With turndown service."

"At this hour?" Emma's brow furrowed.

"That's odd," Agatha murmured, noting the position of the

sun still high in the sky—hours before any reasonable turn-down service would begin.

Scarlett composed herself before opening the door just wide enough to speak with the manager. After a brief exchange, she closed it, leaning against the wood as if suddenly exhausted.

"He says Khumalo wants to see me this afternoon," she murmured. "They've found new evidence."

As she spoke, Agatha noticed a folded piece of paper that had been slipped under the door. She bent to retrieve it, a chill running down her spine as she read the typewritten message:

"I know you're talking. Stop now."

The paper trembled in Agatha's hand as she showed it to the others. Scarlett sank into a chair, her face ashen.

"We need to leave," Scarlett whispered, her composure crumbling. "It's not safe. None of this is worth—"

A sharp knock on the door made them all freeze again. Mike's growl deepened, the fur along his spine bristling as he positioned himself protectively in front of Agatha.

"Who is it?" Scarlett called; her voice strained.

"It's Victor. Is everything alright in there?"

The women exchanged wary glances. Scarlett hesitated before opening the door just wide enough to reveal Victor Reynolds standing in the hallway, concern etched on his features.

"I saw the lodge manager heading this way," he explained, glancing over his shoulder. "Thought I'd check on you. You seemed upset earlier."

Scarlett stepped back reluctantly, allowing him to enter. Victor's gaze traveled over the scattered evidence on the table, then to their tense faces. His brow furrowed.

"I see I've interrupted something," he said quietly.

"We're just having tea," Lorraine offered lamely, gesturing toward the cooling cups.

Victor raised an eyebrow. "With blackmail notes as reading material?" He nodded toward the threatening notes still visible on the table. "Look, I don't mean to intrude, but..." He sighed, reaching into his pocket. "I received one too."

He handed Agatha a folded piece of paper. The message was similar to Scarlett's, typed on the same letterhead. "I know what you did. Payment expected by noon tomorrow."

"When did you get this?" Emma asked, studying the note.

"This morning. Slipped under my door." Victor ran a hand through his hair. "I didn't think much of it at first—figured it was a prank. But after what happened to Eleanor and Nigel..."

Agatha handed the note back, watching Victor's expression carefully. Either he was a remarkably good actor or his concern was genuine. Mike had stopped growling but remained alert, his dark eyes fixed on Victor.

"Have you taken this to Inspector Khumalo?" she asked.

Victor shook his head. "Not yet. I wanted to investigate a bit on my own first. I've seen someone lurking around the cabins at night—a man about Elias's height and build."

"Elias?" Lorraine repeated, feigning surprise. "The staff member?"

"Yes. He always seems to be hovering in hallways, listening to conversations." Victor glanced at Scarlett. "I've noticed him paying particular attention to your movements."

Scarlett wrapped her arms around herself. "He's been black-mailing me too."

Victor's eyes widened. "About what?"

She hesitated, looking to Agatha for guidance. Agatha gave a slight nod.

"My books," Scarlett admitted, her voice barely audible. "I... haven't been writing them myself for the past seven years."

Victor seemed genuinely stunned. "A ghostwriter? That's

what this is about?" He sank into a chair. "Eleanor and Nigel were killed over a ghostwriting arrangement?"

"It appears so," Agatha said carefully, noting his reaction. "We believe Elias discovered the secret and has been blackmailing Scarlett. He may have been working with Eleanor and Nigel."

Victor was quiet for a moment, processing this information. "I should leave you to your discussion," he finally said, rising from his chair. "But please, be careful. If Elias is involved in these deaths..."

"We will," Emma assured him.

After Victor left, closing the door behind him, the women exchanged looks.

"Do we trust him?" Lorraine whispered dramatically.

"I don't know," Agatha admitted. "He seemed sincere, but so do all good liars."

"We need more concrete evidence about Elias," Emma said, returning to the blackmail notes. "These are compelling, but they don't prove he's behind the murders."

Scarlett nodded, gathering the papers back into her lockbox. "So what do we do next?"

Agatha's mind was already forming a plan. "We need to get into Elias's quarters. See what he's hiding."

"And how exactly do we do that?" Scarlett asked.

"We'll need help," Agatha replied. "Someone with access to the staff areas."

"Marie," Emma suggested. "She might be willing to help. She seemed frightened when I mentioned Elias earlier."

Lorraine clapped her hands together. "Oh, how delightfully clandestine! Breaking into a suspect's quarters—it's just like in those novels where the amateur sleuth finds the crucial clue in the villain's sock drawer!"

"This isn't a novel, Lorraine," Agatha reminded her, though

she couldn't help smiling at her friend's enthusiasm. "If Elias is indeed behind these murders, he's dangerous."

"All the more reason to catch him, ma chérie!" Lorraine declared, her eyes sparkling with determination. "When do we start?"

∽

THEY FOUND Marie in the linen room, folding sheets with mechanical precision. When they entered, she glanced up, her expression guarded.

"Ms. Royale," she greeted Agatha. "Did you need something for your cabin?"

"Actually, Marie, we need your help with something else," Agatha said quietly, closing the door behind them. "It's about Elias."

Marie's hands stilled; a white sheet clutched between her fingers. "What about him?"

"We know he's been blackmailing guests," Emma explained gently. "Including Scarlett Beaumont."

"I don't know anything about that," Marie said quickly, resuming her folding with increased vigor.

"Marie," Agatha said, "two people are dead. If Elias is involved, more people could be in danger."

The young woman's shoulders slumped. "He... watches people. Listens to conversations. Keeps notes." She glanced nervously at the door. "I've seen him sneaking around cabins at night."

"We need to see his quarters," Agatha said. "Can you help us get access?"

Marie hesitated, weighing her options. "He'll be on duty in the dining room for the next hour. His room is at the end of the east staff corridor." She pulled a master key from her pocket. "This will open it. But if he catches you..."

"He won't," Emma promised.

Marie handed over the key reluctantly. "Be careful. Elias isn't... he isn't what he seems." She paused, her brow furrowing. "Mr. Elkins was asking about you earlier, Ms. Royale."

Agatha frowned. "Mr. Elkins? I don't think I know a Mr. Elkins."

Marie's eyes widened, as if realizing her mistake. "I'm sorry —I meant Mr. Reynolds. Victor. I get names confused sometimes." She laughed nervously. "Too many guests to keep track of."

Agatha exchanged a glance with Emma, noting the slip but deciding not to press it now. "What did Victor want to know?"

"Just asking if you'd been in your cabin all morning. Nothing unusual." Marie's gaze darted to the door again. "You should go now if you want to catch Elias while he's busy."

THE EAST STAFF corridor was deserted when they reached it, the afternoon lull providing perfect cover. Lorraine stationed herself at the corner as lookout while Agatha and Emma approached Elias's door.

"This feels illegal," Emma whispered as Agatha slid Marie's key into the lock.

"Probably because it is," Agatha admitted. "But I'd rather face trespassing charges than let a murderer go free."

The room beyond was small and meticulously organized. A single bed with military corners dominated one wall, while a desk covered in neat stacks of papers occupied the other. The space was devoid of personal touches—no photos, no decorations, nothing to indicate the personality of its occupant.

"Where do we start?" Emma whispered.

"The desk," Agatha replied, already moving toward it. She carefully lifted the top sheet of paper, revealing a handwritten list of names—guests at the retreat, each with annotations beside them.

"Look at this," she murmured. "'Eleanor Price – knows about S.B. arrangement. Payment received.' 'Nigel Thompson – demands increased, threatening exposure.'"

Emma peered over her shoulder. "Are these... records of blackmail?"

Agatha nodded, continuing to scan the list. "'Victor Reynolds – suspicious, watching too closely.' That's interesting."

"Check this out," Emma said, opening a desk drawer. She pulled out a small notebook filled with dates, times, and cabin numbers. "He's been tracking everyone's movements."

Agatha flipped through the pages, noting detailed observations about each guest's routines, conversations overheard, and potential vulnerabilities. It was the work of someone meticulous, patient, and deeply disturbing.

"Wait," Emma whispered suddenly, holding up a stack of photographs. "These are pictures of Scarlett with another woman—must be Naomi. They look like they were taken covertly."

Agatha studied the images—Scarlett and Naomi in deep conversation at a café, exchanging what appeared to be manuscripts, arguing in a parking lot. "He's been stalking them for months." A disturbing thought struck her. "What if Elias isn't just a staff member? These aren't casual snapshots—they're calculated surveillance. He's been tracking their movements, documenting their interactions." She examined the dates stamped on the back of several photos. "His job here at the lodge —it could be the perfect cover. Access to everyone's rooms, ability to move around unnoticed, hearing private conversations..."

A soft, urgent whistle from the doorway made them both freeze. Lorraine appeared; her eyes wide.

"He's coming!" she hissed. "Elias is on his way back!"

Agatha quickly gathered a few key pieces of evidence, including the list and several photos. "We need to hide!"

"Where?" Emma whispered frantically, looking around the small space.

The sound of footsteps in the corridor grew louder. There was nowhere to go.

"Under the bed," Agatha decided, already dropping to the floor. Emma followed suit, both of them squeezing into the tight space just as the door handle turned.

From their hiding place, they could see only feet entering the room—Elias's polished black shoes, followed by a second pair of sensible flats.

"You said it was urgent?" a woman's voice asked. Naomi.

"They know," Elias replied, his voice tense. "I saw them in Scarlett's cabin with all the evidence spread out."

"That's not possible," Naomi snapped. "I've been careful. No one could—"

"Well, they do," Elias cut her off. "That Royale woman and her friends. They're getting too close."

Agatha held her breath, straining to hear over the pounding of her heart.

"Did they see the contract?" Naomi asked.

"I don't think so. But they know about the blackmail, and they're connecting it to the murders."

There was a long pause before Naomi spoke again. "Keep an eye on them. Make sure they don't talk to Khumalo. I need to figure out what to do."

"And if they do talk to him?"

"Then we'll both have bigger problems, won't we?" Naomi's voice had an edge to it. "Just do as I say and keep quiet. This will all be over soon."

The conversation continued in lower tones that Agatha couldn't quite make out. She glanced at Emma, whose face reflected the same realization: Naomi and Elias were working together.

After what felt like an eternity, the door opened again. Elias's shoes moved toward it.

"I'll handle it," he was saying. "Just stay away from them for now." The door clicked shut behind them.

Agatha and Emma waited several long moments before crawling out from their hiding place.

"We need to get out of here," Emma whispered.

"Not without proof," Agatha replied, quickly scanning the room again. Her eyes landed on a hollowed-out book on the nightstand. Pulling it open, she found a stack of notes written on the same letterhead as the blackmail messages.

"Got it," she said, slipping a few into her pocket.

They carefully put everything else back in place and eased the door open. The corridor appeared empty, but as they stepped out, a loud crash sounded from the direction of the dining room, followed by Lorraine's unmistakably dramatic voice.

"Oh, mon dieu! How clumsy of me! An entire tray of dishes, ruined! Please, everyone help me clean this disaster!"

Emma suppressed a smile. "Our diversion, right on cue."

They hurried away from Elias's room, rounding the corner just as staff members rushed toward the commotion Lorraine had created. Outside, in the relative safety of the gardens, they found her waiting, a triumphant smile on her face.

"Was that performance not magnifique? I channeled my

inner French catastrophe!" She dusted her hands theatrically. "Please tell me my sacrifice of dignity was not in vain?"

Agatha patted her pocket where the stolen notes resided. "It was worth it. We have proof Elias has been blackmailing multiple guests, and—"

"And he's working with Naomi," Emma finished.

Lorraine's eyes widened. "That quiet writer who's always scribbling in her notebook? Oh, the plot thickens!"

"This changes everything," Agatha said thoughtfully. "We need to figure out what connects them and why they'd be targeting Scarlett."

"And why they'd go to such lengths to hide whatever secret they're protecting," Emma added, her brow furrowed in concentration.

"We need to get back to Scarlett," Agatha said. "Show her what we found."

As they made their way across the grounds, Mike suddenly appeared from around a cabin, trotting toward them with purpose.

"There you are, you naughty boy," Agatha scolded gently, kneeling to ruffle his fur. "Where have you been?"

Mike barked once, then turned to look over his shoulder. Victor was walking along a nearby path, his posture relaxed as he chatted with another guest. He caught sight of them and waved, his smile friendly.

"Ladies," he called. "Enjoying the afternoon?"

"Just getting some fresh air," Agatha replied smoothly.

Victor nodded, continuing on his way, but not before giving Mike a curious glance. The dog had gone still, his attention fixed on Victor's retreating figure.

"What is it, boy?" Agatha murmured, noting his unusual behavior.

Mike whined softly, pressing against her leg.

"It's almost as if he doesn't trust our charming Mr. Reynolds," Lorraine observed. "Or should we say, Mr. Elkins? What was that slip of Marie's about, anyway?"

"I don't know," Agatha admitted. "But I think we should find out."

They found Scarlett where they'd left her, pacing nervously in her cabin. Her relief at their return was palpable.

"You were gone so long, I thought—" She stopped short when she saw their expressions. "What did you find?"

Agatha spread the stolen notes on the table. "Evidence that Elias has been blackmailing multiple guests, not just you." She recounted what they'd overheard between Elias and Naomi.

Scarlett's face hardened. "I knew it. Naomi's been behind this all along."

"It seems that way," Emma agreed. "But something doesn't add up. Why would Naomi kill Eleanor and Nigel if they were all in on the blackmail together?"

"Maybe she wanted all the money for herself?" Lorraine suggested.

Agatha shook her head. "There's still a missing piece to this puzzle." She glanced at Scarlett. "Marie mentioned someone named 'Mr. Elkins' earlier, then quickly corrected herself, saying she meant Victor. Do you know anything about that?"

Scarlett frowned. "Elkins? No, I've never heard Victor called that."

Just then, a sharp knock on the door made them all jump. Mike growled, positioning himself between Agatha and the door.

Scarlett checked the peephole, her face paling. "It's Inspector Khumalo."

The Inspector's expression was grim when they let him in. He surveyed the room, his eyes lingering on the notes scattered across the table.

"Ms. Beaumont," he began formally, "I need to speak with you about some evidence we found in Nigel Thompson's effects." He pulled an evidence bag from his pocket, containing blackmail notes identical to the ones they'd just stolen from Elias's room.

"The handwriting analysis confirms these were not written by Mr. Thompson or Ms. Price," Khumalo continued. "But they match notes found in Ms. Price's room that appear to be from the same blackmailer."

Scarlett's hands trembled slightly. "Inspector, I need to tell you something. I've been receiving similar notes."

Khumalo's eyebrow raised. "From whom?"

"I believe from Elias, one of the staff members," Scarlett replied. "And I have reason to think he's working with Naomi Ndlovu."

The inspector's expression remained neutral, but his eyes sharpened with interest. "That's a serious accusation, Ms. Beaumont. I'll need you to come to the station to give a formal statement." He glanced at the notes on the table. "And I'll need to take those as evidence."

As Khumalo gathered the documents, Agatha slipped the notes she'd taken from Elias's room into her pocket. Something told her they might need their own evidence if things went wrong.

"Will you be wanting statements from all of us?" Emma asked.

Khumalo nodded. "Eventually. But for now, Ms. Beaumont will do." He turned to her. "Are you ready?"

Scarlett looked to Agatha, who gave her an encouraging nod. "Yes, I'm ready."

As they left, Agatha couldn't shake the feeling that they were missing something crucial. Marie's slip about "Mr. Elkins,"

Mike's reaction to Victor, the connection between Naomi and Elias—it all pointed to a larger conspiracy.

"We need to find out more about Victor," she told Emma and Lorraine once Khumalo and Scarlett had gone. "There's something about him that doesn't add up."

"Where do we start?" Emma asked.

Agatha's expression was determined. "With Marie. I think she knows more than she's letting on."

As they left Scarlett's cabin, the sun was beginning to set, casting long shadows across the lodge grounds. In one of those shadows, a figure watched them go, their face hidden in darkness.

29

VICTOR'S ALIBI

"I still can't believe it," Emma said, her gaze fixed on the distant acacia trees silhouetted against the setting sun. "Every time we think we've figured it out, something new throws us off track."

The three friends sat on the veranda of Agatha's cabin, nursing cups of tea as the African evening descended around them. Mike lay at Agatha's feet, his ears perking up occasionally at distant animal calls.

Lorraine sighed dramatically, her hand pressed against her forehead. "Mon Dieu! This is more twisted than that Brazilian soap opera I used to watch. Everyone is a suspect, yet no one seems guilty enough."

Agatha remained silent, turning over the facts in her mind. Scarlett's confession had been a breakthrough, but something still wasn't sitting right. The pieces weren't fitting together perfectly.

"We need to talk to Victor again," she said finally, setting her teacup down with a decisive clink. "He's been hovering around the edges of this whole thing. Maybe he knows more than he's letting on."

"Or maybe he's the killer," Lorraine suggested, her eyes widening with excitement. She leaned forward, lowering her voice to a theatrical whisper. "The quiet, observant writer who watches from the shadows, waiting for the perfect moment to strike!"

Emma rolled her eyes. "Lorraine, not everything is a plot from your mystery novels."

"But you have to admit," Lorraine persisted, "he does have that mysterious quality about him. Always watching, always... so calm."

"We'll talk to him tomorrow," Agatha decided, stifling a yawn. "After a good night's sleep, we'll have clearer heads."

The morning sun streamed through the windows of the lodge's dining area as Agatha and her friends selected pastries from the breakfast buffet. The events of the previous day had left them all drained, though Lorraine still maintained enough energy to critique the selection of jams.

"The apricot is divine, but the strawberry is an abomination," she declared, spreading a generous amount on her croissant. "Clearly store-bought."

Emma was about to respond when she nudged Agatha. "Look who just walked in."

Victor Reynolds stood in the doorway, scanning the room before his eyes settled on their table. With purpose in his stride, he approached them.

"Good morning, ladies," he said, his expression carefully neutral. "I heard you've been asking about me."

Agatha stepped aside, inviting him in with a gesture. "We have. There are still some questions we'd like to ask you."

Victor entered, his gaze sweeping over Emma and Lorraine before settling back on Agatha. There was something different about him today—a strange tension in his shoulders, a wariness in his eyes.

"Before you start interrogating me," he said, taking the seat Agatha offered, "I think it's time I cleared things up."

Lorraine straightened, practically vibrating with anticipation. "Ooh, a confession?"

Victor smiled faintly. "Not quite, Ms. Dubois. More of an explanation." He ran a hand through his hair, suddenly looking tired. "I know I've been acting... suspicious. But there's a simple reason for that."

Emma crossed her arms. "We're listening."

"I wasn't at the lodge during either murder," Victor stated, his voice steady. "I couldn't have been the one who killed Eleanor or Nigel."

Agatha leaned forward. "That's quite a claim. Can you prove it?"

Victor nodded, pulling out his phone. He scrolled through it before turning the screen toward them. "During Eleanor's murder, I was video chatting with my family back home. My daughter was celebrating her birthday." The screen showed screenshots from the video call—a smiling Victor, clearly in a different location, surrounded by what appeared to be family members. "My sister-in-law took screenshots during the call and sent them to me. See the timestamps?" He pointed to the corner of the images, which matched the estimated time of Eleanor's death.

"And Nigel?" Agatha pressed.

Victor swiped to another set of photos. "I was at a small village about thirty miles from here. I'd arranged to meet a local storyteller for research. These photos were taken throughout the day and evening. The lodge's driver can confirm he took me there and brought me back the next morning."

Emma and Agatha exchanged glances. If Victor was telling the truth, he couldn't have committed either murder.

"Why didn't you tell us this before?" Emma asked.

Victor sighed. "Because I found something after Eleanor's death, and I wasn't sure what to do with the information."

Lorraine leaned forward so eagerly she nearly spilled her tea. "Found what? Don't leave us in suspense!"

"When I returned to the lodge after Eleanor was killed, I was asked to help clear her room. The staff was short-handed, and Inspector Khumalo wanted it done quickly." Victor hesitated. "While packing her things, I found some notes in her notebook. They appeared to be blackmail notes."

Agatha's pulse quickened. "Blackmail notes? About what?"

"About Scarlett," Victor said quietly. "Eleanor had discovered Scarlett's secret and was using it against her."

"What secret?" Emma asked, though Agatha suspected they already knew the answer.

"That Scarlett wasn't writing her own books," Victor confirmed. "Eleanor had proof that Scarlett was using a ghost-writer while claiming full authorship. It would have destroyed her career if it got out."

"So Eleanor was blackmailing Scarlett!" Lorraine exclaimed with theatrical surprise, pretending she hadn't already known this fact. She caught Agatha's subtle eye roll and added with a dramatic flourish, "Well, that certainly gives her a motive, non? We mustn't overlook the obvious!"

Victor nodded. "Yes, but there's more. I also overheard a conversation between them at breakfast the day before Eleanor died. Eleanor was pushing Scarlett, demanding more money. Scarlett looked terrified."

Agatha considered this information. It aligned with what Scarlett had confessed, which lent credibility to Victor's account.

"Why didn't you take this to Inspector Khumalo?" she asked.

Victor's expression grew troubled. "Because I wasn't supposed to be looking through Eleanor's personal items. And honestly, I wasn't sure what to make of it. I knew it would make Scarlett look guilty, but something about it felt... off."

"Off how?" Emma pressed.

"The notes weren't just about Scarlett," Victor explained. "There were references to Nigel, too. It seemed like they were working together to blackmail her."

Agatha felt a chill run down her spine. "And then they both ended up dead."

The room fell silent as they absorbed this information. Outside, the savannah stretched out beneath the bright morning sun, the occasional call of birds punctuating the stillness as early risers among the wildlife began their day.

"I should have come forward sooner," Victor admitted. "But I've been a writer long enough to know that the obvious solution isn't always the correct one. I wanted to understand what was really happening before pointing fingers."

Agatha studied him carefully. His story was plausible, and the evidence he provided seemed legitimate. But something still nagged at her—a feeling that they were missing a crucial piece of the puzzle.

"What about Naomi?" she asked suddenly. "Where does she fit into all this?"

Victor hesitated, his fingers drumming lightly against his knee. "That's what I couldn't figure out. Naomi and Scarlett have history, certainly. But Naomi has been just as evasive as Scarlett throughout this whole ordeal."

"Perhaps because she's the ghostwriter," Emma suggested.

"Perhaps," Victor agreed. "But there's something else you

should know." He reached into his pocket and pulled out a folded piece of paper. "I found another threatening note in my cabin this morning."

He unfolded it and placed it on the table. It was a note, written in block letters:

KEEP YOUR MOUTH SHUT OR YOU'LL BE NEXT.

"Someone doesn't want me talking to you," Victor said quietly. "Which makes me think we're getting closer to the truth."

Lorraine's eyes widened. "Mon Dieu! A threat! How deliciously dramatic!"

"Lorraine," Emma scolded, though there was no real heat in her voice.

Agatha picked up the note, examining it carefully. The paper was high-quality, with a faint watermark visible when held to the light. "This isn't ordinary paper," she observed. "It looks like stationery from a business or organization."

Victor nodded. "I noticed that too. It seems familiar somehow, but I can't place it."

A sudden bark from Mike drew their attention. The schnauzer had been resting under their table but now stood alert, his ears perked up as he stared intensely toward the entrance of the dining room.

"What is it, boy?" Agatha whispered, following his gaze.

They all turned discreetly to look. A shadow passed quickly by the doorway, and they glimpsed someone hurrying away from the dining area.

"Someone was listening," Emma murmured, keeping her voice low.

Victor set down his coffee cup, his expression grim. "I should go. It seems our conversation has attracted unwanted attention."

"Be careful," Agatha warned. "If someone is threatening you, they might be dangerous."

Victor lingered at the door, his hand resting lightly on the frame. "I'll be fine. My cabin's close, and the staff are patrolling the grounds." He smiled faintly. "Besides, I'm not the one stirring up trouble with all these questions."

His gaze softened as it met Agatha's. "For what it's worth, I believe you, Ms. Royale."

Agatha's chest tightened. "Thank you," she said quietly.

After Victor left, the three friends sat in thoughtful silence. Mike returned to Agatha's side, resting his head on her lap.

"Do you believe him?" Emma asked finally.

Agatha stroked Mike's fur, considering the question. "His alibi seems solid, and his story matches what Scarlett told us. But there's still something we're missing."

Lorraine popped the last bite of a pastry into her mouth. "Maybe we should focus on this threatening note. If we can figure out where the paper came from, we might find our killer."

"That's actually not a bad idea," Emma said, looking surprised at herself for agreeing with Lorraine.

Agatha nodded slowly. "Tomorrow, we'll see if we can identify the stationery. And I think it's time we had another chat with Naomi. If she is Scarlett's ghostwriter, she might be more involved than we realized."

As they prepared for bed that night, Agatha couldn't shake the feeling that they were getting closer to the truth. Victor's alibi had unexpectedly cleared him, shifting their focus elsewhere. But in this web of secrets and lies, she wasn't sure who to trust anymore.

One thing was certain—someone at the lodge was a killer, and they weren't finished covering their tracks.

30

A CLUE IN THE LETTERHEAD

The morning arrived with a blaze of golden light streaming through the cabin window, but Agatha had been awake for hours, her mind churning over Victor's revelations. Mike stretched at the foot of her bed, his little schnauzer face yawning widely before he hopped down to begin his morning patrol of the room.

"At least one of us got some sleep," Agatha muttered, running a hand through her hair.

After a quick shower and a change of clothes, she grabbed Victor's threatening note and headed for the lodge. The air was already warm, carrying the scent of dry grass and distant smoke —someone was cooking breakfast over an open fire. Her stomach growled in response, reminding her that mysteries were better solved on a full stomach.

She found Emma and Lorraine already at their usual table, Emma nursing a cup of coffee while Lorraine arranged an impressive array of pastries on her plate.

"I see you've discovered the kitchen's latest batch," Agatha said, sliding into the chair beside Emma.

Lorraine beamed, holding up a sticky bun. "Magnifique! The

chef added a touch of cardamom. One must fuel properly for a day of detective work, ma chérie."

Emma rolled her eyes but couldn't hide her smile. "Did you bring the note?"

Agatha nodded, placing the folded paper on the table between them, careful to keep it partially concealed from curious onlookers. "I've been thinking about this all night. The paper quality is distinctive—it's not something you'd find in the lodge's stationery drawer."

Emma picked it up, examining it more closely in the morning light. "You're right. This is high-quality business stationery. See how the paper has that subtle texture? And there's definitely some kind of watermark or letterhead that's been carefully cut off."

Lorraine leaned forward, powdered sugar dusting her chin. "Ooh! Like in 'Murder at Midnight' when the threatening note turned out to be written on the victim's own personal stationery!"

"You might be onto something," Agatha admitted. "If we could figure out where this paper came from, it might tell us who wrote the note."

Emma pulled out her phone and started typing. "I'm going to search for some of the publishing houses represented at the retreat. Maybe one of them uses this kind of stationery."

While Emma researched, Agatha scanned the dining room. Naomi sat alone at a corner table, picking at her breakfast while reading something on her tablet. Scarlett was nowhere to be seen—probably hiding in her cabin after yesterday's confession. Victor sat at the bar, chatting with the bartender, seemingly unconcerned despite the threat he'd received.

"Anything?" Agatha asked Emma.

She shook her head, frustration evident in her furrowed

brow. "There are too many possibilities. Without seeing the full letterhead, it's hard to narrow it down."

Lorraine dabbed at her mouth with a napkin. "Perhaps we need a different approach. What if—" Her words cut off abruptly as her eyes widened, fixed on something over Agatha's shoulder.

Agatha turned to see Inspector Khumalo approaching their table, his expression serious as always.

"Good morning, ladies," he greeted them with a slight nod. "Ms. Royale, I'd like a word if you don't mind."

Agatha's stomach tightened. "Of course, Inspector."

He gestured toward a quiet corner of the veranda. "In private, please."

She exchanged glances with Emma and Lorraine before following him. Mike trotted at her heels, unwilling to leave her side.

Once they were out of earshot, Khumalo turned to face her. "I understand Ms. Beaumont has made some interesting claims about her relationship with the deceased."

So he knew about Scarlett's confession. Agatha wondered briefly if she had gone to him herself or if someone else had informed him.

"Yes," she confirmed. "She told us about being blackmailed by Eleanor and Nigel over her use of a ghostwriter."

Khumalo nodded. "And Mr. Reynolds has provided an alibi for both murders that checks out. Which leaves us with Ms. Ndlovu, who found herself conveniently absent during both incidents, though witnesses place her in the lodge during Nigel's death."

"Do you think she's the murderer?" Agatha asked.

Khumalo's expression remained impassive. "I think there's more to this case than any of us initially suspected. Including you, Ms. Royale."

Agatha bristled slightly. "I'm just trying to clear my name, Inspector."

"By inserting yourself into an active murder investigation," he pointed out, though there was a hint of something like respect in his voice. "But I must admit, your amateur sleuthing has uncovered details my team might have missed."

She wasn't sure whether to feel flattered or offended by his backhanded compliment.

Khumalo's expression softened slightly as he looked down at Mike, who was watching him with curious eyes. "Your little friend here seems to have quite good instincts about people. Perhaps better than some of my officers." He bent down briefly to let Mike sniff his hand before straightening again.

"Inspector," Agatha began hesitantly, "am I still a suspect in all this?"

Khumalo's smile was small but genuine. "Ms. Royale, I would be remiss in my duties if I told you that you were completely in the clear." He held up a hand as she began to protest. "Not because I personally believe you're guilty, but because a good detective never removes anyone from the suspect list until the case is closed." His eyes crinkled at the corners. "Even if that person happens to be doing half my job for me."

Agatha couldn't help but smile back. "I'll take that as a compliment."

"As you should." Khumalo's voice turned serious again. "But please remember to be careful. Whoever murdered Eleanor and Nigel is still here, among us. And they've already killed twice."

Before she could respond, Mike let out a small whine, drawing her attention back to their table where Emma was waving frantically.

"If you'll excuse me, Inspector," Agatha said. "It seems my friends need me."

He nodded.

"We'll speak again soon, Ms. Royale. I'm sure of it." As she turned to go, he added, "And do try to stay out of trouble. I'd hate to see your little detective partner there lose his human."

When she returned to the table, Emma was practically vibrating with excitement. "Agatha, look at this," she whispered, her voice tense with discovery.

She had laid the threatening note beside her phone, which displayed a webpage open to a publishing company's contact information. The letterhead on the screen matched the faint impression visible on the note when tilted toward the light— same font, same spacing, same elegant simplicity.

"These notes are written on letterhead from a publishing house in New York," Emma said quietly, her finger tracing the subtle pattern. "Someone carefully cut off the top part, but they couldn't completely remove the watermark."

Agatha leaned closer, her heart beginning to race. "What publishing house?"

Emma turned her phone toward her. "Meridian Press. They're a boutique publisher specializing in thrillers and mysteries."

A quick search online made Agatha's breath catch in her throat. "Oh my gosh... that's Naomi's new publisher!"

Lorraine's grin was triumphant. "I knew it. It's always the innocent ones."

The three of them turned simultaneously to look at Naomi, who was still absorbed in her reading, completely unaware that she had just become their prime suspect.

"We need to be careful," Agatha cautioned, lowering her voice. "If Naomi is behind this, confronting her directly could be dangerous."

Emma nodded, her expression serious. "Should we take this to Khumalo?"

Agatha considered their options. The letterhead was suspicious, certainly, but it wasn't definitive proof. Naomi could easily claim she had nothing to do with the note, that someone had stolen her stationery or was framing her. They needed more.

"Not yet," she decided. "Let's see if we can find a connection between Naomi, Eleanor, and Nigel beyond just the publishing industry. There has to be something more personal driving all this."

Lorraine sighed dramatically. "Mon Dieu, another day of detective work! My nerves can barely stand the excitement." Despite her theatrical complaint, her eyes sparkled with anticipation.

As they finished breakfast and prepared to continue their investigation, Agatha couldn't shake the feeling that they were finally on the right track. The letterhead was their first solid clue pointing to a specific suspect. But experience—both from her bookshop mysteries and this increasingly complicated case—had taught her that the obvious answer wasn't always the correct one.

She glanced across the dining room at Naomi once more. The woman looked up suddenly, as if sensing Agatha's gaze, and their eyes met. For a brief moment, Naomi's expression shifted from surprise to something darker—anger? Fear? Guilt?—before she quickly looked away.

Whatever her involvement, one thing was becoming clear: the web of deception surrounding these murders was far more tangled than any of them had initially suspected.

And they were getting closer to the heart of it.

31

CONFRONTING SCARLETT

The afternoon sun beat down mercilessly as Agatha, Emma, and Lorraine made their way toward Scarlett's cabin. The path was lined with scraggly acacia trees that offered little shade, and the red dust kicked up with each step, leaving a fine coating on their shoes.

"Are we sure this is a good idea?" Emma asked, her voice low. "If Naomi is really behind all this, maybe we should be talking to her instead."

Agatha shook her head. "We have the letterhead—with her publisher's watermark. That connects her to the threatening notes. And don't forget—we overheard her conversation with Elias. I don't think there's any doubt left, Emma."

Agatha shook her head. "Scarlett admitted to being black-mailed. She's the only one who's been willing to talk openly. If Naomi is involved, Scarlett might know how."

"Besides," Lorraine added with a dramatic flourish of her hand, "confronting a suspect directly is classic detective work! Though I do wish we had one of those little pistols that fits in an evening purse. Very chic, very practical."

Emma rolled her eyes. "We're not confronting anyone with a gun, Lorraine."

"Of course not, ma chérie. I was merely making an observation about accessorizing for detective work."

As they approached Scarlett's cabin, Agatha noticed the curtains were drawn despite the bright day. They climbed the three wooden steps to the small porch, and Agatha knocked firmly on the door.

Silence.

She knocked again, louder this time.

"Perhaps she's napping?" Lorraine suggested, peering through a narrow gap in the curtains. "I can't see anything."

Emma tried the handle. "It's unlocked."

Agatha hesitated, then pushed the door open slowly. "Scarlett? It's Agatha Royale. We need to talk."

The cabin was dim but not dark, the heavy curtains unable to fully block the bright African sun. Scarlett sat in an armchair facing the door, her expression wary. She looked exhausted, dark circles under her eyes standing out starkly against her pale skin.

"I thought you might come," she said quietly. "After my confession to Inspector Khumalo this morning."

"You went to see him?" Emma asked, surprised.

Scarlett nodded, gesturing for them to enter. "It was time to come clean about the blackmail. I couldn't keep living with the guilt."

Agatha closed the door behind them and took a seat on the small sofa opposite Scarlett. Emma joined her, while Lorraine perched on the arm of the sofa, ever dramatic in her posture.

"Did you tell him everything?" Agatha asked.

"I told him about Eleanor and Nigel blackmailing me." Scarlett's fingers twisted nervously in her lap. "About the ghostwriting. About how I was afraid they'd destroy my career if the truth got out."

"But you didn't kill them," Agatha stated, watching Scarlett's face carefully.

"No." Scarlett met her gaze steadily. "I didn't. I was terrified and angry, but I'm not a killer."

Agatha pulled out the threatening note they'd found and placed it on the coffee table between them. "Do you recognize this?"

Scarlett leaned forward, her brow furrowing as she studied the paper. "No. What is it?"

"Someone left it for Victor. A warning to keep quiet."

Scarlett picked it up, turning it over in her hands. "I don't understand. What does this have to do with me?"

Emma shifted forward. "We think it's written on letterhead from Meridian Press. Naomi's new publisher."

Scarlett's eyes widened. "You think Naomi is behind all this?"

"We're not sure," Agatha admitted. "But we need you to tell us everything about your relationship with her. Is she your ghostwriter?"

The question hung in the air between them. Scarlett's shoulders slumped as she sank back into her chair.

"Yes," she finally whispered. "She is—or was. It started seven years ago. My third book was due, and I had the worst writer's block of my life. My marriage was falling apart, I was drinking too much, and my publisher was threatening to drop me if I didn't deliver."

"So you hired Naomi to write it for you," Emma supplied.

Scarlett nodded. "She was talented but unknown. I offered her good money—more than she'd get for her own book as a debut author. She wrote it, I put my name on it, and it became

my biggest bestseller yet." Her laugh was bitter. "Ironic, isn't it?
The book I didn't write was my greatest success."

She traced a finger along the rim of her teacup, her gaze
distant. "What amazed me most was how perfectly she captured
my voice—better than I could myself. She'd studied my earlier
work meticulously, analyzed my sentence structures, my
metaphors, my character development patterns. She knew
which words I favored and which I avoided. She even replicated
my tendency to use semicolons when I'm building tension."

Scarlett sighed, setting down her cup with a soft clink. "We
developed a system. I'd provide a concept, character sketches,
maybe a rough outline. Then she'd disappear for weeks and
return with chapters that sounded so much like me that sometimes I'd forget I hadn't written them." Her voice dropped to
almost a whisper. "Soon critics were praising my 'evolved style'
and 'newfound depth'—all while I was doing less and less of the
actual writing."

Her fingers twisted nervously in her lap. "I told myself it was
a business arrangement that benefited us both. She got financial
security; I got my career back. But there were moments when I'd
be at a signing, hearing readers gush about passages I'd never
crafted, themes I'd never conceived... that's when the shame
would hit hardest."

"And then what happened?" Agatha prompted.

"We continued the arrangement. She wrote three more
books for me. But then Eleanor somehow found out. She threatened to expose me unless I paid her."

"How did Eleanor discover your secret?" Lorraine asked,
leaning forward eagerly.

Scarlett's expression darkened. "Nigel. He was Naomi's
editor before he dropped her. He must have recognized her
writing style in my books." She shook her head. "Eleanor

approached me at a conference six months ago with proof—emails between Naomi and me discussing the books."

"And Nigel joined in on the blackmail," Emma guessed.

"Not at first. But when he found out what Eleanor was doing, he wanted a cut." Scarlett's voice cracked. "They were bleeding me dry."

Agatha considered this information. It all fit with what they already knew, but something still bothered her.

"Scarlett," she said carefully, "why did you bury that bottle we saw you with the other night?"

The color drained from Scarlett's face. "You saw that?"

Agatha nodded. "You and Naomi seemed to be working together. She gave you something, and you buried it. What was it?"

Scarlett closed her eyes briefly before answering. "Sleeping pills. The same kind that were found in Nigel's system."

Emma gasped. "You had the murder weapon?"

"Not exactly," Scarlett said quickly. "After Eleanor died, Naomi came to me in a panic. She said she'd bought some herbs for me—which was true, I had asked her to get them for research—but she was worried they might look suspicious now that someone had been killed. Then when Nigel died and Inspector Khumalo mentioned sleeping pills, she gave me a bottle she had in her cabin. Said she was afraid someone might plant it in her room to frame her."

Agatha's brow furrowed. "Research? What kind of research involves potentially poisonous herbs?"

Scarlett hesitated, then squared her shoulders. "I'm writing again. My own work, not ghostwritten. For the first time in years, I've found my voice again." Her expression softened with genuine pride. "It's a psychological thriller about a botanist who specializes in toxic plants. I've been doing extensive research into traditional remedies and herbal properties to make it authentic."

She crossed to her desk and pulled out a thick notebook filled with handwritten notes and sketches of various plants. "See? Everything meticulously documented—effects, traditional uses, historical context. I even have interview notes from a botanist in Johannesburg."

Emma leaned closer, examining the detailed work. "That's impressively thorough."

"I needed to understand it all completely," Scarlett continued, her voice gaining confidence. "After relying on someone else's talent for so long, I wanted to prove to myself that I could create something real again." She closed the notebook gently. "I asked Naomi to get those herbs from the local market because I wanted to study their properties firsthand—texture, smell, how they break down when steeped."

"But the sleeping pills weren't part of your research," Agatha pointed out.

Scarlett shook her head. "No, those came later. After Nigel's death, Naomi showed up at my door looking terrified. She thrust this bottle at me and begged me to get rid of it. She said they were the same brand found in Nigel's system and she was afraid of being framed." Scarlett's eyes dropped. "I should have taken them straight to Khumalo, but I was scared. So I buried them instead."

"Suddenly my innocent herb research looked suspicious too," she admitted. "Everything looked incriminating in this new context. I panicked and made it worse by hiding evidence."

"So you buried it to protect her?" Agatha asked incredulously.

"I buried it because I was scared!" Scarlett's voice rose. "I didn't know what to think. Naomi has been good to me, despite everything. She never threatened to expose our arrangement, even when I know it hurt her career. I felt I owed her."

"Or maybe," Emma said slowly, "you were afraid of her."

A look of fear flickered across Scarlett's face. "I don't know what you mean."

"I think you do," Agatha pressed gently. "Naomi had plenty of reason to hate Eleanor and Nigel. They ruined her career while you profited from her talent. Maybe she decided to take matters into her own hands."

"And you helped her cover it up," Emma added.

"No!" Scarlett stood abruptly, pacing the small room. "I didn't know anything about Eleanor's murder until it happened. And I was in my cabin all night when Nigel was killed. You can check with the security guard—I called him to fix my air conditioning unit at midnight."

Agatha studied her, trying to determine if she was telling the truth. "Why haven't you told Inspector Khumalo about the buried bottle?"

Scarlett stopped pacing, her expression pained. "Because I don't know what to believe anymore. If Naomi did kill them... I don't want to be the one to condemn her. Not when I've used her for my own success all these years."

The room fell silent for a moment, the only sound the distant call of birds from the savannah beyond the lodge.

Finally, Agatha stood. "You need to tell Khumalo everything, Scarlett. About the bottle, about Naomi—all of it. If you don't, you could be charged as an accessory."

"She's right," Emma said, her tone softening. "This isn't something you can hide."

Scarlett looked defeated, sinking back into her chair. "You're right. I'll go to him today."

As Agatha and her friends prepared to leave, Mike, who had been quietly exploring the cabin, suddenly began barking aggressively at Scarlett. His hackles were raised, teeth bared in a most uncharacteristic display.

"Mike!" Agatha called, surprised. "What's gotten into you?"

The little schnauzer wouldn't stop, backing Scarlett into her chair with his growls.

"Get him away from me!" Scarlett cried, pulling her feet up onto the chair.

Agatha grabbed Mike's collar, gently pulling him back. "I'm so sorry. He's never acted like this before."

As they left the cabin, Mike still grumbling under his breath, Lorraine shivered despite the heat. "Mon Dieu! Did you see how he went after her? Perhaps our little detective knows something we don't."

Agatha frowned, glancing back at Scarlett's cabin. Mike had always been an excellent judge of character. His unusual behavior toward Scarlett bothered her more than she wanted to admit.

"Let's head back," she said finally. "We need to decide what to do next."

As they walked away, Agatha couldn't shake the feeling that there was still something important they were missing. The pieces were coming together, but the picture they formed didn't quite make sense.

And time was running out.

32

THE NET CLOSES

The afternoon sun hung low in the sky, casting long shadows across the lodge grounds as Agatha, Emma, and Lorraine sat on the veranda, processing their conversation with Scarlett.

"Do you believe her?" Emma asked, stirring her iced tea absently, the ice cubes clinking against the glass.

Agatha frowned, watching Mike, who lay at her feet still occasionally grumbling in the direction of Scarlett's cabin. "Parts of it. The ghostwriting arrangement makes sense. But there's something she's not telling us."

"What bothers me," Lorraine said, uncharacteristically serious, "is that bottle she buried. If she's innocent, why hide evidence?"

"Fear," Emma suggested. "Or maybe loyalty to Naomi."

"Or guilt," Agatha countered. "Mike certainly didn't trust her, and he's rarely wrong about people."

They fell silent as Inspector Khumalo approached their table, his expression unreadable as usual. He nodded a greeting before taking the empty chair beside Agatha.

"Ms. Royale," he began, "I've just finished speaking with Ms.

Beaumont. She's told me everything—including your visit to her cabin."

Agatha met his gaze steadily. "We were trying to understand her connection to Naomi."

"So she mentioned." Khumalo's dark eyes studied each of them in turn. "She also told me about the bottle she buried—the one you all discovered was missing. My officers managed to track it down based on Ms. Beaumont's description of where she buried it."

"And?" Emma pressed.

"The forensic team's preliminary tests confirm it didn't contain herbs as Ms. Ndlovu claimed—it contained sleeping pills. The exact same brand found in Nigel Thompson's system." Khumalo's voice remained professional, but Agatha detected a hint of respect in his tone. "Ms. Beaumont's testimony, combined with the evidence you three have uncovered, has painted a much clearer picture of these events."

"So you believe Scarlett is innocent?" Agatha asked.

"I've verified her alibi for the night of Nigel's murder," Khumalo said, folding his hands on the table. "The maintenance log confirms a service call to her cabin at 11:48 PM for the air conditioning unit, and the security guard remained until 1:45 AM while the technician completed extensive repairs. The medical examiner places Nigel's death between 1 and 3 AM, and staff members confirmed seeing the maintenance activity at her cabin throughout that critical timeframe."

"Ms. Ndlovu's whereabouts that night are less certain," Khumalo admitted. "Several guests recall seeing her in the lodge bar until around midnight, but no one can confirm her location after that."

Agatha exchanged glances with Emma. "So Naomi doesn't have an alibi for the time of Nigel's murder."

"Correct." Khumalo adjusted his position slightly. "Now, Ms. Royale, I believe it's time we clarified your situation as well."

Agatha's heart skipped a beat. "My situation?"

"Yes." A small smile played at the corners of Khumalo's mouth. "In light of recent developments, I can officially inform you that you are no longer a person of interest in Eleanor Price's murder."

Relief washed over Agatha, though she tried not to show it too obviously. "Thank you, Detective."

"Don't thank me yet," Khumalo cautioned. "You're still involved in this investigation, and I expect you to exercise appropriate caution. The person responsible for these deaths is clearly dangerous and resourceful."

As if on cue, Mike suddenly sat up, his ears pricked toward the lodge entrance. They all turned to see Victor Reynolds approaching, his face drawn with concern.

"Inspector," Victor nodded to Khumalo before turning to Agatha. "I need to speak with you. It's important."

Khumalo rose from his chair. "I'll leave you to it. But remember what I said, Ms. Royale—caution." With a meaningful look, he headed back toward the main building.

Victor took the seat Khumalo had vacated, running a hand through his hair in a gesture of agitation. "I've received another note," he said without preamble.

"When?" Agatha asked sharply.

"Just now. It was slipped under my cabin door while I was showering." He handed Agatha a folded piece of paper, similar to the first. "This time, they're not being subtle about the threat."

Agatha unfolded the note and read aloud softly, "Stop digging or you'll be buried next. Final warning." The paper was the same high-quality stationery as before, with the same faint trace of a letterhead at the top.

"I'm being blackmailed too," Victor admitted, his voice low and strained. "Just like Scarlett."

"By whom?" Emma asked.

Victor glanced around before answering. "I think it's Naomi. I found this in my mailbox yesterday." He pulled another note from his pocket and handed it to Agatha.

This note was longer, more detailed, and contained a clear demand for money in exchange for silence about some unspecified secret. It was written on the same letterhead paper.

"What is she blackmailing you about?" Lorraine asked bluntly.

Victor hesitated, then sighed. "It's complicated and frankly embarrassing. I worked at Meridian Press years ago, before I became a full-time author. There was an... incident. A manuscript I edited turned out to be plagiarized, but it wasn't caught until after publication. The scandal nearly destroyed my career. I've kept it quiet ever since."

"And Naomi knows about this?" Agatha pressed.

"She must know someone at Meridian. Former editors or staff members often gossip about old scandals." Victor shook his head. "The publishing world is surprisingly small—everyone knows everyone's business eventually. I never connected her to the blackmail until I saw that letterhead."

"We should take this to Khumalo," Emma said firmly. "This is clear evidence against Naomi."

Agatha nodded, but before she could respond, her attention was drawn to a commotion near the lodge entrance. Inspector Khumalo and two uniformed officers were heading toward the guest cabins with purposeful strides.

"Something's happening," she said, standing for a better view.

They watched as the small procession turned down the path toward Naomi's cabin. Minutes later, they emerged with

Naomi between them, her expression a mixture of shock and fury.

"They're arresting her," Emma whispered.

Without discussion, the four of them moved to a spot where they could observe without interfering. As Naomi was escorted past, her eyes locked with Agatha's, and the look of pure venom in them made Agatha take an involuntary step back.

"You wannabe mystery writer." Naomi spat, struggling against the officers holding her arms. "You ruined my life!"

"Ms. Ndlovu," Khumalo's voice was stern, "anything you say can and will be used against you."

"I didn't kill anyone!" Naomi shouted as they led her away. "You're making a terrible mistake!"

When they had disappeared into the main lodge, Agatha turned to Victor. "You should show Khumalo that blackmail note immediately."

Victor nodded, his expression troubled. "I will. But I can't help feeling that something isn't quite right about all this."

"What do you mean?" Emma asked.

"It just seems too... convenient. Naomi suddenly becoming the obvious suspect." He shook his head. "Maybe I'm over-thinking it."

"Or maybe you're not," Agatha said slowly, a nagging doubt forming in her mind. "What exactly did Khumalo say when you provided your alibi?"

Victor looked surprised by the question. "He seemed satisfied. Said the time stamps on the photos and the driver's testimony cleared me of suspicion."

"And you never mentioned working at Meridian Press during your conversations with him?"

"No." Victor's brow furrowed. "It never came up. Why?"

Agatha exchanged glances with Emma and Lorraine before answering. "Just making sure we're not missing anything."

As Victor excused himself to speak with Khumalo, Lorraine leaned close to Agatha. "You don't believe him, do you?"

"I'm not sure," Agatha admitted. "Something about this doesn't feel right."

Emma nodded. "Naomi being the killer is too neat. Too obvious."

"Exactly." Agatha watched Victor's retreating figure thoughtfully. "And in my experience with mysteries, when the solution seems too obvious..."

"It usually is," Emma finished for her.

Lorraine sighed dramatically. "Mon Dieu! Just when I thought we could finally relax and enjoy what's left of this disastrous vacation." She straightened her posture, a determined glint in her eye. "So, what do we do now?"

Agatha's gaze drifted toward the cabins where Victor had disappeared. "We keep digging. There's still a piece missing from this puzzle, and I think we need to find it before we leave Botswana."

As the sun began to set over the savannah, casting a golden-red glow across the landscape, Agatha couldn't shake the feeling that they were approaching a dangerous turning point. The net was closing—but around whom, she wasn't entirely sure.

33

THE TWIST

"I still can't believe they arrested Naomi," Emma said, stirring her coffee the next morning. Dark circles under her eyes betrayed a restless night. "The evidence seemed solid, but her reaction..."

"Was too genuine," Agatha finished, nibbling at a piece of toast without much appetite. "She seemed genuinely shocked, not guilty."

Three days had passed since Naomi's arrest. The retreat, originally scheduled to continue for another week, was being cut short in light of recent events. Most guests were making arrangements to leave within the next forty-eight hours.

Lorraine swept into the dining area, her dramatic entrance turning heads despite the somber atmosphere. "Mes amies! I have wonderful news!" She dropped into the chair beside Agatha, her eyes sparkling with excitement. "I've secured us seats on tomorrow's flight to Johannesburg. We can be home by the weekend!"

Emma smiled, reaching over to squeeze Lorraine's hand. "That is good news. I think we're all ready to put this nightmare behind us."

Agatha nodded, but her expression remained troubled. "We should probably visit Victor before we go, to say goodbye. He's been through a lot too."

"And he did help clear your name," Emma added.

"Oui, a proper goodbye is the civilized thing to do," Lorraine agreed, snagging a croissant from Agatha's plate. "Besides, I want to thank him for that recommendation letter he offered to write for my future cooking blog."

The morning passed quickly as they packed their belongings, the simple task of folding clothes and organizing souvenirs bringing a sense of normalcy that had been absent for days. By early afternoon, their suitcases were ready, and they decided to make their farewell visit to Victor.

"I should bring Mike for a quick walk first," Agatha said, reaching for his leash. "He's been cooped up all morning."

"We'll meet you at Victor's in fifteen minutes," Emma suggested. "Cabin twelve, right?"

"That's the one. The blue door at the end of the path," Agatha confirmed, clipping the leash to Mike's collar.

After a brisk walk around the lodge grounds, with Mike stopping to investigate every interesting scent, Agatha headed toward Victor's cabin. As she approached, she noticed Marie exiting with her cleaning supplies.

"Good afternoon, Marie," Agatha called.

The young housekeeper startled slightly, then smiled. "Ms. Royale. Are you here to see Mr. Reynolds?"

"Yes, my friends and I are leaving tomorrow, so we wanted to say goodbye."

Marie nodded. "He's not in at the moment, but he shouldn't be long. He mentioned going to the main office to arrange his own departure." She gestured to the partially open door. "You can wait inside if you'd like. I've just finished cleaning."

"Thank you," Agatha said, stepping onto the small porch.

"By the way, how are you doing? This has all been quite traumatic."

Marie's expression clouded. "It's been... difficult. But I'm glad they've caught the person responsible." She hesitated, then added, "Ms. Ndlovu always seemed so quiet. It's hard to believe she could do something so terrible."

Agatha studied Marie's face carefully. "Do you believe she did it?"

Marie averted her eyes. "It's not my place to say, madame. I should go—other cabins to clean." With a quick nod, she hurried away, her cleaning cart rattling slightly on the uneven path.

Agatha watched her go before pushing the door open and stepping inside. Victor's cabin was larger than hers, with a separate sitting area and a small desk positioned near the window to catch the natural light. Mike trotted in behind her, immediately beginning his customary inspection of the new space.

She had just settled into one of the armchairs when Emma and Lorraine arrived, letting themselves in with a quick knock.

"No Victor?" Emma asked, glancing around the empty cabin.

"Marie said he went to the main office. He should be back soon." Agatha gestured for them to sit. "Make yourselves comfortable."

Lorraine wandered around the cabin, admiring the decor. "He has quite good taste for a man. These cushions are certainly a step up from the scratchy things in my cabin."

As Emma and Lorraine chatted about the differences in their accommodations, Agatha noticed Mike sniffing intently at Victor's desk. His tail was straight, ears perked—the stance he took when he found something interesting.

"What is it, boy?" she asked, moving to join him.

Mike nudged the partially open bottom drawer with his nose, looking up at Agatha expectantly.

"Agatha," Emma cautioned, "should you be going through his desk?"

Agatha hesitated, her hand hovering over the drawer. "Probably not, but Mike seems pretty insistent." She opened it wider, revealing a stack of papers and a small notebook.

Lorraine glanced toward the door nervously. "If you're going to snoop, ma chérie, do be quick about it."

Agatha carefully lifted the top papers, finding nothing unusual until she reached the bottom of the stack. Her breath caught as she recognized the high-quality stationery—identical to the blackmail notes, but in a full pad rather than cut sheets. The letterhead at the top read "Meridian Press" in elegant font.

"Emma, Lorraine," she whispered urgently. "Look at this."

Emma moved to her side, her eyes widening. "That's the same letterhead. Why would Victor have Meridian Press stationery?"

"He said he used to work there," Agatha reminded her, "but this isn't old stationery. Look at the date—it's from this year."

Lorraine joined them, her dramatic flair momentarily subdued by genuine concern. "Do you think... could Victor be lying about his connection to Meridian?"

A cold suspicion formed in Agatha's mind. She turned to Emma. "Hand me your phone. I want to check something."

Emma passed her phone over, and Agatha quickly typed "Victor Reynolds Meridian Press" into the search bar. The results appeared instantly, but none mentioned any professional connection between Victor and the publishing house.

She refined her search, trying various combinations until finally typing "Victor Reynolds name only." The search yielded several author profiles and interviews, but nothing suggesting an alias or alternative identity.

"What are you looking for?" Emma asked, watching over her shoulder.

"I'm not sure," Agatha admitted. "But something Marie said has been bothering me. Actually, something she didn't say." She tried one more search, this time for "Meridian Press executives' history."

The results brought up a page listing the company's leadership over the years. Agatha scrolled through it quickly until a name caught her eye: "Victor Elkins, Editorial Director, 2010-2015."

"Elkins," she murmured. "Where have I heard that name before?"

Emma and Lorraine exchanged confused glances. "What is it?" Emma prompted.

"I remember now," Agatha said slowly. "When I was talking with Marie a few days ago, she slipped and called Victor 'Mr. Elkins.' She tried to cover it up, but I knew I'd heard it clearly."

"You think Victor Reynolds is really Victor Elkins?" Lorraine asked, her voice uncharacteristically hushed.

"It would explain why he has Meridian Press stationery," Emma reasoned. "But why use a different name?"

The sound of the front door opening cut their speculation short. They turned to see Victor standing in the doorway, a look of surprise registering on his face when he saw them gathered around his desk.

"Making yourselves at home, I see," he said, his tone light but his eyes sharp.

"We were just waiting for you," Agatha explained, trying to sound casual as she discreetly slipped the stationery pad back into the drawer. "Marie said we could wait inside."

"Of course." Victor stepped into the cabin, closing the door behind him. "I'm glad you stopped by. I wanted to say goodbye before you left."

Mike, who had been quietly observing from the side of the

desk, suddenly began growling, his hackles rising as he stared at Victor.

"Mike," Agatha admonished, though her own unease was growing. "I'm sorry, he's not usually like this."

Victor's smile didn't reach his eyes. "Dogs can be unpredictable. Especially when their owners are nervous." He moved toward the small kitchenette. "Can I offer anyone a drink before you go? I have some excellent scotch."

"Actually," Emma said, casting a meaningful glance at Agatha, "we should probably finish our packing. We just wanted to say goodbye."

"So soon?" Victor's voice had an edge to it now. "But we were just getting to know each other." He turned back to face them, and Agatha noticed his posture had changed subtly—more alert, more guarded.

"Victor," Agatha said carefully, "or should I call you Mr. Elkins?"

The change in his expression was immediate—a flash of shock, quickly replaced by cold calculation. He let out a small, humorless laugh.

"I always knew you were clever, Agatha. Too clever for your own good."

Emma stepped closer to Agatha, her voice barely audible. "We should go."

"I don't think so," Victor said, casually positioning himself between them and the door. "Not until we've had a proper chat about what you think you know."

Lorraine, to her credit, maintained her composure remarkably well. "We don't know anything," she assured him with an exaggerated wave of her hand. "Just a case of mistaken identity, non? These things happen all the time."

"The problem is," Victor said, ignoring Lorraine's attempt at lightness, "I can't afford mistakes. Not when I've come this far."

Agatha's mind raced, trying to fit the pieces together. "You knew Eleanor and Nigel from Meridian Press, didn't you? Not as colleagues—as enemies."

Victor's smile was cold. "Very good. Eleanor and Nigel were responsible for the plagiarism scandal that destroyed my reputation in publishing. They knew the manuscript was suspect but pushed it through anyway because it was guaranteed to sell. When it all fell apart, they made me the scapegoat."

"So, you killed them for revenge," Emma said, her voice steadier than Agatha expected.

"I prefer to think of it as justice," Victor corrected. "They ruined my life, forced me to change my name, start over from nothing. And then they had the audacity to turn up at this retreat, flaunting their success." His expression hardened. "They deserved everything they got."

"But why frame Agatha?" Lorraine asked. "She had nothing to do with any of this."

Victor smirked, his demeanor shifting into something cold. "I used you from the beginning, Agatha. Lindsey was right—you were gullible and easy to fool."

Agatha's breath caught. "Lindsey?"

Victor grinned cruelly. "Oh yes. My dear sister, Lindsey Elkins. She suggested I invite you here when I told her about Eleanor and Nigel. You were the perfect scapegoat."

The name hit Agatha like a physical blow. Lindsey Elkins—the woman her ex-husband had left her for. The affair that had shattered her marriage and upended her life. That Lindsey was Victor's sister seemed too cruel to be coincidence.

"Lindsey," Agatha repeated, her voice barely above a whisper. "Your sister is the woman who had an affair with my husband?"

Victor's smile widened. "Small world, isn't it? Lindsey has always detested you. When I mentioned setting up this retreat and needing someone to take the fall, she immediately suggested you. Said you were nursing literary aspirations as a mystery writer but were too naive for your own good. The perfect patsy."

Lorraine let out a dramatic gasp. "Mon Dieu! So she ruins your marriage, steals your husband, and then tries to frame you for murder? That woman needs more than therapy—she needs an exorcism!" She turned to Emma with wide eyes.

"Remind me to never date Agatha's ex-husband's relatives. They clearly have a flair for the homicidal."

Despite the gravity of the situation, Emma couldn't suppress a brief, startled laugh.

Victor's jaw tightened at the interruption. "This isn't a joke."

"No," Lorraine agreed, straightening her shoulders. "But neither is our friendship, monsieur murderer. And you've clearly underestimated it."

Agatha's hands curled into fists, a surge of righteous anger giving her courage. "So this entire thing—the invitation, the retreat—it was all just to frame me for murder?"

"How else do you think a retreat like this would invite a bookshop owner from nowhere America?" Victor sneered, his polite facade finally dropping away. "You're not even talented enough to finish writing or publish a book. Did you really think you were invited on merit?"

"She has finished a book," Emma cut in sharply, stepping closer to Agatha's side. "It just isn't edited yet. And she's twice the writer you'll ever be."

His cold, calculated laugh sent chills down Agatha's spine. "Your typewriter proved the perfect murder weapon," he added with smug satisfaction. "And it would have worked perfectly if you hadn't been so unexpectedly resourceful. I suppose Lindsey underestimated you."

Wait a minute," Agatha said, realization dawning. "The typewriter was a surprise gift from Emma and Lorraine. You couldn't have known about it beforehand.

Victor's eyes gleamed. "I make it my business to know everything. Marie was quite helpful in keeping me informed about all the little details—including your friends' surprise gift."

"So you stole it from my cabin and staged it at the murder scene?" Agatha said, the pieces finally falling into place.

"That's not how the police see it," Victor countered with a dismissive smile. "As far as they're concerned, you brought it there yourself. The perfect evidence." He shrugged. "Then, when that plan started falling apart, I had to shift the blame to someone else. Naomi was perfect—a struggling writer with a grudge against both Eleanor and Nigel." His lips curled into a self-satisfied smirk. "The plan was working beautifully—until you and your friends decided to play detective." His gaze hardened, voice dropping to a dangerous level. "And now, I'm afraid we have a problem."

As he reached behind him, Agatha realized with horror that he was going for a weapon. Without thinking, she shouted, "Mike, now!"

The little schnauzer, who had been tensed and ready, launched himself at Victor, latching onto his pants leg with surprising ferocity. Victor cursed, stumbling backward as he tried to shake the dog off.

"Run!" Agatha yelled to Emma and Lorraine, who didn't need to be told twice.

They bolted for the door, Agatha pausing only long enough to call Mike back. The dog released Victor's leg and darted after them as they burst out of the cabin into the late afternoon sunlight.

"Help!" Emma shouted as they ran toward the main lodge. "Somebody help us!"

To their immense relief, Inspector Khumalo emerged from

around the corner, accompanied by two uniformed officers. His expression shifted from surprise to alertness as he took in their panicked state.

"What's happening?" he demanded.

"It's Victor," Agatha gasped, fighting to catch her breath. "He killed Eleanor and Nigel. He just admitted everything. He's Victor Elkins, not Reynolds. He was going to hurt us too!"

Khumalo didn't waste time with questions. He issued rapid orders to his officers, who immediately headed toward Victor's cabin, weapons drawn.

"Stay here," he instructed the three women before following his officers.

Agatha, Emma, and Lorraine huddled together on the lodge steps, shaking with the aftermath of adrenaline. Mike pressed himself against Agatha's leg, a steady, reassuring presence.

"Do you think he'll try to run?" Emma whispered.

"He won't get far," Agatha said with more confidence than she felt. "Not with Khumalo's team after him."

Minutes stretched into what felt like hours before they finally saw the officers returning, Victor between them in handcuffs. His face was a mask of cold fury as he was led past them toward a waiting police vehicle.

Inspector Khumalo approached after Victor had been secured. "We found a gun in his cabin," he informed them grimly. "And a significant amount of incriminating evidence, including notes detailing his plan to frame Ms. Ndlovu after his original plan to frame Ms. Royale failed."

"So Naomi was innocent all along," Agatha said, more as a confirmation than a question.

"It appears so. We'll be releasing her shortly." Khumalo's expression softened slightly. "You three have had quite an ordeal. I suggest you go inside and rest while we handle the formalities." As he turned to go, Agatha called after him, "Inspector? Thank you for believing us."

Khumalo nodded once. "Thank your dog. If he hadn't alerted us with his barking when you ran out, we might not have responded so quickly."

With that, he walked away, leaving Agatha, Emma, and Lorraine to process everything that had happened.

"It's finally over," Emma said, sounding dazed.

Lorraine collapsed dramatically onto a nearby bench. "Mon Dieu! I need a very large glass of wine and possibly an entire baguette to recover from this!"

Despite everything, Agatha found herself smiling as she bent down to ruffle Mike's fur. "You're the real hero of this story, aren't you, boy?"

Mike wagged his tail, looking thoroughly pleased with himself.

As they made their way inside, Agatha couldn't help but reflect on the irony. She had come to this retreat hoping to gather inspiration for writing mysteries, never expecting to find herself in the middle of one. But as harrowing as the experience had been, she knew one thing for certain—her first book would be one heck of a story.

"What are you thinking about?" Emma asked, noticing Agatha's contemplative expression.

"I'm thinking," Agatha replied with a small smile, "that Bristol Lake is going to seem very quiet after this."

Little did she know how wrong she would be.

34

HOMEWARD BOUND

The rich golden light of the African sunrise bathed the airstrip as Agatha, Emma, and Lorraine stood watching their luggage being loaded onto the small aircraft that would take them to Maun, where they would connect to their flight to Johannesburg.

The morning air was cool, carrying the distinctive scent of the savannah—earthy and wild, tinged with the promise of approaching heat.

"I never thought I'd be so happy to see such a tiny plane," Lorraine said, adjusting her oversized sunhat against the morning glare. "Even if it does look like it's held together with duct tape and positive thinking."

Emma smiled, her posture relaxed for the first time in days. "After everything we've been through, a bumpy flight seems like the least of our worries."

"And at least we know no one on this plane is a murderer," Agatha added, checking Mike's travel crate for the third time to ensure his comfort. The little dog wagged his tail, entirely unconcerned about the journey ahead.

A familiar voice called to them from across the tarmac. "Ms. Royale!"

They turned to see Inspector Khumalo approaching, his tall frame silhouetted against the rising sun.

"Inspector," Agatha greeted him. "I didn't expect to see you this morning."

Khumalo nodded respectfully to each of them. "I wanted to personally see you off." He handed Agatha a small envelope. "And to give you this."

She opened it curiously. Inside were three small, polished wooden medallions, each etched with a traditional Botswanan design and attached to a colorful woven cord.

"What are these?" she asked, running her finger over the intricate pattern.

"Honorary medallions," Khumalo said, his smile warm and genuine. "Just a small tradition we started at the local station— for those who help us solve the tough ones. It's not official, but it means a lot to us."

"But we're not police officers," Emma said, already reaching for a medallion with a grin.

"No," Khumalo agreed, "but your assistance was instrumental in resolving this case. Without your observations about the letterhead and your courage in confronting Reynolds—or Elkins, as we now know him—we might never have uncovered the truth."

Lorraine clutched her medallion to her chest dramatically. "I shall treasure this forever! My first official recognition as a detective!" She leaned in to kiss Khumalo on both cheeks, leaving him momentarily flustered. "Merci beaucoup, monsieur l'inspecteur!"

Recovering his composure, Khumalo turned back to Agatha. "Ms. Ndlovu asked me to convey her gratitude as well. She's already left for Gaborone to meet with her publisher about salvaging her reputation."

"And Victor?" Agatha asked.

"Mr. Elkins is facing multiple charges of first-degree murder, attempted murder, fraud, identity theft, and evidence tampering." Khumalo's voice was grave. "He won't see freedom again for a very long time, if ever."

Agatha nodded, feeling a complex mix of relief and sadness. "And his sister? Lindsey?"

"We've confirmed she was directly involved in planning this. During questioning, Victor revealed that Lindsey specifically suggested inviting you to the retreat." Khumalo looked at her with sympathy. "It seems she holds quite a grudge against you, though her brother was less forthcoming about why."

Agatha felt a chill despite the warming morning air. "Lindsey Elkins was the woman my ex-husband left me for," she explained quietly. "She's always resented me, even though she was the one who had the affair with my husband."

Emma placed a hand on Agatha's arm. "It still doesn't sit right with me—how deliberate it all was."

"According to Victor's confession, Lindsey knew about your aspirations to write mystery novels," Khumalo continued. "She described you to her brother as 'gullible' and said you would be 'easy to set up.' They're both being charged as co-conspirators."

Lorraine's usual dramatic flair was replaced by genuine anger. "That witch! To think she would go to such lengths just because of her own guilt!"

"At least they're both facing justice now," Agatha said, taking a deep breath to steady herself. The reminder that Lindsey had been involved in the plot to frame her added a personal dimension to the trauma they'd experienced. It wasn't just a random targeting—it was revenge, cold and calculated.

The pilot approached, signaling that it was time to board.

With final handshakes and promises to stay in touch, they said goodbye to Inspector Khumalo and climbed the short stairs into the aircraft.

As they settled into their seats, Emma looked out at the golden landscape below. "Botswana gave us elephants, drama, and a mystery involving a typewriter. Honestly, I'm not sure how we'll ever top that."

"Life is full of surprises, ma chérie," Lorraine said, then added with a theatrical sigh, "Though I do hope our next surprise involves less dust and more room service."

Agatha chuckled, grateful as always for Lorraine's flair. As the engines hummed to life and the small plane began to taxi down the runway, she glanced out the window one last time. Somehow, despite everything, she felt lighter. Changed, even. And maybe—just maybe—ready for whatever came next. "I wonder what awaits us back home," she said, almost to herself.

"Same old Bristol Lake," Emma replied with a fond smile. "Quiet streets, friendly faces, and absolutely no murders to solve."

Lorraine snorted. "How terribly boring. Perhaps we should start a detective agency to liven things up?"

"No thank you," Agatha said firmly. "One murder investigation is enough for a lifetime."

The plane lifted off, rising above the golden savannah. Agatha watched the landscape fade from view, a small smile on her lips—and a story already forming in her mind.

EPILOGUE

Two days later, they stood on the familiar sidewalk of Bristol Lake's Main Street, breathing in the comforting scents of home—fresh pastries from Eliza's bakery, flowers from the corner florist, and the distinctive smell of books and coffee wafting from Agatha's bookshop.

"It feels like we've been gone for years instead of weeks," Emma said, smiling at the familiar sights.

Gladys hurried toward them from across the street, her silver hair escaping from its neat bun in her excitement. "You're back! Oh, we've missed you terribly!" She pulled Agatha into a tight hug before doing the same to Emma and Lorraine. "And you're all over the news! 'Local Bookshop Owner and Her Friends Solves Double Murder in Botswana'—it's the biggest story to hit Bristol Lake since the Mayor's son got stuck in that carnival ride last summer!"

"News?" Agatha repeated, bewildered. "How did that get out?"

"That inspector fellow gave an interview to Reuters," Gladys explained, buzzing with energy. "Said you three were instrumental in catching a dangerous killer. The whole town's been talking about nothing else for days!"

"Mon Dieu!" Lorraine exclaimed. "We're celebrities! I must refresh my makeup immediately."

Emma rolled her eyes affectionately. "So much for a quiet return."

As they made their way toward Agatha's bookstore, Gladys filled them in on everything they had missed, most of which involved small-town gossip and the ongoing drama with the town council's debate about expanding the farmers' market onto Central Avenue.

"Oh, and the biggest news of all," Gladys said, lowering her voice conspiratorially, "the old Acadia Theater has been sold! To Hollywood people, if you can believe it. They're planning to renovate it back to its original glory—red velvet seats, vintage marquee, the whole thing. They're promising it'll be like stepping back in time for a classic theater experience."

"Really?" Agatha asked, intrigued. The Acadia had been abandoned for years, its once-grand Art Deco façade slowly crumbling into disrepair. "Who bought it?"

"Some production company run by these two sisters," Gladys replied. "Monroe something. Very hush-hush about their plans. They've already started work—brought in a whole team from New York."

As they reached the bookstore, Agatha was pleased to see that Celeste had kept everything in perfect order during her absence. The window display featured mystery novels, with a handwritten sign proclaiming "Our Owner Lives the Genre!"

"That girl has a wicked sense of humor," Emma chuckled.

Inside, the familiar smell of books enveloped Agatha like a warm embrace. Celeste looked up from the register and broke into a wide grin.

"You're back!" she exclaimed, hurrying around the counter

to greet them. "I've been fielding calls all week from people wanting signed copies of your books—which don't exist yet, but I took pre-orders anyway."

"Pre-orders?" Agatha repeated, feeling slightly dazed. "Celeste, I haven't even written anything."

"Well, you'd better start," Celeste advised with a grin. "You've got thirty-seven paid pre-orders already."

Before Agatha could process this information, the shop door opened again, and a striking woman entered. She appeared to be in her early forties, with sharp features and an air of refined impatience. Her tailored navy pantsuit and sleek bob haircut screamed big-city sophistication, making her stand out dramatically in the small-town setting.

"Excuse me," she said, her voice clipped and efficient, "I'm looking for the owner."

"That would be me," Agatha replied, stepping forward. "Agatha Royale. How can I help you?"

The woman gave her a swift, assessing glance. "Clara Monroe. My sister and I purchased the Acadia Theater." She handed Agatha a business card. "We're hosting a small reception next Friday to introduce ourselves to the community's business owners. Your presence would be appreciated." Her tone made it clear this was less an invitation than a command.

"Thank you," Agatha said, somewhat taken aback by the woman's brusque manner. "I'll try to attend."

Clara nodded curtly. "See that you do. We're particularly interested in establishing relationships with cultural venues in town." She glanced around the bookshop with a critical eye. "Even the... quainter ones."

"I'll send formal invitations before the event," she added, checking her sleek silver watch. "We're still finalizing some details."

With that, she turned and left, the door closing firmly behind her.

"Well!" Lorraine exclaimed into the silence that followed. "She's about as warm as a penguin's bottom, isn't she?"

"Lorraine!" Emma scolded, though she was clearly fighting a smile.

Gladys, who had observed the exchange with wide eyes, leaned in excitedly. "Vivian Monroe? As in *the* Vivian Monroe? The famous actress from the '80s?" At their blank looks, she continued, "She starred in all those psychological thrillers before she disappeared from Hollywood. There were all sorts of rumors—nervous breakdown, secret marriage, even witness protection! No one's seen her publicly in over twenty years!"

"And now she's in Bristol Lake," Agatha mused, turning the business card over in her hand. "How strange."

Mike, who had been quietly exploring his old territory, suddenly appeared at Agatha's feet, looking up at her with intelligent eyes that seemed to say, "Here we go again."

Agatha met Emma and Lorraine's gazes, seeing in them the same mix of curiosity and apprehension she felt herself. After Botswana, they should have had enough of mysteries to last a lifetime. Yet something about Vivian Monroe's appearance in their quiet town tugged at Agatha's newfound investigative instincts.

"I'm not sure I'm going to like having Hollywood types taking over the Acadia," Emma said thoughtfully. "Especially ones with attitudes like hers."

"I'm not sure I like her," Lorraine agreed. "Though her shoes were absolutely divine."

Agatha smiled, slipping the business card into her pocket. "Let's reserve judgment until we know more. After all, everyone deserves the benefit of the doubt."

As they settled back into the comfortable rhythm of small-town life—Agatha tending to her bookshop, Emma resuming her work at the local library, and Lorraine planning an elaborate "welcome home" dinner for them all—none of them could have guessed that Vivian Monroe's arrival in Bristol Lake was about to plunge them into another mystery, one that would make their Botswanan adventure seem like merely the first chapter in a much longer story.

For now, though, they were home, safe, and together. And for Agatha, watching Mike curl up contentedly in his favorite spot by the bookshop window, that was more than enough.

She smiled, running her fingers along the spines of her beloved mystery novels. Perhaps it was time to finish writing one of her own.

LORRAINE'S FAMOUS FRENCH BEIGNETS

When Lorraine commandeered the kitchen during their Botswana adventure, these beignets brought comfort during a time of tension and suspicion.

Ingredients:

- 2 cups all-purpose flour
- 1/4 cup granulated sugar
- 1 tablespoon baking powder
- 1/2 teaspoon salt
- 1 large egg, beaten
- 3/4 cup whole milk
- 2 tablespoons melted butter
- 1 teaspoon vanilla extract
- Vegetable oil for frying
- Powdered sugar for dusting

Instructions:

1. In a large bowl, whisk together flour, sugar, baking powder, and salt.

2. In a separate bowl, combine egg, milk, melted butter, and vanilla.
3. Add wet ingredients to dry ingredients and stir until just combined. Let the dough rest for 10 minutes.
4. Heat oil in a deep pan to 350°F.
5. Drop tablespoons of dough into the hot oil, cooking 3-4 beignets at a time.
6. Fry until golden brown, about 2 minutes per side.
7. Drain on paper towels, then dust generously with powdered sugar.
8. Serve warm with Lorraine's dramatic flair: "Voilà! Beignets magnifiques!"

EMMA'S CALMING CHAI TEA

A soothing beverage for when the mystery gets too intense, inspired by Emma's practical and calming presence.

Ingredients:

- 2 cups water
- 2 cups milk
- 4 black tea bags
- 8 cardamom pods, slightly crushed
- 8 whole cloves
- 2 cinnamon sticks
- 1-inch piece of fresh ginger, sliced
- 1/4 teaspoon black peppercorns
- 2-3 tablespoons honey (adjust to taste)

Instructions:

1. In a medium saucepan, bring water to a boil.
2. Add cardamom, cloves, cinnamon, ginger, and peppercorns. Simmer for 5 minutes.
3. Add tea bags and simmer for another 2 minutes.

4. Add milk and bring to a gentle simmer (do not boil).
5. Remove from heat and strain into mugs.
6. Sweeten with honey to taste.
7. Sip slowly while contemplating the next mystery to solve.

As Agatha would say: "Sometimes the best detective work happens over a perfect cup of tea."